# Into the Blue

(The Blue Crystal Trilogy)

Book Three

Pat Spence

# Into the Blue

*In memory of my dad, Alan Spence, who loved a great adventure.*

*The chill ascends from feet to knees*
*The fever sings in mental wires.*
*If to be warmed then I must freeze*
*And quake in frigid purgatorial fires*
*Of which the flame is roses, and the smoke is briars.'*

East Coker, The Four Quartets, T.S. Eliot

# CONTENTS

## PART TWO: FOUND

## PART THREE: THE BLUE

# PROLOGUE:

*Deep in the subterranean layers beneath the Dolomite Mountains in Northern Italy something stirred. Eyes that had slept for thousands of years flickered open and pupils strained to see in the darkness. Waking breath came in fits and starts, as stale air was cast out and clean air drawn in through quivering, straining nostrils. Limbs that were twisted and bent through lack of movement straightened as blood and oxygen brought them to life. Electrical impulses leapt across synapses, reawakening a dormant nervous system.*

*As consciousness dawned, curled claws extended from cold fingers, gouging trails across the cold rock. Slowly, the figure raised its head, looking for a way out, seeing the pile of boulders that sealed the entrance, turning the cavern into an underground tomb. With a howl of frustration, it leapt to its feet, throwing rocks aside with superhuman strength, clearing the passageway that had been blocked for millennia. Speedily, it moved through the underground tunnel system, climbing upwards through winding pathways hewn into rock.*

*The trail opened into a large cave, sunshine flooding the entrance. Shielding its eyes at the unaccustomed glare, the creature moved forward, stepping out into clear mountain air.*

*Curling its toes over the narrow ledge, it looked down into a vast ravine disappearing thousands of metres below. For a minute, it basked in the sun like a butterfly emerging from a chrysalis, then inhaling deeply, stepped forward.*

*Sleek and beautiful, dark and deadly, the demon flew, summoned by a centuries-old voice, ready to perform its master's bidding.*

# PART ONE: LOST

## 1. Staying alive

To the outside eye, all was normal. Seth, Tash and I continued to attend college and live at home, while the de Lucis family remained at Hartswell Hall, living their glamorous lives, staying young and beautiful. The sun shone, the grass grew and the plants in the Hall gardens continued to thrive.

But, of course, everything was different. In an instant, life had changed beyond all recognition. The blue crystal was missing and we were in free-fall.

My friends were kept alive by small blue crystals hanging round their necks on silver chains. It was a short-term salve, not a permanent solution to the evil threatening to poison their systems. Without the big crystal, death was imminent. And the de Lucis family didn't fare any better. Their days, and the days of all those like them, were numbered. Without the blue crystal to rejuvenate their bodies, in less than three years they would age rapidly, turning to bones and dust in minutes, and their species would be wiped out forever.

Their life force had been snatched from them and they had no idea how it had been taken or where it had gone.

## 2. **Paradise Lost**

It was English Literature and Miss Widdicombe was trying her best to keep us interested.

"Today, we're going to look at Paradise Lost by Milton," she said brightly."

"Great," said Seth, sprawling in his chair, dark fringe spilling over his face as he flicked through the textbook. "Looks like a bundle of laughs."

"If you want laughs, Seth, I suggest you look in the mirror," she retorted drily, holding up her textbook. "This is one of the greatest poems in English Literature. It recounts the fall of Satan, one of the brightest angels, also known as Lucifer or the Shining One." She beamed at us. "Any idea what he did to be thrown out of heaven?"

"Turned himself into a serpent and got Eve to eat the apple," said Seth, sprawling even lower in his chair.

"That's right. He committed original sin and, as a result, lost his glory, his jewels, his brightness, everything. He was forced to live in the shadows, experiencing 'endless misery' in a place known as hell, tormented by thoughts of 'lost happiness and lasting pain'. But in Paradise Lost, he rises again, joined by his legions of demons who can assume whatever shape they choose."

As she spoke, I felt a prickling at the back of my neck. I recalled the words of the Fallen Angel, how he'd once shone brighter than all the others, how he'd been cast out and forced to live in darkness, stripped of all his jewels. He said the crystal had once belonged to him, before Viyesha found it, and told me he would seize it again, rising out of bondage with his legions of followers.

My mind was reeling. Could it have been Lucifer that I'd encountered? No wonder my friends were in such a bad way. I'd been protected by the blue crystal's power, but they'd had nothing. They'd been exposed to pure evil, Tash in the Fallen Angel's lair and

Seth when a feeder had attacked him. Now, without the blue crystal to heal them, they stood no chance. They were lost.

There again, without the blue crystal, we were all lost.

\* \* \*

At break time, we met up in the cafeteria. Theo and Violet sat at a table, Joseph with them. Although not a student, he was too worried and protective of Tash to let her out of his sight for any length of time.

"Any news?" I asked Theo, as we approached the table. I sat next to him and he closed his hand over mine, protective and calming. Instantly, I felt sparks of energy transfer from him to me and the blue crystal hanging round my neck tingled, vibrating against my breastbone. I looked at him and smiled, seeing the blue flecks in his eyes shining and sparkling. Then his eyes clouded over.

"Nothing," he whispered. "There's no news."

"It's obvious, isn't it? This Fallen Angel dude must have it," said Seth, sliding on to the seat next to Violet. Sparks of energy flew from her body and she looked up at him from beneath her eyelashes. As usual she looked like a fashion model, in a white scoop-neck crop-top, blue denim jacket, white skinny jeans and white platform sandals.

"Hi beautiful," he said, pecking her on the cheek.

"Hi Seth," she purred.

"Seth, you are such a cliché," I protested.

"It's okay. I don't mind," simpered Violet and I looked away in exasperation, unable to stomach Seth's posturing and Violet's flirting.

"Are you okay, Tash?" asked Joseph, standing up and putting his arm around her. He led her to a chair.

"I'm okay," she said quietly. "Just tired."

Her face, already pale, had a sickly pallor and her eyes, usually sparkling and green, were flat and colourless. She'd lost weight and her usual figure-hugging jeans hung off her. Joseph looked distressed.

"You shouldn't have come in today. You should have stayed at the Hall and let Pantera look after you."

"Like she's really gonna look after me," she answered sarcastically. "I'm not exactly her favourite person."

"I think you're confusing yourself with me," I pointed out. "I'm the one she can't stand. She only dislikes you by association."

"It's immaterial who likes who," said Theo flatly. "Without the crystal, none of us stand a chance. Seth and Tash can only keep going for so long. There's not enough power in the crystal pendants to heal them. The evil is spreading like poison."

"Cheers, Theo," said Seth, raising an eyebrow. "Say it like it is, why don't you? You really know how to make us feel good. Actually, I'm feeling okay right now." He grinned at Violet.

I looked at him closely. He might say he was okay, but there were tell-tale dark circles under his eyes and a sallow tone to his skin.

"You don't seem to get the seriousness of the situation," said Theo tightly. "As usual, you're being an asshole. The crystal has vanished into thin air and without it we're all dead."

"I get it, okay?" answered Seth. "But there's nothing I can do right now. And if I don't have long to live, I want to make the most of every moment with Violet. So, why don't you back off, Goldilocks?"

"Okay, you two. This isn't achieving anything," said Joseph. "Violet, can't you sense anything? Any feeling as to where the crystal may be?"

She stared at him blankly. "No, nothing. It's like it's fallen into a black hole."

"If the Fallen Angel has it, surely he'd have made a move by now," I said. "It's been a week and nothing's happened. Don't you think it more likely that Badru has the crystal? I mean, he sent Bellynda La Drach, his second in command, to safeguard it. It would make sense if she'd taken it."

"Except she's still here," pointed out Joseph. "If she had it, she'd have gone hot foot back to Badru. She's been searching as hard as anybody.

"Perhaps she's bluffing," suggested Seth.

"To what end?" asked Theo. "Why would she take the crystal and then pretend to look for it? Any more dumb suggestions?"

"Stop it, please, everyone," said Tash, closing her eyes and frowning. "This is making my head hurt. I'm sure Viyesna will know what to do."

"I'm taking you back to the Hall," said Joseph, firmly. "You need to rest."

Gently, he helped Tash to her feet and led her from the cafeteria.

"Catch you later," he called over his shoulder.

I stared at Theo.

"If the Fallen Angel doesn't have the crystal and neither does Badru, maybe there's another force at work."

"Emily," he said soothingly. "We'll find the crystal. I haven't waited all this time to lose everything again. I'll do whatever it takes to find it."

"Fighting talk," declared Seth, grinning. "I'd high five you if I had more energy. Kissing Violet's about all I can manage." He lent forward and put his arm round Violet's shoulders, drawing her to him. I saw a flicker of blue energy move across her body.

I raised my eyes at Theo. "I don't know what's got into him. He's behaving like a lovesick puppy."

"That's because he is one," said Theo. "I pity any boy who falls under Violet's spell. They don't stand a chance. He's lovesick and she's high maintenance. Not a good combination."

"Then it's up to us, Theo," I said defiantly. "Joseph's preoccupied with Tash, Seth's obsessed with Violet. You and I will have to help find the crystal."

"No Emily. It's up to me. You're not strong enough. You need to stay out of danger."

I smiled and nodded in agreement, but I knew the stakes were too high not to get involved. Wild horses couldn't stop me, whatever the consequences.

## 3. **Suspicion 1**

Viyesha stood in the clock tower room, holding the empty silver casket in her hands, Leon by her side.

"I keep asking myself how it happened," she said, tracing a finger where the crystal had been. "I don't understand how it could be taken without me knowing. Surely I would have felt something, been aware something was amiss? I felt nothing."

She looked at her husband, anguish and desperation written across her beautiful features. Gently, he put his arm around her shoulders.

"Something isn't right, Viyesha. You've been the keeper of the crystal for so long, you would have sensed its removal, felt it was being carried away."

"Exactly, Leon, so why did I feel nothing? And how could it be removed from under Bellynda La Drach's vigil? She's a sentinel. It was her job to guard the crystal. That's why she came."

"It would seem the crystal was taken as we let our guard down," said Leon slowly, going through events in his mind. "The feeders were destroyed, the Fallen Angel banished. We thought all was well. But something or someone was watching in the shadows, waiting for their opportunity."

"But who?" demanded Viyesha. "And how did they take it?"

"I don't know," he answered. "We were aware of no outsiders in the Hall. Whoever took it had to act quickly. Presumably, they knew where the key was hidden and how to operate the mechanism to reveal the hidden alcove."

"But other than the family, who else knew where the crystal was kept?" said Viyesha, running her fingers through her hair. "Seth and Tash were too ill to do anything and Emily was getting over her ordeal with Badru."

"Emily led others to the crystal in the past. Could she have done it again?"

"I don't believe so. She and Theo are in love. She wants to be initiated. She wouldn't put their future at risk."

"But she missed her chance this full moon. Maybe she took the crystal in the hope of initiating herself? She's made some rash decisions in recent weeks."

"True. But she wouldn't jeopardise Theo's life. She's loyal to the family."

"How about Pantera and Aquila? Can we trust them? And Bellynda, for that matter? Maybe Badru instructed her to remove the crystal and take it to him."

"Then why is she still here? She's distraught at its disappearance. I believe she's kept news of the crystal's disappearance from Badru, rather than admit her failure. Besides, the morning it was taken, she was resting after sustaining injury in the battle. And as for Pantera and Aquila… They've been with the family since the beginning. I trust them implicitly. They would never do anything to harm us. Even as we speak, they're out looking for the crystal."

"There is another," said Leon. "What about Juke? He said he was going to the airport to pick up Emily's mother, but he had the opportunity. And he knew where the crystal was kept. He could have taken it before he left."

"But it was thanks to him we overcame the Fallen Angel," said Viyesha. "He led the battle, proving he was on our side."

"Perhaps he was clearing the way to take the crystal for himself. Making out he was on our side so suspicion wouldn't fall on him."

"He could certainly hold the crystal without any effect," said Viyesha. "But he's a force for good. He has angelic powers. I cannot think it was him."

"Even the brightest beings succumb to temptation," said Leon bitterly. "As we well know."

"True." Viyesha sighed and walked to the window, looking out at the Hall gardens where the leafy shrubs basked in the warm sunshine.

She turned back to Leon. "We must watch Juke. I'll instruct Aquila and Pantera. At this moment, he's our most likely suspect."

\* \* \*

In the secret garden on the far northwest side of the Hall grounds, three figures met in the shadow of the wall, safe behind the ancient locked gate.

"Do you have it?"

"I do."

"Then where is it? And how come Viyesha can detect nothing?"

The tallest figure laughed triumphantly.

"Because it's shrouded. I've hidden the crystal in a web of anti-matter. Just one of my many tricks. Most effective when one requires total concealment."

"But where is it?"

"Somewhere safe. That's all you need know."

"Very well. But what's our plan? We cannot keep the crystal hidden forever."

"I propose a simple trade," said the figure that had so far remained silent. "Let the girl know we have it and tell her it will be restored to the family on one condition."

"And that is?"

"That she breaks off all contact with Theo. Leaves him and goes back to her ordinary life. Lives and dies as a mortal."

"She'd never agree to that. She's too stubborn. Or too stupid."

"I disagree. I think she would. She knows Theo will eventually die without the crystal. By walking away, she can save him. The ultimate act of love."

"And Ahmes will be avenged."

"Exactly. The pretender will be removed and Theo will continue to pay for the terrible wrong he committed. He will suffer, but the family will have the crystal. It's a perfect solution."

"You're sure she'll walk away from him? The girl is self-absorbed. She may put herself first."

"You're forgetting the added leverage of her friends." A cruel smile curled over the features of the tallest figure. "They're dying. They have a week, maybe two, before they succumb to the evil in their systems. If she walks away as we ask, she saves her friends' lives."

"Leave it to me," said the tallest figure. "I will make contact. I'll put a proposition to her she cannot refuse."

## 4. The Window Cleaner

Mrs Trelawney stood back and surveyed her house. It was a large, five-bedroomed red-brick, Edwardian property set in its own grounds in The Roundheys, the village's only private road. Having thrown heart and soul into its refurbishment, she was immensely proud of her achievement. Now she gazed lovingly at the fruit of her labours, marvelling at the redness of the brickwork, the carved detail around the windows and the splendid chimneys, imposing and commanding. No doubt about it, this was the best house in the village.

A frown flitted across her even features as the sun emerged from behind a cloud, bathing the house in brilliant light, highlighting smudges and marks on the windowpanes.

"You need a window cleaner," remarked the postman, walking up the driveway and handing her a stack of letters.

"Thank you, Roger," she said in a clipped voice, snatching the letters out of his hand. "It's on my list." She retreated to the house, mortified at the local postie finding fault with her beloved house.

She shut the front door behind her and leaned against the wall, letting out a sigh. The indignity! First, having dirty windows, and secondly being told so by the local postman.

"A window cleaner! Where can I find a window cleaner?" she muttered. "Do I Google one? Do window cleaners have websites? I'll ask Mrs Livingstone next door. She'll know."

No sooner had the thought entered her mind than the doorbell rang, making her jump. She opened the front door and peered out. On the doorstep was the most handsome man she had ever seen. He was tall and sun-tanned, with smooth olive skin, high cheekbones and angular features. His long black hair was tied back in a ponytail and brown sensuous eyes gazed at her from beneath dark-fringed eyelashes. She couldn't help but notice the well-defined muscles clearly visible beneath his taut T-shirt and felt herself flushing. Unbelievably, there was a ladder and a bucket of soapy water on the step beside him.

"Good morning," he said smiling, revealing perfect white teeth between firm, kissable lips. There was no mistaking the Italian accent and she felt her flush deepen. His gaze was both sensual and probing, and she had the feeling he was looking inside her. It was most unsettling.

"Good morning," she answered, a little more breathily than she had intended.

"Forgive me, signora, but I notice your windows, they need cleaning. Can I be of assistance?"

Murmuring a little prayer of thanks, she answered, "You can indeed. That's amazing, just as I need a window cleaner, you appear."

He smiled charmingly and held out his hand.

"Barolo di Biscione at your service, Signora."

"Pleased to meet you, I'm sure," she said, shaking his hand.

He had beautifully cool, sculptured hands that looked too elegant for cleaning windows. They were the fingers of a concert pianist, tapered and long, with well-manicured nails. His grip was firm and made her go weak at the knees.

"Shall I get started?" he asked, causing butterflies to turn in her stomach.

"If you would, please," she whispered.

Flashing his brown piercing eyes at her, he turned and picked up his bucket.

"I'll be inside," she informed him." Give me a shout if you need anything."

For the next half hour, he worked tirelessly, washing and rinsing the windows then polishing them dry, all the while taking note of everything he saw. He noticed the carefully arranged colour schemes, the matching accessories and expensive pieces of artwork. In the kitchen, he saw a shopping list with Prosecco and Cabernet Sauvignon underlined, and on the table a newly opened bottle of wine and fluted glass alongside, pink lipstick clearly visible on the rim. In the main bedroom, he saw an open wardrobe, revealing sequined eveningwear, blouses in every colour and a shoe collection to die for. With each revelation, he smiled to himself, piecing together a picture of the lady of the house.

"She loves the good life, she's vain and likes a drink," he murmured to himself. "Correction, she needs a drink. A human with a flaw. Just what I like."

He smiled again, thinking of the houses he'd visited that week and all he'd seen. He knew what went on behind closed doors in the village. He knew their insecurities and dependencies, their secrets and weaknesses. And that's all it took. One small weakness and he was in. A chink in the moral armour, an Achilles heel offering a small portal for him to enter.

Now all he had to do was secure an invitation over the threshold.

Surveying his work and deciding it was a job well done, he knocked on the front door.

"I'm finished, bella signora," he said. "The windows, they gleam and sparkle like jewels in a crown. You may inspect if you wish."

"No, no. I'm sure you've done a good job," Mrs Trelawney fluttered. "I'll pay you. How much is it?"

"£20, signora."

"Marvellous value. Why don't you step inside while I find my purse?"

Needing no further bidding, he stepped over the threshold, while Mrs Trelawney went in to the kitchen to retrieve her handbag. The moment she was out of sight, his handsome features began to change, his nose melding to his mouth as if made of wax, his lips elongating, ears shrinking back, and skin turning scaly and black. His neck stretched upwards, his arms fused to his side and his body shrank inwards, becoming long and tubular. The transformation took no more than a second and, once complete, the creature glided towards the kitchen door, raising itself up and opening its mouth wide to reveal savage white fangs.

"Won't be a second," called Mrs Trelawney.

The creature waited, ready to strike, as her heels sounded on the ceramic floor, walking back towards the hallway. Her fingers appeared around the door, and as she pulled it open, the creature widened its mouth further, ready to devour its unsuspecting prey. Luckily for Mrs Trelawney, she stepped into the hallway just as the postman, finding the front door ajar, knocked loudly.

"Mrs Trelawney, sorry to bother you. Forgot to give you this parcel. Could you sign for it?"

Instantly, the creature snapped back into human form, arms reappearing, neck shooting inwards and mouth shrinking to normal proportions.

"Why, Barolo, what are you doing lurking outside the kitchen door?" asked Mrs Trelawney coyly. "Here's your £20. And thank you, Roger. Leave the parcel in the porch. I'll sign in a second."

She waved dismissively in the postman's direction.

Smiling seductively at Mrs Trelawney and pocketing the £20 note, Barolo di Biscione made his exit.

"Thank you, bellissima signorina, I am much obliged. Shall I return this time next week?"

"I'm sure the windows won't need cleaning quite so quickly," answered Mrs Trelawney. "But why not? I'll see you in a week."

She watched him go, gazing longingly at his powerful shoulders and tight jeans.

"Sign here," instructed the postman.

"Yes, Roger," she answered in an irritated tone. "Just let me admire the view, won't you?"

She watched the window cleaner walk away from the house, hips snaking seductively, one hand clutching his ladder, the other holding his bucket of soapy water. Reluctantly she turned her attention to Roger.

## 5. **Transferring Energy**

After college, Theo and I, accompanied by Violet and Seth, walked up the gravelled driveway towards Hartswell Hall, its soft honeycombed stonework restored after the battle with the feeders.

"How are you feeling, Seth?" I asked, aware he was quieter than normal and his shoulders were hanging more than his usual stoop.

""I'm good. Never better, thanks, Em," he responded lightly. "The forces of evil are no match against Super Seth, Man of Iron." He flexed his muscles to prove his point.

"They're certainly not affecting your bravado," noted Theo. "It's okay to say you're not feeling great, you know, Seth. That crystal round your neck won't work forever. We need to know if you're feeling worse."

"Two words for you, Theo, my friend," answered Seth. "Get lost. I don't need you to make me feel bad. All right?"

"That wasn't what I was getting at," Theo snapped back. "Believe it or not, dumb ass, I'm trying to look out for you."

"I choose not to believe, pretty boy."

"Okay, you two. Break it up. This is not helping."

I exchanged a worried glance with Violet. She linked arms with Seth and spoke to him softly. "Theo's only looking out for you. We're all worried."

"I promise I'll let you know if I start feeling bad again," answered Seth. "For now, the crystal necklace seems to be working. Can't believe I'm wearing a necklace. How girly is that? If the rugby team find out, my reputation's dead."

"If we don't find the big crystal, we're all dead," said Theo. "That girly necklace is keeping you alive, don't you get it?"

"Theo," I said gently. "Let him be. We're all on edge. Let's find Tash."

By now we were approaching the Hall's impressive frontage, with its huge, metal-studded oak door. From high above, the stone gargoyles looked down, jaws open, sneering and snarling. I felt a shiver run down my spine.

Viyesha met us in the reception area. As always, she was immaculate in a close-fitting blue jump suit, showing off her figure to perfection, accessorized with a large, blue-jewelled bracelet and matching necklace, her hair pinned back in a chignon, emphasizing her large blue eyes and high cheekbones. Her beautiful face looked strained and troubled, and when she bent to kiss my cheek I didn't experience the feelings of peace and serenity she normally radiated. Her energy was depleted.

"Emily, how are you? You seem well."

"I'm fine, Viyesha. I don't know why, but my ordeal in the crypt hasn't affected me at all."

"I'm pleased to hear it. Seth, how are you?"

"Cool, Mrs de Lucis," he answered in an upbeat voice. "Raring to get out and find this crystal."

She smiled thinly. "Not so fast, Seth. You must leave that to us. It's too dangerous and your immunity is too compromised."

"How's Tash?" asked Theo. "Joseph brought her home. She wasn't good."

Viyesha looked troubled. "She's not. She's weakening fast and there's little we can do. I've put her in one of the guest bedrooms. Joseph's with her."

She turned to Seth. "I think it would be a good idea if you and Tash stayed at the Hall, so we can look after you. Would your parents be agreeable?"

"Sure," said Seth, his eyes brightening at the thought of staying in the same place as Violet. "Mine are on holiday for a fortnight and Tash's mum is visiting relatives. They won't even know."

"It's settled then. You'll stay here," she declared.

"I need to see Tash," I demanded, alarmed at her words. "Can I go up?"

"She's in the red suite," answered Viyesha. "You should prepare for the worst, Emily. She may not have long. Without the big crystal, we can only make her comfortable. I'm sorry. We may need to get her mother back from holiday."

Within two minutes, we were knocking at the door of the red suite. Joseph answered, pale and weary, silently opening the door and letting us in. Tash lay, tiny and insubstantial, in an enormous four-poster bed, a rich red quilt pulled up beneath her chin. Even the reflected colour of the quilt did nothing to hide the deathly pallor that hung around her face. She lay motionless, her eyes closed.

"Tash," I cried, my voice breaking as I realised how ill she'd become.

I sat on the edge of the bed, willing her to wake. Her eyes flickered open and a tiny smile played across her lips.

"Emily, I'm glad you're here, " she whispered. She struggled to free her hand from beneath the bedclothes.

"Lie still, Tash," instructed Joseph. "Conserve your energy."

Somehow she managed to pull out her hand and gripped mine, holding tight.

"I'm scared, Emily. I don't want to die, especially now I've found Joseph."

A small teardrop trickled down her cheek. I gently wiped it away.

"Hush, Tash. Don't cry. You're not going to die. We're going to find the crystal. You'll soon be feeling better."

"How can you find it? You don't know where it is. There's nothing you can do for me."

"Viyesha and Leon have a fairly good idea where it is," I lied. "It's only a matter of time before we get it back. As long as you remain quiet and still, you'll be okay. Now, give me your other hand. I have an idea."

Slowly, she brought it from beneath the quilt and placed it in mine. I sat, holding both her hands, concentrating as hard as I could. The others watched without saying a word. Mentally, I visualised the small crystal pendant on my breastbone sending torrents of energy cascading into Tash, and felt it vibrate, getting warmer. The more intensely I concentrated, the stronger the energy became and a blue glow began to surround Tash's body as her energy field grew strong and vibrant. With every ounce of strength I possessed, I pushed the energy out of my fingertips into Tash, seeing her aura shine bright blue.

I held it as long as I could, before slumping back, breaking the connection. But it seemed to have done the trick. Her skin looked a little less pale, her eyes opened wider and some of their green sparkle was back. She smiled at me.

"Thanks, Emily. I don't know what you did, but I feel a lot better."

"I don't suppose it will last long," I admitted, "but it's given you a boost."

"How did you do that, Emily?" asked Theo, impressed. "You just performed energy transference."

"I don't know," I answered. "I just did it."

I saw Theo, Violet and Joseph exchanging glances.

"What?" I asked.

Violet shook her head. "It doesn't matter. It's just that we can only transfer energy from the big crystal. Somehow, you drew energy from the small crystal round your neck and passed it on to Tash. We don't understand how you did it."

"How about some for me, Em?" asked Seth, hopefully.

I shook my head. "Sorry, Seth. I don't think I could do it again. Not right now. I'm spent. Anyway, I thought you were feeling okay."

"Oh, yeah. I am. Strong as an ox, me. Strong, bad n' buzzin'."

But I knew he was feigning. The circles under his eyes were darker and lines of tiredness were etched into his face. His energy field was in rags, giving him no protection, and what little energy his crystal pendant provided was fading fast. It was only a matter of time before weakness claimed him.

"If it's okay with you, I'm gonna crash," he said to Violet. "I'm bushed and I've got to be up to scratch for the rugby match at the end of the week."

"Of course," she said. "Why don't you use the Hartswell Suite at the end of the corridor? Come on, I'll show you."

She took his hand and led him from the room, closing the door behind her.

Joseph sat on the bed by Tash. "You look brighter," he said, smoothing her hair from her forehead.

"I feel as if I've been plugged into a battery," she said, giving me a smile. "Thanks, Emily."

"Try and sleep," advised Joseph. "Harness the energy while you rest. What do you say?"

"Okay." She slipped her hands beneath the covers, closed her eyes and within seconds was fast asleep, her breath regular and gentle.

"I'll stay with her," said Joseph. "I want to be here if she wakes."

Theo and I went downstairs into the ballroom. We sank into one of the large purple sofas, the flickering flames from the huge open fire creating patterns of light and shadow on our faces. Theo looked young and handsome and I had never loved him more. Softly, he put his arm around me and pulled me towards him. Our lips met and his energy consumed me, powerful and caressing, transporting me to another place. Just for a moment, it was like before, when everything was okay and I stood on the threshold of an exciting new life.

Too soon I was aware of someone entering the room and we crash-landed back to reality. Viyesha stood before us, reminding me that nothing was okay and the door to my new life had just slammed in my face.

"Can I join you?" she asked, approaching the sofas.

"Of course," answered Theo.

She sat opposite us and regarded us for a moment.

"How are Seth and Tash?"

"Seth's lying down," answered Theo, "and for the moment Tash is okay, thanks to Emily's intervention. She boosted Tash's energy from her own energy field."

"Indeed?" asked Viyesha, regarding me quizzically.

I shrugged. "It was nothing. I'm not sure how I did it. I held her hands and passed on some of my energy. It seemed to come from the blue crystal necklace. I know it won't cure her, but it made her feel better."

"You're certainly a girl of surprises, Emily," said Viyesha. "To have such power and control after all you've been through is most unusual." She stared at me, as if weighing me up. "You're right, of course. It won't help her survive. It's like giving an aspirin when she needs a transplant, but anything that makes her feel better is good."

Her words hit hard, bringing home the hopelessness of our situation.

"It's bad, isn't it?" I asked. "You must have some idea who has taken the large crystal, Viyesha. Somewhere we can start to look. Theo and I are ready to go. Just tell us where."

Viyesha shook her head. "That's just the thing, Emily, I don't know. I don't know how it was taken, who took it or where it can be. I have no sense of where it's being kept, near or far away, whether it's being contained or used. It seems to have disappeared into another dimension."

"Like Dreamtime? Why don't we ask Juke to take a look? He knows all about other dimensions."

A hard look came over Viyesha's face. "I don't think that's a good idea."

"Why not?"

She hesitated. "I know he's your mother's boyfriend, but how well do you know him?"

"He won the battle for you. He saved the crystal. You can't suspect Juke."

"Maybe he saved the crystal for himself?" said Viyesha. "We don't know, Emily. He's a newcomer to the village, he knows where the crystal was kept and he has the power to remove it."

I thought hard. "Juke's a decent person. My mother adores him. It's not him."

"Until we can prove that, you need to be careful, Emily," said Theo, sliding his hand over mine.

"So you think it's Juke as well?" I demanded, snatching my hand away. "You're wrong. So wrong."

"Emily, we're just saying be careful. Juke is very believable. But we don't know anything about him, other than what he's told us. He might be highly dangerous. You and your mother could be in grave danger."

I stared angrily out of the window into the gardens, where the tall Cedars of Lebanon swayed majestically in the early evening breeze. The ground beneath me kept shifting, making me stumble just as I thought I'd found my feet. Was anything as it seemed in Theo's crazy, mixed-up world? Was Juke who we thought he was? Or was it all a lie?

He'd said he was a world traveller, an urban angel. And I knew he had supernatural powers. But perhaps the relationship with my mother was a front allowing him to get close to the de Lucis family. Maybe he wasn't what he claimed to be and stealing the crystal had been his aim all along. Perhaps there was something ugly beneath that crinkly, friendly, worldly-worn exterior.

I resolved to watch him closely. One slip and I'd be on to him.

## 6. **Attack**

Theo offered to walk me home, but I needed to get away and clear my head. I had to step back and think rationally, so many crazy things had been happening recently.

"I'll be fine," I told him, kissing him on the cheek and stepping onto the Hall's gravelled driveway. "I need to be on my own for a bit. Juke's spending the evening with my mother, I want to go home and be with them."

"I don't like you walking home on your own."

"Theo, it's daylight. What can possibly happen? I'm wearing the blue crystal. If I sense danger, I'll put my hand around it and summon you. You'll know straight away. Besides, whoever's taken the crystal has what they want. They don't need to use me as leverage any more. I'll be okay."

Reluctantly, he agreed. "All right, but text me when you get back, okay?"

"Yes, okay."

I waved goodbye and began walking down the driveway, my head buzzing with thoughts of Juke and wondering if Viyesha's suspicions were possible. Soon I was out of sight of the Hall's windows, walking alongside the rose garden, with the wall to the secret garden just visible in the distance. I was so lost in thought I failed to register a rustling in the bushes to my left until it was too late. The first indication that I wasn't alone was when a black bag was pulled over my head from behind. I fought to get away from my attacker but I was powerless. Strong arms fastened me in an iron grip and I felt myself being lifted from the ground. I kicked and shouted, but it was no good. The black bag must have been laced with a powerful sleeping agent because I lost consciousness almost immediately.

When I awoke, the black bag was still over my head, preventing me from seeing. I tried to move my arms but realised they were tightly bound behind my back. My legs stretched out in front of me, also bound, and I had the impression I was sitting on rough ground. The smell of damp vegetation assaulted my nostrils.

"Who's there?" I called, desperately shaking my head from side to side and trying to dislodge the black bag. "What do you want?"

The black bag was pulled tight from behind, cutting into my throat and raising my chin into the air. I fought to breathe, fighting panic.

"Stop talking and listen," said a rough voice in my ear.

The bag was pulled even tighter and I felt myself choking.

"Stay quiet, okay?"

"Okay," I managed to whisper.

Thankfully, the grip on the bag released slightly and I was able to breathe, despite my head still being pulled backwards.

The voice spoke again. "Without the blue crystal the de Lucis family will cease to exist. Your beloved Theo will not survive and your friends will be dead within days. Do you understand?"

I nodded as best I could.

"The only hope for your friends is to bathe in the light of the crystal. It's within your power to save them if you do as I say. So listen carefully."

I nodded again.

"We have the crystal," the voice rasped into my ear. "We will release it on one condition. Sever all connection with Theo. Walk away. Do you understand?"

"Finish with Theo?" I gasped. "Never!"

"Then you are a fool and have just signed the death sentence for your friends and the de Lucis family."

"No," I cried, pulling my head forward and trying to free myself.

My captor jerked my head backwards fiercely and now I was in agony, the ligaments of my neck stretched to breaking point. I fought to breathe.

The voice spoke viciously. "Are you really so stupid? I will tell you one last time. Tell Theo you've changed your mind and don't want to be with him. Tell him the idea of eternity is too much and you wish to remain mortal. Walk away from him and don't look back. Finish with him forever."

The hand pushed my head forward roughly, causing me to cough.

"Why?" I started to ask.

There was a short, sharp slap to my head, causing me to cry out.

"It's not for you to ask. Do as I bid and all will be well."

"How do I know you have the crystal?" I persisted. "I need to know."

"Very well," the voice spoke quietly and I felt something thrust in to my hands, tied tightly behind me. I touched the smooth facets of a large crystal with my fingertips and instantly a sensation of relaxation swept through my body as if the sun was bathing me in its warm, sweet light. I'd experienced this before and there was no doubt in my mind it was the blue crystal. But it was over in a split second. I felt a hand pull the crystal away.

"It is the crystal, you agree?" the voice demanded.

"Yes," I answered weakly. "But who are you and why do want me to leave Theo? I don't understand."

"No more questions," the voice whispered malevolently in my ear.

I persisted. "How come you're hiding the crystal from Viyesha? Why can't she detect it?"

"Viyesha is not as all-seeing and all-knowing as she thinks. There are others more powerful than she," said the voice dismissively. "Now, do we have a deal?"

"Yes," I answered faintly. "I'll do as you ask if you return the crystal."

I felt sick at the thought of what I must do.

"Tell no one of this encounter," the voice hissed in my ear. "If you do, we will disappear and the de Lucis family will never see the crystal again. When the time comes for them to renew, they will crumble to dust. And your friends will be dead within forty-eight hours." The unseen hands pulled the black bag even tighter so I was nearly losing consciousness. "You hold their lives in your hand. You have until sundown tomorrow."

I felt a sudden blow to my head and everything went black.

When I awoke, the black bag had been removed and my arms were free. I looked around. It was still early evening, the sun visible in the sky, tingeing the clouds with a delicate pink. I was lying on soil, thick vegetation and bushes surrounding me. Quickly, I sat up and untied my legs, rubbing my ankles to restore the circulation, my neck feeling bruised and sore where the bag had been pulled tight. Unsteadily, I rose to my feet and looked through the leaves. To my right, I saw a red-brick wall, about two metres high, and realised I was in the secret garden. Trying to stop my hands from shaking and forcing myself to breathe slowly, I followed the wall until I reached the ornate wooden gate. To my relief, it was open. I looked warily for signs of my attacker, but all was quiet except for the welcome sounds of bird song. I ran through the gate and into the rose garden, barely noticing the scents of Joseph's prize blooms.

My first thought was to find Theo and tell him what had happened, run back to the Hall where I'd be safe and hope Viyesha could make sense of what had occurred. My hand closed around my crystal pendant. I had to let Theo know I was in danger. Then I stopped, drawing back my hand as my attacker's words echoed in my head. I couldn't tell Theo. I couldn't tell anyone. I had the power to save my friends and the de Lucis family, but the price was high. I had to sacrifice the one thing that meant more to me than anything. I had to give up Theo.

Bitter tears fell from my eyes as I thought about what lay ahead. I had to renounce all claims to a future with Theo, all thoughts of happiness and living for eternity. I had to face the future alone, living and dying as an ordinary mortal, watching my face and body grow old. And in a further, cruel twist, I had to endure my friends bathing in the light of the crystal as they were initiated at the next full moon, looking forward to eternity with their newfound loves.

It was too much to bear. With a breaking heart, I ran down the gravelled driveway, away from Hartswell Hall, away from the one true love of my life. I knew I would see him one last time, but it would be to tell him I was leaving, and I knew the unbearable suffering that would cause. Just as he'd found me after centuries of waiting, I was about to abandon him. It was the only way I could save him. And what hurt more than anything was that I would never be able to tell him why I was doing it. He would live for eternity, never knowing why I'd walked away. My suffering would be finite, but his would last forever.

I wondered again who would possibly want to cause Theo and me so much pain. None of it made sense.

## 7. **Questions**

I ran all the way home, arriving red-faced and breathless to find my mother standing on the front step, about to let herself in.

"Hi Emily," she called. "I've just got back from work. We had a rush order and I stayed late to process it. Are you all right?"

"Yes, I'm fine." I forced myself to smile and act naturally. "I've just run back from Theo's. I'm not as fit as I thought I was."

She laughed and unlocked the front door, letting us in to the hallway.

"Where's Juke?" I asked, trying to sound casual. "Did he work late, too?"

"No, he was on the early shift. He finished at two. I haven't seen him all afternoon. He should be round later. I said I'd cook dinner for half seven."

"Okay, cool. I'm going to my room. I have some college work."

I went up to my bedroom and lay on the bed, re-living the horror of my ordeal. My neck felt stiff and sore, my arms hurt from being tied so tightly behind my back, and there was a lump on the back of my head where I'd been hit. I was pretty tough and had been through worse, but emotionally I was a mess. My future had been snatched away and there was no one I could confide in or ask for advice.

I wondered again about the identity of my attackers. It seemed they'd taken the crystal as a means of getting me out of the way, which ruled out the Fallen Angel and a host of other enemies. But it would suit Aquila and Pantera, I reflected. They'd never hidden how much they detested me. There again, why would they put the family through such an ordeal? And Viyesha had said they were looking as hard as anyone to find the crystal. Was it just a front? And how about Juke? Viyesha's words were still ringing in my head. Although I couldn't believe he was my attacker, he hadn't been at work and potentially had a motive for separating me from Theo. He knew the dangers of getting initiated. Perhaps he was trying to protect me. Perhaps he wanted my mother and me to have a normal life and knew I'd never walk away from Theo unless I had no choice.

The more I thought about it, the more it made sense. I didn't believe Juke was bad. Or that he wanted to harm anyone. That's why he hadn't taken the crystal for his own gain. Given his relationship with my mother, keeping me safe was a priority. There again, the attack had been violent, which wasn't Juke's style. I touched my neck, feeling once again the pain of having my head forced back. Juke was kind and thoughtful. I couldn't imagine him behaving like that. But was anyone really as they seemed in Theo's world? Perhaps Juke thought it was the only way.

A glimmer of hope came into my heart. If it was Juke who'd taken the crystal as a means of keeping me safe, I could try to bring him round to my point of view. Once he knew I was serious in my intentions and fully aware of the dangers of initiation, he'd realise there was no changing my mind. Then he could return the crystal to Viyesha, save the family and my friends, and I could be with Theo.

Suddenly my situation didn't seem quite so hopeless. I began to wish more than anything that Juke was my attacker. Strange as it may be, I could get my head around that. I needed to ask him some questions.

At seven thirty, the doorbell rang and I ran down the stairs to let him in. There he stood, in his old bush jacket, a battered old bush hat on his head, guitar on his shoulder. His eyes lit up when he saw me, twinkling and blue, small laughter lines criss-crossing his tanned, leathery skin.

"Emily, my favourite girl," he said, leaning forward and kissing my cheek.

Immediately, I felt his energy skim past me, like a delicate silver skin, wispy and transparent. It was like being brushed with a fairy wing.

"Hi Juke. Come in. Dinner's about to be served."

Now I felt confused. Was it possible this warm, friendly being could be my cruel attacker? It didn't seem possible. And the voice was completely different. Juke spoke in soft, mellifluous tones, while my attacker had been rasping and rough. Still, appearances were deceptive. I knew Juke was a warrior of phenomenal strength. He could be violent when he had to be, so I mustn't let his soft exterior fool me. Juke showed me what I wanted to see.

I led him through to the breakfast room, where my mother was serving a meal of smoked salmon, new potatoes and green salad.

"Hi darling," she said, seeing Juke behind me and placing the food on the table. "Come and sit down. That's perfect timing."

We sat around the table and I wondered how best to question Juke. I couldn't ask too many questions with my mother present. After all, she knew so little of Theo's world and had no idea about Juke's true identity.

"I gather you weren't at work this afternoon," I began, handing him the salad bowl.

"No, that's right. I was on the early shift. I finished at two."

"And where did you go?"

"Emily." My mother sounded annoyed. "Stop asking questions. Can't we have a civilised meal without you interrogating Juke?"

"I'm not interrogating him. I'm making conversation. So, what did you do this afternoon, Juke? Just out of interest."

He watched me, amused.

"This afternoon, I went for a walk down by the lake, I sat under a tree and played my guitar for a while, and then I had a snooze in the sunshine. After that, I went back to my lodgings, had a shower. And then I came here. Does that answer your question?"

"Did anybody see you?"

"No, I was on my own. Anything else you'd like to know? Like what I had for breakfast this morning?"

"Emily," said my mother, sounding annoyed. "That's enough. What's wrong with you?

I was spared having to speak by the phone ringing in the hallway. My mother left the room to answer it and I seized my chance.

"Juke," I said directly, "you know I'm planning to be with Theo and get initiated at the next full moon, don't you?"

"Whoa, Emily. I'm aware of your intentions and it's something I need to talk to you about, but now's not the time. Can we do this later?"

"Do you want to stop me?" I persisted. "Do you want to prevent me from being with Theo, staying this age for eternity and possibly dying in the attempt?"

Juke opened his eyes wide. "Better keep your voice down, Emily. These are big issues and there's a lot to discuss."

But I was on a roll. I could hear my mother talking in the hallway and took my chance.

"How far would you go to stop me, Juke? You know the world of the de Lucis family better than anyone. D'you think it would be better if I wasn't with Theo? I'm fully aware of the dangers ahead and it's what I want more than anything. I just wonder how far you'd go to stop me."

"What are you accusing me of, Emily? If I thought it was the right thing to do, sure I'd stop you. But if it's your destiny, you have to play it out."

Now I was confused. He was neither admitting nor denying anything. I was prevented from saying more by my mother's reappearance. I felt Juke's eyes on me but couldn't return his gaze. I concentrated on my meal.

"Sorry about that," said my mother. "That was my friend Mo from The Roundheys. Honestly, she gets worse. Apparently, there's this new window cleaner in the village and he's got looks to die for. Like a film star. All the women are desperate to have their windows cleaned."

I wrinkled my nose. "Oh pur-lease. It sounds like that coke ad. You know, when all those sad middle-aged women are drooling over that scantily-clad workman. Pathetic."

"Nothing wrong with appreciating beauty," said my mother, "especially when it's called Barolo de Biscione. Apparently, he's quite the Italian stallion."

"Say that again," demanded Juke, a strange look on his face.

"Which bit? Italian stallion or Barolo de Biscione?" joked my mother. "I might have got the name wrong. It's something like that. Don't say you're jealous, Juke," she joked, seeing his expression.

He laughed, forcing his face to relax, but I could see he was rattled. Momentarily, his energy field went dark and even when it returned to silver, it was streaked with black.

"As long as he's only eye candy," he joked. "Just do me a favour. Let me check him out first before you have your windows cleaned." He made an attempt to smile, but his eyes were cold.

"You are jealous!" said my mother with satisfaction, placing her hand over his. "Don't worry, Juke. I only have eyes for you. You're my one and only. Now, how about dessert?"

"No, thanks. I'm stuffed," I said. "Plus, I don't want to watch you two making out. I'm going up to my room."

I shot Juke a penetrating glare as I walked passed him. I had no idea if he'd been my attacker. He had motive and he had opportunity, but it didn't fit somehow. Juke would tell me straight if he thought I was doing the wrong thing. And there was no way he'd put the lives of my friends in jeopardy. Not even for a day. I wondered whether to tell him about the attack. He'd know what to do. But if I did, the attacker might disappear with the crystal. In which case, everyone would die. At least this way, we'd all survive, albeit Theo and I broken-hearted.

But was I really capable of walking away from Theo? I felt sick at the thought.

And now something else had been thrown into the mix. Juke's reaction to the handsome window cleaner had been very strange. What was that all about? It wasn't jealousy, as my mother thought. I'd seen the way his energy field had reacted. It had turned black and that was more representative of danger. Or anger. He knew something we didn't. And it wasn't good. Perhaps the Italian window cleaner had been my attacker. I needed to find him fast.

If I didn't find out the identity of my attacker, I had no option but to walk away from Theo and break his heart. The lives of my friends depended on it.

If they died, I'd have their blood on my hands. And that was something I couldn't live with.

Now or ever.

## 8. **Suspicion II**

It was nightfall when Juke walked up the gravel pathway to Hartswell Hall. He rang the ornate bell on the grand oak front door, hearing it echo deep within. The door opened to reveal Leon. He stood back, allowing Juke into the reception area.

"It's late, Juke. Is everything all right?"

"I need to speak with you and Viyesha. Something's going on."

Leon eyed him suspiciously.

"Very well. I'll get her. Wait in the ballroom."

He showed Juke into the large, elegant room, the fire burning brightly in the hearth.

"Please, have a seat." He indicated the large sofas situated around the fire. "I'll be back shortly."

He left the room and Juke sat uneasily, watching the flames. If what he suspected was happening, they were all in grave danger and needed to act quickly.

Leon returned with Viyesha.

"Juke," she murmured softly, stepping forward to meet him. "Please don't get up. Leon said you wished to speak with us."

She looked stunning in a dark blue halter-neck shift dress, the crepe fabric clinging to her figure, emphasizing her elegance and poise. Her hair played loose around her shoulders.

"Hi Viyesha." Juke half rose from his seat, then sat back on the sofa. Leon and Viyesha sat opposite.

"I don't want to alarm you," he began, " but something's going on in the village."

"Before we talk about that, I think there is perhaps a more urgent subject we need to address," said Viyesha.

"There is?" asked Juke, looking puzzled.

"The question of our crystal," said Leon coldly. "Where is it, Juke? What have you done with it?"

"Steady, Leon," cautioned Viyesha, putting her hand on her husband's arm. "We cannot make accusations until we know for certain."

"What d'you mean?" asked Juke. "What's happened to your crystal?"

"You mean you don't know?" said Leon angrily.

"No, I don't know, mate. And I don't like your tone of voice." Juke got to his feet, facing Leon. "I helped you, don't forget. Without me, you wouldn't have seen off the feeders or the Reptilia or the Fallen Angel. Why would I help you one day and take your crystal the next?"

"Getting rid of the opposition, so you could step in and take it?" said Leon, standing to face Juke. "You knew where the crystal was kept, you had the opportunity and, more to the point, you can handle it."

"Then why am I still here?" asked Juke incredulously. "If I'd taken it, as you suggest, why am I not thousands of miles away? So much for the vote of confidence, mate. I step in to help and this is the thanks I get."

"Gentlemen, please," said Viyesha, her honeyed tones calming the waves of anger that shot between the men. "Juke, I'm sorry. Maybe we've misread the situation. The truth is, our blue crystal has disappeared and we have no idea where it is or who has taken it. This has immediate implications for Seth and Tash. Without the crystal, we cannot stem the flow of evil in their systems and it's only a matter of time. For ourselves, we have longer, but without the crystal our species will die. We cannot renew and we cannot survive. We are desperate and don't know where to look. You are a stranger in our midst. It was possible that you had taken it."

Juke looked at her in silence for a moment then spoke. "Okay, I get it that you're scared and in a bad situation. But pointing the finger at me is misplaced. I don't have your crystal and I had nothing to do with its disappearance. How d'you know the Fallen Angel hasn't got it?"

"We don't," admitted Leon. "But there's been no opportunity for him to take it. The crystal has been too well guarded. On the other hand, you were here. It seemed a logical conclusion."

"But a wrong one," said Juke pointedly. "Somebody else has taken it. Someone with the means to remove it from under your noses. How do you know it isn't one of your own household that's working for the Fallen Angel?"

"But who?" asked Leon. "There's only the family and our retainers. They've been with us for centuries. Their loyalty is unquestionable."

"Which brings us back to square one," said Viyesha. "For some reason, I can't get a sense of where it is. It's as if it's ceased to exist."

"It could have been shrouded," said Juke. "If so, you'd never detect it."

"Shrouded? What's that?" asked Viyesha.

"Hidden within anti-matter," explained Juke. "Makes it disappear to all intents and purposes." He frowned. "You need knowledge of dark energy to create a shroud, which means you're looking for someone from the dark side. And I have an idea who that might be."

"You do?" ask Viyesha, leaning forward.

"It's the reason I was attracted here in the first place. There are dark forces at work in this village. And now there's a new threat. Ever heard of a biscione?"

"Biscione? The Italian serpent!" exclaimed Viyesha.

"The same," said Juke. "I think there's one here in Hartswell. As yet, I've no idea why he's here or how much damage he's done."

"A biscione?" queried Leon.

"They're from the Italian mountains in the north," said Juke. "A particularly nasty type of man-eating demon. When they've eaten their prey, they absorb the soul and spit out the rest. The empty husk looks and sounds like the original person, but it's not. It's become a new biscione, with an insatiable appetite for human souls. If they're not stopped, they'll spread like wildfire through the village."

"Giving the Fallen Angel an army much more powerful than feeders," said Viyesha in dismay.

"Have you seen this biscione?" asked Leon.

"Not yet," admitted Juke. "But he's in the village and I'm on his trail."

"But surely, if the biscione had the crystal, he'd have taken it to the Fallen Angel. He wouldn't stick around," queried Leon.

"None of it makes sense," said Viyesha, rubbing her forehead with a well-manicured hand. "We're going round in circles. My immediate concern is for Seth and Tash. Without the crystal, they'll die within a couple of days and there's nothing we can do. Although Emily helped Tash today."

"She did?" asked Juke. "How?"

"Some kind of energy transference. It made Tash feel a lot better."

Juke smiled, a faraway look coming into his eye. "She's an amazing girl. There's no doubt in my mind that her rightful place is with you, Viyesha. And Theo. As long as we can get the crystal back. And believe me, I will fight with every ounce of energy I possess to help you. I need to ensure Emily's future. Now, first things first. I must find this biscione and any others he's created, and destroy them as quickly as possible."

Viyesha put a hand on Juke's arm.

"Thank you, Juke. Once again, you are riding to our rescue." She paused. "Forgive me for asking, but why is Emily's future so important to you?"

He stared at her with a strange expression in his eyes, and shrugged.

"It's a long story, Viyesha. For now, let's just say I need to keep her safe."

He got to his feet and tipped his hat.

"Stay vigilant. These are dangerous times. You need to watch everyone. I feel the crystal is near, which means we can still save Seth and Tash. I'll be in touch as soon as I have anything to report."

Viyesha and Leon watched silently as he left the ballroom. As soon as they heard his feet crunch on the gravel outside, Viyesha turned to her husband.

"Can we trust him?" she asked quietly. "Is there really a biscione in the village? Or is it a smokescreen to cover his tracks?"

"We can't trust anyone," answered Leon darkly. "Until we know more, everyone is under suspicion."

## 9. **Baby Barrowsmith**

Baby Barrowsmith waved off her husband early the next morning, thinking what an idiot he was. There he went, in his Hugo Boss suit, Fratelli Borgioli shoes, hair gelled back, driving his 911 Porsche Carrera, imagining he had flair and panache, when all the while he was a middle-aged cliché. Paunchy, pasty and pathetic.

"Bye darling," he called from the driving seat. "Get your hair done, why don't you? Looks a mess. Charge it to my account."

He put his foot down and the Porsche shot off the driveway, turbo-charged engine roaring. She watched him go with contempt.

"Bye, dickhead. Hope you meet with a horrible accident. Leave all that lovely life assurance money to me."

That would suit her just fine. She hated him. He was a capitalist pig of the first order. Not for the first time, she berated herself for marrying a man twenty-five years her senior. He was approaching old age, while she wasn't yet in the prime of life. Still, the marriage had its advantages. Like the ready funds whenever she needed them, the life of leisure and luxury, his long absences giving her plenty of time to amuse herself...

She smiled, tossing back her peroxide-blond curls and smoothing down her tight-fitting red dress over her hips. She glanced in the large gilt mirror hanging in the hallway, pleased to see the latest bout of surgery had worked so well. Her lips were large and pouty, her eyes just that little bit wider and her skin stretched taut over her cheekbones, giving her the look of an over made-up adolescent.

"I'd pass for nineteen any day," she murmured to herself, wondering if another tummy tuck was in order, or perhaps a buttock enlargement.

"I'll think about that tomorrow," she declared. "What I need today is a little fun. Now, who is it to be? Stan the DIY man? He's always up for a little squeeze between the sheets. Gary the gardener?

He can trim my hedge any day. Or why don't I call David, the financial adviser? My assets certainly need attention."

She picked up the phone, fingers playing on the keypad.

From his vantage point down the road, Barolo di Biscione watched with delight. She was prime prey and gagging for it. Just his type. His eyes lit up, as he placed his ladder on his shoulder and grasped his bucket of soapy water. Cockily, he sauntered towards her house, walking casually up the driveway.

"Well, hello," she said, eyes nearly falling out of her head. "Who are you?"

"Barolo di Biscione," he answered flirtatiously, "window cleaner extraordinaire at your service."

She noticed his dark good looks and how he mentally undressed her with his black flashing eyes. Seductively, she ran her fingers over her hips.

"Just what I need," she answered, looking up at him through her eyelash extensions. "My upper windows are really smudgy, they really need sorting out."

"I am just the man for the job, signorina," he said, taking her hand and kissing it with his full, firm lips.

"Hm, I like a man who's not backward in coming forward," she said playfully. "Why don't you start at the top and work down?" She winked at him.

He smiled and sizzled at her a little more, making sure she got a good eyeful of his strong biceps and well developed pecs straining beneath his T-shirt. Carefully, he placed his ladder against the upstairs windows and began to climb up, aware of her watching him from beneath.

"Nice," she murmured to herself. "I think I'll slip into something more suitable."

She went inside and up to the main bedroom, where she carefully selected a lacy leopard skin negligee, making sure she put it on just as he appeared outside the window, his handsome face showing through the soap suds.

He devoured her with his eyes. Such wanton abandon, such lack of morality. He couldn't have asked for a tastier snack. Within ten minutes, he'd completed the upper and lower windows, and was gently knocking on the front door, waiting for an invitation inside.

"You're a fast worker," she said, opening the front door wide and admiring his lean, firm body, his gently tapering fingers and beautiful black hair. "Come in."

Needing no further bidding, he stepped over the threshold and she closed the door firmly behind him. Hips sashaying seductively, she led the way into the kitchen. No point in going straight up to the bedroom, that would be too easy. Play a little hard to get.

"I'll make you a cup of coffee," she said, turning to look at him over her shoulder. "Do you take sugar...?"

She never finished her sentence, her words replaced by an ear-piercing scream as she saw the horror she'd let into the house. Instead of a handsome young window cleaner, tanned and ripped, a monstrous snake filled the hallway. Its huge serpentine head bore down on her with an enormous mouth full of jagged teeth, opening wider than she ever thought possible. She smelled its ancient, fetid breath and an instant later its jaws closed around her beautiful blond curls. She didn't stand a chance. In one deft movement the creature devoured her. Engorging its neck to accommodate its prey, the creature shuddered and swallowed, and then she was gone. For a minute, it sat back, letting the inner workings of its digestive system sift through its meal, taking what it required. Then opening its mouth wide once more, it regurgitated the bits it had no further use for.

First came the tiny painted toenails, then the long tanned legs, followed by the curvy body still in its leopard-skin print negligee, two graceful arms and finally the pretty face with its head of blond hair. Once again Baby Barrowsmith stood in the hallway, looking for all the world as she had a minute earlier. But with one important difference. This version had no soul. It looked like Baby and it sounded like Baby. But it was a husk, an empty vessel that answered only to its new master, Barolo di Biscione.

Blinking its black eyes in pleasure, the biscione snapped back into human form and once again, the handsome, young window cleaner stood in the hallway, sexy and seductive, lethally attractive.

"Hi Baby," he said. "How was that for you? For me it was amazing."

She looked at him with blank eyes. "Barolo," she murmured, her voice soft and pliant. "I'm here for your bidding."

"Bellissima," breathed Barolo appreciatively. "You know what you must do, Baby. Feed that hunger. Create more bisciones and bring me souls. The more the merrier. Best get started, we need to work quickly."

She smiled, revealing perfect white teeth, looking just like Baby, but now a deadly tool for the most malevolent of demons. Preparing the way for the return of its master.

For Hartswell-on-the-Hill, the horror had begun.

## 10. **Barolo**

I woke up early feeling edgy and dull. A ferocious headache threatened to split my head in two and I hid under the bed sheets, not wanting to think about the day ahead, thinking about my attack the day before.

Was it possible my attacker had told the truth? That they had the crystal and were willing to return it as long as I forfeited my relationship with Theo? Even in the cold light of day, I still couldn't make sense of it. Why was it so important to get me out of the picture?

I was a threat to nobody. I had no special powers. It would neither benefit nor hinder the de Lucis family if I was with them or not. The only person it would affect was Theo. His suffering would be terrible. Maybe that was their aim. But why would anyone wish to prolong Theo's agony, when he'd already spent centuries alone, carrying his guilt? Surely he was due some happiness? Perhaps it was linked to Ahmes, his bride of a few hours, so long ago. Theo believed I was her reincarnation, but I had no memory of it, and if I was honest, I didn't buy into all that past life stuff. Maybe I had a passing physical resemblance to her, but that was as far as it went.

Viyesha seemed to think the thief could be Juke, but that didn't seem likely. If he'd taken it, why was he still here? And by all accounts he didn't need it. Theo had told me of his amazing transformation when he battled the Reptilia dragons, how he'd replicated into an army of sword-wielding, shining angels, singlehandedly destroying them all. Violet said he'd called himself an urban angel and it was obvious he possessed phenomenal supernatural power. A being such as he would have no need of the crystal. Or would he?

What did I really know of this strange world I was about to enter and the beings who inhabited it? Correction – the strange world I would never enter.

I thought of my friends. They were getting weaker by the hour. I couldn't stand by and watch them die. Not when I had the power to save them. And how would Theo and his family survive without the crystal? Instead of regenerating at the next Blue Moon, they'd cease to exist.

But how could I tell Theo I'd changed my mind? He wouldn't believe me. He knew how much I loved him. How could I sound plausible? And how could I walk away from him and never look back? That was my worst nightmare.

My thoughts went round in circles until it was impossible to think straight. Only one crystal-clear thought shot through my mind with the precision of a laser beam. If I finished with Theo, the crystal would be returned and my friends would live. I couldn't look beyond that. It was academic who'd taken the crystal and why they'd done it. It didn't matter and I didn't have time to work it out. I had to act quickly, which meant I had to finish it with Theo today. Before sundown.

With a heavy heart, I got up and pulled on my old blue jeans and faded blue Granddad top. I didn't shower or wash my hair and I didn't put on make-up. What I was about to do was grubby and underhand. I was going to lie to Theo. I was going to tell him I couldn't leave my human life behind and couldn't be with him for another moment, let alone eternity. I didn't want to feel clean and fresh.

After today, I didn't know what life held for me, apart from emptiness and a grey, meaningless future. Trying to think positively was futile. I knew what I had to do and I would do it. But to go through with it I needed to turn myself into some kind of zombie without thought or feeling.

I reached for my iPod and looked through my downloads, choosing 'Can You Feel My Heart?' by Bring Me The Horizon. I put in my earphones and turned the volume to max, losing myself in the jagged music and agonising lyrics.

I was so lost in hopelessness and misery, screaming the words as loudly as I could, I failed to hear my mother knocking at my bedroom door. The first I knew, she was pushing open the door and speaking. Reluctantly, I turned down the volume and pulled out the earphones.

"What?" I asked, sounding annoyed and irritated.

"Sorry to disturb you, I'm sure," she replied. "I thought you might be interested in my news."

"Not really," I said dismissively. "Got more important things on my mind."

She grinned. "More important than the most gorgeous man you've ever seen? Well, maybe not as gorgeous as Theo or Juke, but a real piece of eye candy."

"What are you talking about?" I asked dully.

Whatever it was, it was unimportant and I wasn't interested.

"I'm talking about the new window cleaner," she said with satisfaction. "You know the one I mentioned last night? The Italian stallion that all the women in the village are talking about? Well, he's here, cleaning our windows. Right now."

She grinned excitedly, with the enthusiasm of a loon.

"Is that it?" I asked scornfully. "Mum, I'm really not in the mood for a middle-aged woman's fantasy, okay?"

"Okay, pardon me for breathing. Just thought you'd like to take a look, that's all. Oh, speak of the devil…"

I heard the clattering sound of a ladder placed against my bedroom window.

"Get out, Mum. How embarrassing is that?" I quickly pushed her out of the room and rushed over to the window to draw my curtains. But I was too late. I found myself looking into the face of possibly the most handsome man I'd ever seen. Dark soulful eyes looked in at me, framed by jet-black hair and smooth olive skin, with a muscular arm raised to the window. I couldn't help myself. I stared and he stared right back at me, drinking in every detail. At least that's what it felt like. I felt a horrible sense of unease, compounded by him running his tongue over his upper lip. It wasn't lasciviously done, more unconsciously, as if he'd been faced with a tempting meal. Then he smiled and that was it. I shot out of my bedroom as fast as I could. How cringing was that? There was no way I was going to stand in my room while he gave me the once over, however handsome he was.

I went into the bathroom and pulled down the blind. At least he couldn't see me in here. I sat on the toilet lid and picked up my iPod, putting in the earphones once again and turning up the volume. I was soon lost in the music, the heavy metal drowning out my thoughts and doubts.

All but one small persistent thought that kept getting in the way, until I could ignore it no longer.

Juke had been rattled to hear about the new window cleaner. He didn't trust him and if I knew anything about Juke it was that his judgement was good. Forget about him possibly stealing the crystal. I knew it wasn't him. He had my best interests at heart. And my mother's. Gut instinct told me. It also told me the handsome new window cleaner was bad news. Quite how bad I didn't know, but I couldn't leave it to chance. I had to warn my mother and get him to go. I heard the ladder being placed up against the bathroom window and knew I didn't have long.

Unlocking the door, I raced down the stairs and found my mother drinking coffee and reading the paper in the breakfast room.

"Mum, we have to get rid of that window cleaner," I blurted out.

She frowned at me, puzzled. "What are you talking about? He's doing a great job."

"It's not that. It's something else," I said, unsure how to articulate my fears.

"What do you mean? He's gorgeous. It's not every day you get a window cleaner as handsome as that."

"I don't know," I faltered. "I don't think Juke liked him."

"Jealous!" said my mother. "Typical man!"

She grinned at me. "Look, I'm hardly about to start a relationship with the window cleaner, all right? Why don't you go back upstairs to whatever it was that was so important five minutes ago and let him do his job? And if I want to invite him for coffee afterwards, that's my business. Okay?"

She had that steely tone to her voice and I knew when to back off. I had to think of something else. I walked out of the breakfast room and into the hallway. Next thing I knew, I was opening the front door, stepping outside and walking round the house. I found his ladder propped up against the back of the house and looked up. There he was, working hard, bucket of soapy water in one hand and rag in the other. I thought window cleaners were supposed to have those extendable rods these days, so they didn't have to climb up ladders. He was obviously a traditionalist. As if he could hear my thoughts, he turned suddenly and looked down at me. For a split second, I didn't see him. I saw a vile serpent-headed snake, with a crested head, black glittering eyes and a wide, open mouth full of jagged teeth. It was only for a split second, but the image was so violent and unexpected, I cried out , stepping backwards, trying to get away. As quickly as it had appeared, the image vanished and I was looking once again into those smoky seductive eyes and winning smile.

"Hallo," he called down. "And who are you?"

"Er, Emily," I said blankly.

"Emily! What a beautiful name. Is that your mother inside the house?"

"Yes," I answered unwillingly, terrified by the apparition I'd just seen

"I thought so," he answered, "you have her same beautiful looks. Bellissima!"

I stared up at him in horror. And then I knew. He wasn't a handsome window cleaner at all. He was a hideous monster on a par with the feeders. Perhaps even more dangerous. What's more, he could tell by the look on my face that I knew. And that wasn't good. To make matters worse, I could hear my mother coming round the side of the house.

"Emily, what are you doing?" she asked, a twinkle in her eye. "Couldn't stay away, could you?"

I smiled weakly. How could I tell her that her new bit of eye candy was some weird serpent-demon?

"Barolo," she called up. "Coffee's ready if you'd like to come in."

"Ah, signorina, that would be most welcome."

He smiled at me, his eyes glinting in the sunshine, and started to climb down the ladder. This was all happening too fast and I knew instinctively he mustn't come into our house. I knew from all the horror stories I'd ever read that you never invited a demon over the threshold. Vampire, demon, witch, it was all the same. You were asking for trouble if you invited them in.

I thought quickly. Should I rub the crystal round my neck and summon Theo? He'd know what to do, but I wasn't ready to see him yet. I had to get my story right. Juke would know what to do, but he wasn't here and I didn't have time to call him. This was something I must handle myself.

I darted back round the house and into the hallway, waiting for them to follow me.

"Sorry about my daughter," I could hear my mother saying. "She acts a little strangely at times. Now tell me about yourself. Where are you from? And how did you find your way to Hartswell-on-the Hill?"

"I come from Northern Italy," he answered. "Some'ow I find my way to this beautiful village."

By now, they were outside the front door and I still didn't know what to do. I ran to the cupboard beneath the stairs and climbed inside, hiding alongside the vacuum cleaner, mops and brushes. I left the door open a crack so I could see what was happening.

"Come into the breakfast room," my mother was saying. "There's fresh coffee brewing."

The front door opened and they were walking into the hallway.

"If you don't mind, could you take off your shoes," she asked him. "Come through when you're ready. I'll pour the coffee."

She disappeared into the breakfast room and he stooped to undo his shoes. As soon as her back was turned, he stood up, abandoning all thought of removing his shoes, and smiled horribly in my mother's direction. In my mind's eye, I saw his skin begin to buckle and change, his neck extend and his head grow larger, until he was one huge snake-like body with enormous open jaws and vicious pointed teeth. I stared, not knowing what to do. I couldn't let him get to my mother. In one quick movement I pushed open the cupboard door and charged into the hallway, shouting loudly. At the same time, I was aware of someone coming in through the front door and before I could stop myself, we'd collided.

It was Juke. I don't think I'd ever been so glad to see him in my whole life.

"Juke, thank God," I cried out.

"Whoa, Emily," he cried, stepping backwards. "What's going on?"

"It's him! The window cleaner!" I gasped, turning to point at Barolo.

I stopped, not knowing what to say.

"Is there a problem, Emily?" came his charming voice.

Barolo stood there smiling. I blinked, wondering if I was hallucinating with all the stress I'd been under. I looked at Juke, pleading with my eyes for him to understand. And now my mother walked back into the hallway.

"Juke, great to see you," she beamed. "I was just making a coffee for Barolo. Why don't you join us?"

"No!" I shouted.

My mother looked at me angrily. "Emily, what is the matter with you? Where are your manners?"

I couldn't speak and looked down at the carpet, mortified.

"Actually, you know what? I need to get going," said the window cleaner. "Thanks for the offer of coffee. Perhaps another time? Don't worry about paying. I'll see you again. Ciao."

He walked quickly down the hallway, giving Juke a wide berth, and was out of the front door in an instant. I stared at Juke, willing him to act. We heard the window cleaner picking up his ladder outside.

"Honestly, Emily, I don't know what's got into you," my mother said crossly. "Must be your hormones. If you can't be polite, just go away and give me and Juke some peace. Juke?" She realised she was talking to an empty hallway. "Where is he?"

I ran to the open door and saw Juke standing on the front pathway, looking down the road.

"Where's he gone, Juke?" I whispered, aware of my mother behind me.

"Vanished," he said under his breath. "I've lost him."

Then my mother was coming out of the door and he couldn't say more.

"Are you coming in for a coffee, Juke?" she asked in an annoyed tone.

"Sure," he smiled broadly. "Sounds good."

She led the way back into the house and he followed.

"You know what he is, don't you?" I whispered behind him.

He turned for an instant. "Stay away from him, Emily. He's more dangerous than you know."

Then he was following my mother into the breakfast room and I was left in the empty hallway, staring after him. At least I knew I hadn't been hallucinating and, for the moment, my mother was safe.

Now I focused on the challenge ahead. I knew what I had to do.

The sooner the crystal was restored to the de Lucis family and they were in possession of their full powers the better.

## 11. **Leaving Theo**

Slowly, I walked up the driveway towards Hartswell Hall. I'd texted Theo and told him I needed to see him. Thankfully, it was a Saturday and I didn't need to worry about college. He'd said Seth and Tash had spent the night at the Hall and neither of them was good. It wasn't what I wanted to hear, but it spurred me on.

Theo was waiting for me on the Hall steps when I arrived. He smiled, his face lighting up when he saw me. He was wearing a white linen shirt and faded blue jeans, highlighting his tousled, blond hair and deep blue eyes. I felt my breath catch in my throat. How could I give him up? I'd never loved anyone as much as I loved him. He'd given my life meaning, provided me with a future, made me feel wanted and adored. How would I cope when he wasn't in my life any more? My mouth felt dry and my pulse pounded in my head with the ferocity of a sledgehammer. I didn't know how he was going to react when I told him we were finished.

"Hi Emily," he bounded down the steps towards me. "Am I glad to see you."

He put his arms around me, drawing me close so I could feel his heart beating against his chest. I held on to him, feeling like a traitor. He had no idea I was about to change his life forever, taking him back to a dark place he thought he'd left behind, but which was about to become his new reality.

Strange how you remember the most incidental things at key moments in your life. I was aware of the clear, blue sky, pure and unrelenting as if it had been airbrushed in, contrasting with the Hall's honey-coloured stonework. From above the main entrance, a leering gargoyle peered down at me, its cruel stone mouth pulled back in a snarling grin as if mocking my predicament, and right in my line of vision, a lock of Theo's hair shone white-golden in the bright summer sunshine. I drew back and looked deep into his eyes, determined to commit to memory their blue intensity, interspersed with flecks of green, gold, grey and black. It was like looking into a kaleidoscope, where the pieces kept moving into new and intriguing patterns, beguiling and beautiful.

"Are you okay, Emily?" he asked.

"I love you, Theo," I murmured softly. "Never forget that. I love you with every atom of my being. Now and for always."

"I love you too," he said, puzzled. "Is something wrong?"

I laughed bitterly. "Everything's wrong, Theo. You know that. It's all gone wrong and it can't be mended. Unless...."

"Unless what?" he asked edgily.

"Should we take a walk?" I suggested.

"If you like." Now there was an element of suspicion in his voice. "I thought you'd come to see Seth and Tash."

I shrugged. "What's the point? I know how they are. They're dying. Why would I want to remind myself of that?"

"Not necessarily," he answered. "There's every chance we'll recover the crystal in time. Aquila and Pantera are out looking. Bellynda too. And my mother believes she can feel it nearby. She had a very strong premonition this morning. All is not lost, Emily. We will save your friends."

I looked at him pityingly. "Nice words, Theo. But that's all they are. Words. We both know what the reality is. Come on, let's walk."

He looked at me strangely and we began walking along the gravelled driveway, the crunching stones highlighting the silence that hung between us. I led the way around the side of the Hall, into the formal rear garden edged by the ha-ha, framing the outlying farmlands and fields in a distant tableau.

Theo took my hand and I felt a surge of energy coursing through my veins. It was like being plugged into my very own life support system. And now I was about to turn it off. The thought went through me like a bolt and I felt nausea rising. This was going to be the hardest thing I'd ever done. We walked around the house until the Clock Tower came into view, the place where the crystal was kept. It seemed as good a setting as any for delivering my blow. At least I would be reminded why I was doing this.

I looked up at the golden clock faces on the three sides of the tower, each adorned with exotic renditions of the horoscope, and thought how far we'd come since the day Theo and Joseph gave me a guided tour of the gardens. I'd had no idea then what lay ahead. None of us did. Would I have continued if I'd known? Yes, I think I would. I wouldn't have missed knowing Theo for the world.

But now it must come to an end. I stopped and turned to face him, my heart beating fit to burst. I felt shoddy and underhand.

"Theo, I'm sorry, but I have to end things between us. It's not working."

He frowned, not comprehending my words.

"What are you saying, Emily? We've already agreed. We're going to be together. It's what we both want."

I took a deep breath and exhaled slowly.

"No, It's not. The last few days have made it clear to me. I'm not ready to give up my human life. I don't think I ever will be. I'm sorry."

Theo looked first incredulous, then angry.

"You mean you're just going to walk away from me? After all we've been through? After I've waited centuries to find you again?"

"Theo, I'm not Ahmes. I never was. I never knew you in a past life. That's all in your head. I'm Emily. I live now, in the 21$^{st}$ century, and I'm not ready to become immortal. I'm sorry."

"What's brought this on, Emily? Is it your mother? Is it Juke? Have they pressured you? Is it because of your friends? I don't understand. How come we were so good yesterday and yet today it's all over. It doesn't make sense."

"I've been having doubts for some time," I lied. "I guess I'm just not ready to embrace a life of eternal youth. If it's even on offer any more. With the crystal gone, who knows what will happen?"

"Is that it?" cried Theo. "Is it because you're afraid what's going to happen?"

I looked him square in the face.

"Theo, we're from different worlds. It could never work. We're miles apart and could never truly understand each other. I thought I could do it, but I can't. You're better off without me."

"Let me be the judge of what's good for me," he said harshly. "You can't make that decision for me."

I smiled ruefully. "I can and I will. I'm sorry, I can't do this any more."

"What about your friends?" he said angrily. "Are you going to walk away from them too, just as they need you? This doesn't make sense."

"I haven't got the power to save them. They need the crystal, not me."

Now he tried to be reasonable.

"It's only natural you would have doubts, Emily. I get it. I really do. Why don't you think about it? Talk to Viyesha? Maybe have some time apart?"

I looked into his dear face and it was all I could do not to pull him to me and kiss those tender lips, letting our souls entwine as we'd done so many times before. It felt as if a guillotine blade was falling between us, severing the connection and splitting us in two. I felt his pain with every sinew of my being but I had to be strong. I was doing this to save him. To save my friends. It was the only way the crystal would be returned. I had to be strong. I had one last card up my sleeve.

"Theo, if you truly love me, you'll let me walk away. You won't make me do something I don't want to do."

It was a cheap shot, but it was all I had left.

"You know I love you, Emily. You know I'll do whatever you want. And if this is truly what you want, I can't make you stay. I won't stand in your way."

Now he was trying to call my bluff, but I wasn't falling for it.

I looked at the ground, not wanting to look into his eyes for fear he could see I was lying.

"It is, Theo. I'm sorry."

"Stop saying sorry. You've obviously made up your mind. Just go, if that's what you want. Go, Emily. Enjoy your human life and your human death. You're right. You're not Ahmes. She would never have left me. I've made a huge mistake."

The coldness in his voice sent an icy shiver through me. I looked into his eyes, but they were pools of black, dark and unreadable. I struggled to find words, not knowing what else to say. Whatever I said was a lie.

He turned away and started walking towards the rear garden, retracing our steps around the Hall. I watched him go, willing him to turn around, run back to me, or at least look at me for one last time. But he didn't. He just looked straight ahead and then disappeared out of sight, round the side of the Hall.

I stood alone in the shadow of the Clock Tower, numb with shock.

Somehow I left the Hall. I don't recall, but I suppose I must. The first thing I remembered was walking towards the church through the graveyard. It seemed a fitting place for my frame of mind. I recalled the John Donne poem I'd been studying when I first met Theo, those lines about 'absence, darkness, death, things which are not....' Now it seemed more appropriate than ever.

I found myself at my Granddad's grave and dropped to my knees, bitter tears stinging my eyes.

"Oh, Granddad. I wish you were here. I wish I could ask you what to do. Have I done the right thing? Please tell me I had no choice. "

I looked around blindly, waiting for a sign. Something, anything that would tell me I was right. But the gravestone remained cold and still, the dying flowers in the funeral vase dried out and brown. A deathly hush hung over the graveyard.

"Are you there?" I cried out to the dark bushes at the back of the church, imagining a dark figure lurking. "I've done what you asked. I've left him. Now it's time to keep your side of the bargain. Return the crystal!"

There was no sound. No motion. Just the murmur of a breeze gently stirring the leaves. Slowly I got up, unable to see for the tears filling my eyes, spilling down my cheeks.

"Please tell me I've done the right thing," I whispered in desperation.

But everything was silent.

And I knew deep down, I'd had no choice.

## 12. **Betrayal**

Three dark figures met again in the seclusion of the secret garden, the gate locked safely behind them, keeping out prying eyes. Each wore hooded cloaks. The earlier summer sunshine had disappeared, lost behind a bank of dark cloud that filled the sky, threatening rain. The temperature had dropped and an icy chill filled the air. They huddled in the shadow of the red-brick wall.

"You have the crystal?" asked one of the figures.

"Yes, it's here," said the largest figure, holding up a black leather bag with a drawstring top.

"Is it safe?" asked the other figure. "Can I see?"

"By all means," said the large figure, pulling back the drawstrings and opening up the bag.

The other two peered inside, seeing nothing.

"It's empty."

"It's been taken."

The larger figure laughed. "I told you, it's shrouded in anti-matter. To all intents and purposes, in another dimension. Here, let me show you."

Opening the bag, the figure pulled out what seemed to be a mass of sticky black wool, dense and unyielding, and placed it on the ground. Parting the sticky strands, it revealed a deep, dark hole, into which it plunged a hand. The other two figures leaned in closer, trying to see. The larger figure suddenly made a grabbing motion, quickly pulling out its fist, causing the others to draw back. Dripping with black goo and what appeared to be hundreds of tiny black spiders running over its hand, the figure shook them to the ground, where they disintegrated immediately.

"Dark matter," it said in disgust, wiping away the black substance to reveal a bright, shining blue within. It was the blue crystal. Immediately, a powerful blue light shone out. The air became bright and the temperature warmer. Instinctively, the other two figures extended their hands towards the crystal, drawing in its energy, bathing in its light.

"Okay. That's enough," said the first figure. "We don't want Viyesha sensing where it is. As long as it's in the energy shroud, it's hidden."

Immediately, it plunged the crystal back into the black, sticky ball and placed it within the bag. The mid-day light grew dim and a chill hung in the air.

"The girl has acted," said the figure. "She has done as we bid. I witnessed it in the garden. She has severed all connection with Theo."

"Are we really rid of her?" asked the second figure.

"It would appear so," answered the first, "and even better, Theo said if she left him now, after all they'd been through, she couldn't truly be Ahmes. He said he'd made a mistake believing she was Ahmes reincarnated."

"He denied her?" asked the third figure.

"Yes."

"So the memory of Ahmes is restored?"

"Absolutely. Theo is left grieving for Ahmes, his one true love, and the pretender is banished."

"Then, we have achieved what we set out to do. Ahmes' death has been avenged. And now the crystal must be restored to the family. Their suffering was never part of the plan. We must place it back within the Clock Tower. No one will ever be the wiser for our part in this episode. Just as well Badru was never alerted to the crystal's absence."

"Will you take it to the tower?" the second figure asked of the larger figure, who stood a little apart, holding the black leather pouch by the drawstrings, letting it swing back and forth.

"Not so quickly," came the answer. "There are other issues to address, apart from the family's needs."

"What do you mean?" asked the third figure. "What issues?"

"How we will benefit, depending where we place the crystal."

"I don't follow. We place it back with the family, surely?"

"Not necessarily." The larger figure became more animated. "If we return the crystal to Viyesha, things carry on as before. Nothing changes. We are still beholden to Badru."

"And the alternative…?"

"We swap allegiance. The Fallen Angel is growing in power. He wishes to be restored to his former position. Why not ally ourselves with him, give him the crystal, be part of the new order?"

"Never!"

"What you say is impossible. The Fallen One is corrupt, destroyed by evil, condemned to live in the shadows. We cannot be part of his rise to power. We acted to preserve the memory of Ahmes, not betray Badru and the de Lucis family."

"Is Badru so different to the Fallen One?" asked the larger figure. "He is just as corrupt, tainted by vanity and cruelty, with thoughts only of personal gain. Once, his goodness made him strong. Now, his vices make him weak. I say we side with the stronger power. Swear allegiance to a new master and reap the rewards."

As it spoke, the figure moved away from the shadow of the red-brick wall.

"Badru may be corrupt, but Viyesha is goodness personified," protested the second figure. "Our allegiance has always been to her. We cannot side with the Fallen One and give up all that we have held dear over the centuries. Neither can you, Bellynda. Possession of the crystal has turned your head. Hand it back. We can still salvage the situation."

The two smaller figures closed in on the larger figure. She clutched the bag containing the crystal and ran towards the grassy area where the folly stood.

"Never. I have been promised more riches and power than Viyesha or Badru could ever imagine. The crystal will be returned to its true master, he who first discovered the crystal and lost it under such tragic circumstances. He will rise again to glory. I will see to it."

As her voice grew in volume, her form began to change. Black scales covered her body, vast wings sprouting from her back, and her mouth elongating into a ferocious snout. In seconds, the transformation was complete. Her human form was gone, in its place a huge dragon, rising into the air, breathing a plume of fire over the garden. The two figures ran for cover as the fire scorched the ground where they'd been standing.

"Bellynda! No!" called the second figure. "Come back!"

But it was too late. The dragon had already risen into the air, its massive wingspan carrying it upwards, causing a shadow to fall over the folly below. Turning to deliver a final breath of fire and ensure it wasn't followed, the dragon took off into the sky, its massive wings dipping low, carrying it towards the east.

The two remaining figures looked at each other in desperation.

"We should have foreseen this," said Pantera. "The crystal has proven too strong for her. She has let its power seduce her with thoughts of personal gain."

"Ahmes may be avenged," said Aquila, a scowl renting his swarthy features, "but, thanks to our actions, we now have a greater problem. If the Fallen One gets hold of the crystal, he will be unstoppable and the family will have no chance of survival."

"Think quickly, Aquila, what can we do? We cannot let the crystal fall into his hands."

"I will follow Bellynda. See where she goes," answered Aquila. "Her wings may be powerful, but she flies slowly and I can catch up with her. You must find Viyesha. Tell her what has occurred. Explain we meant no harm to the family, only to protect Ahmes' memory. She must not doubt our loyalty."

As he spoke, his figure began to change, becoming smaller and streamlined, dark feathers covering his body, his hooked nose turning into a curved beak. Huge wings extended from his back and in no time the large, black eagle was soaring into the sky, flying in the direction Bellynda had taken, with no time to lose. Pantera watched him fly after the dragon, rapidly becoming a small black dot, insignificant in the huge expanse of sky. She looked around her.

Dark clouds amassed, shielding the sun and giving the impression of nightfall, turning the warm summer's day into a cold, alien landscape.

As quickly as she could, Pantera left the secret garden and ran back to the Hall, knowing she must confess to Viyesha their part in the theft, all too aware that the consequences of their actions could result in the demise of the de Lucis family and everything they held dear.

## 13. **Confession**

Pantera found Viyesha sitting with Leon in the library.

"Madam, I would speak with you," she cried, opening the door without knocking.

"Pantera, what is it? Do you have news?"

"I do, madam, and it is not good. Bellynda has the crystal. As I speak, she is flying towards the Fallen Angel, taking it to him."

"No," cried Viyesha, jumping up. "That is not possible. He cannot have the crystal."

"What's happened, Pantera?" demanded Leon, stepping forward and looking angrily into her face.

"We meant no harm to the family," said Pantera, her voice dropping to a whisper. "We only wished to rid ourselves of the girl."

"You mean Emily?" demanded Viyesha. "It's no secret that you and Aquila dislike her. But I gave instructions she was not be harmed."

"She wasn't Madam," protested Pantera, hanging her head. "We respected your wishes. We simply wanted her to walk away."

"Let me guess," said Leon, rounding on her accusingly. "You, Aquila and Bellynda took the crystal and told Emily you'd return it, on the condition she split with Theo. You used her friends' sickness and the family's survival as leverage. It's so transparent, I can't believe I didn't see it. Am I right?"

"Yes," admitted Pantera, eyes downcast. "That was our plan. We wished the family no harm." She looked up, a distant look in her dark eyes. "We only wanted Theo to remember Ahmes as she was, not as some ridiculous reincarnation in the form of Emily." She spat out the name, as if offensive to her ears.

"But you were all looking for the crystal," said Viyesha. "You were pretending?"

"Yes," admitted Pantera. "The plan would only work if you didn't suspect."

"Why did I not see this?" Viyesha demanded of herself. "I've been blind to what's been going on." She stood face to face with Pantera, looking at her closely. "Pantera, if we have disrespected the memory of Ahmes and not considered your feelings, I am sorry. But you have acted rashly, without considering the consequences. What you have done is unforgiveable. It threatens our survival and ensures the certain death of Emily's friends."

"Did you not think of Theo?" demanded Leon angrily. "The boy has suffered enough. He's been guilt-ridden for centuries, yet you wanted to perpetuate his heartache simply to assuage your grief."

"He was disrespecting Ahmes' memory," muttered Pantera.

"No," shouted Leon. "He was trying to put right the terrible mistake he made long ago. Now, because you're hell-bent on protecting the memory of a girl who died over two thousand years ago, you've imposed a death sentence on us."

Viyesha put her hand up to stop him. "Leon, I understand your anger. But there's no time for this. If Bellynda is taking the crystal to the Fallen One, we need to act quickly."

"Aquila's following her," said Pantera. "We had no idea until ten minutes ago that Bellynda would deceive us and turn to the dark side. She had spoken of aligning herself with the stronger force, but we didn't for one second think she meant the Fallen Angel."

"Do you know where Bellynda is heading?" asked Viyesha.

"No. Only that she is taking the crystal to our enemy."

"Then we have no choice but to wait for Aquila to make contact," declared Viyesha. "Let us hope he is able to return the crystal. If not, we must be ready to act as soon as we know its location."

"So we sit and wait," said Leon, balling his fists in fury and frustration.

"Not exactly," said Viyesha. "We must re-unite Theo with Emily." A sigh escaped her lips. "My poor boy. What must he be going through? And Emily? Sacrificing her future to restore the crystal. Putting the survival of our family and her friends above herself. If nothing else, Emily has proved her loyalty." She shot a glance at Pantera. "You cannot deny that."

"No," admitted Pantera, her answer barely audible. "I cannot."

"And getting Emily on side has more strategic value than you may realise, Pantera," said Leon forcefully. "If we have Emily, we have Juke. He sees her wellbeing as his responsibility. If we alienate Emily, we are in danger of losing him. As we've seen before, he possesses powers over and above ours. His intervention may be crucial to win back the crystal." He glanced at Viyesha. "To think we doubted him when he was loyal all along."

"He doesn't know we still had our doubts," she answered. "We will not speak of it again." She turned to Pantera. "Does Badru know what has occurred?"

"No," answered Pantera. "Bellynda kept it from him that the crystal was missing. We thought that was because she meant to return it within a few days." She smiled bitterly. "Now we know otherwise. Without the Lunari on her tail, she was free to go the Fallen One. Will you tell him?" Fear etched her features at the thought of his retribution.

"No," answered Viyesha. "There's no knowing what he'll do. For the moment, we'll contain the situation and handle it ourselves. Only if we fail will we bring in Badru."

She walked to the window, looking into the distance, thinking deeply before turning to her housekeeper. "You have some explaining to do, Pantera."

"Me, madam?"

"Yes, you," Viyesha turned, her eyes flashing dangerously and her voice raised a tone. "You have caused this situation and you will help remedy it. You need to find Emily and explain what has happened. We need Emily and Theo back together. Do whatever it takes."

"Make sure you explain the reason for your actions," Leon informed her roughly. "You owe Emily that."

"Very well," answered Pantera tightly, her mouth pursed, her dark eyes slits.

"Leon, you must find Juke," continued Viyesha. "Tell him what has happened and make sure he's ready to fight if we need him."

"Except that he's already dealing with another situation," pointed out Leon.

"And that is?" asked Pantera.

"We have a biscione in the village," he answered.

"The man-eating serpent?" said Pantera, her voice low.

"The same," answered Leon. "Apparently under the guise of a handsome window cleaner who's targeting women. According to Juke, bisciones are more virulent and lethal than feeders can ever be. He says they breed prolifically, which means within days we could have an army on our doorstep more deadly than anything we've seen."

"We believe the Fallen One is preparing another attack," said Viyesha. "Whether that will still happen if he has the crystal, I don't know. But whatever happens, we need to stop the bisciones."

"I'll speak with Juke," said Leon, making for the door, "alert him to the situation and find out how bad the biscione problem has become."

"I shall wait for Aquila to return," said Viyesha. "I'll inform Violet and Joseph what has happened. They need to know." She sighed. "Now, more than ever, they need to be with Seth and Tash."

"Let's pray Aquila brings back the crystal," said Leon from the door. "Or that Bellynda has a change of heart." He eyed Pantera disdainfully. "Well done, Pantera. You and your cronies have turned a bad situation into an impossible one. And all for your own twisted ends. Let me make one thing clear, if we don't get the crystal back, you won't live to regret your betrayal. I'll make sure of it."

With a flurry of blue energy, he departed the room, leaving sparks of blue light flashing momentarily in the space where he'd stood.

## 14. **Chase**

Aquila flew on, oblivious to the cold air and gathering darkness, intent only on finding the dragon. Ahead of him, he could see the faint outline of Bellynda's form. She was powerful, but her size meant she was slower and no match for his swift, aerodynamic form. He soon had her in sight, but kept his distance, holding back in case she should sense his presence. A fight mid-air was the last thing he wanted. His eagle's form may be fast and deadly, but it was no match for a dragon's fire. With one breath, she could incinerate him, leaving nothing more than a pile of burnt feathers falling through the air.

He was better to take his time, follow by stealth and see where she was going. There would be limited opportunity to take the crystal and failure was not an option. He had to succeed. The future of the de Lucis family lay with him and he was aware, more than anything, he had to put right a situation he'd helped to create.

He slowed his pace, keeping the dragon in sight, but holding back. All around him, black clouds amassed and he sensed a storm brewing. He had the strength and stamina to withstand anything the weather threw at him, but he needed to conserve energy for the journey ahead and whatever else might follow. He felt the wind pick up, buffeting and slowing him, and heavy drops of rain began to lash his body.

On he flew, following the dark form ahead, its enormous wings propelling it forward into the storm. The sky grew increasingly black, making vision difficult, testing his eagle eyes to the limit. He strained to see, momentarily losing sight of her. Then a bolt of lightning illuminated the sky, thunder cracking like a thousand starting pistols, and he saw her, dark wings rising and falling. She was heading south but where her destination lay he couldn't imagine. Was the Dark One aware she was coming to him? Did he know she bore the crystal and that his desire was so close to being satisfied? Thoughts of the Fallen Angel brought anger to his mind, fuelling his body with adrenalin, driving him into the storm with fresh determination. More lightning rent the sky, white-hot electricity shooting past him and loud thunder cracks splitting the air. All he could do was keep going, head down, wings outstretched, focused on the dark shape ahead.

The storm seemed to be moving away, the lightning strikes getting fewer and the sky growing lighter, when disaster struck.

A bolt of lightning cracked down from above, passing through his right wing with a searing, sickening pain. He glanced to the side, seeing flames shooting from his wing feathers, turning them into a sizzling firework display. For a second or so, he lost all feeling, seeing the wing fall uselessly beside him, and started to spiral.

Momentarily stunned, he fell, gaining speed as gravity pulled him down, like a stone dropping to earth. Then something deep within kicked in and he forced his wing upwards. He was a great black eagle, a king amongst birds, and no damaged wing would alter his purpose. Glancing to the side, he saw a hole in the wing, surrounded by singed, burnt feathers. This was serious but it wasn't the end.

Summoning every ounce of strength, he forced the wing to remain outstretched, making it move through sheer effort of will. It wasn't as aerodynamic with a hole in the middle and he couldn't fly as fast, but he could keep going, and slowly he began to gain ground.

Up ahead, the dragon flew and he locked his gaze on her, like a heat-seeking missile. The pain was intense and the effort immense, drawing on all his powers, but he had no choice. He had to follow the crystal.

Thankfully, she seemed to be slowing and losing height, and through the clouds he saw a landmass appearing. They'd been flying for a couple of hours and he guessed they were somewhere over southeast France. Below him, the snow-capped peaks of a jagged mountain range came into view, and he assumed they were flying over the Alps into Switzerland. On the dragon flew and Aquila followed, numbing his mind to the searing pain that cut through his right wing, willing himself to keep going. They passed over mile after mile of the snow covered peaks and he guessed they were nearing the Dolomites of northern Italy.

No sooner had the thought passed through his mind, than Bellynda began losing altitude, veering sharply down towards the mountain range below. It was clear she had a landing place in sight and Aquila, too, dropped in height, seeing the majestic mountain peaks rush ever closer. Thankfully, he was able to slow down, releasing the pressure on his damaged wing and he hung back, riding the thermals, glad to rest on the warm currents.

He saw the dragon preparing to land on a bleak mountainside, her chosen spot a narrow ledge high above a steep ravine. Slowly he circled, watching as she came in to land, her enormous wings more a hindrance than help, sending boulders crashing into the crevasse below as she balanced precariously on the snowy ledge. Cautiously, she drew in her wings and he noticed she too had been injured, hit by the lightning strike just like him. Her right wing hung at an awkward angle, a large hole preventing her folding it in towards her body, the flesh ragged and raw, drops of dragon blood falling on to the white snow.

Letting her injured wing hang over the lip of the narrow ledge, she edged slowly and painfully forward until she reached the dark opening of a cave leading into the mountainside and disappeared from view.

Aquila circled towards the narrow ledge, watching for any sign of movement from the cave's entrance. He perched precariously on the overhanging lip, dislodging snow that fell silently down the sheer crevasse to the valley floor below. Folding his injured wing into his body as best he could, he walked along the ledge, following the path the dragon had taken, until he was standing at the cave opening.

Inside, he saw the form of the dragon lying towards the back of the cave, seemingly sleeping. Attached to one of her yellow talons was the black drawstring bag containing the crystal.

He inched forward. All he had to do was creep in, grab the drawstring in his beak and fly away.

Once he had the crystal, he could hole up while his wing recovered and return to the de Lucis family as soon as he was able.

## 15. **Heartache**

I returned home feeling empty and lost. I'd done it. I'd broken up with Theo. My heart might be breaking, but I'd saved my friends. Maybe even now the crystal was being used to restore their health. And Theo, although heartbroken, would know that his family's future was safe. It would be small recompense at the moment, when all he could think of was his emotional loss, but in the long term he'd get over me. And now he had a future to look forward to. Which is more than I had.

I walked into each room, looking for my mother, but the house was empty. I hoped she was with Juke, safe from the clutches of the monstrous window cleaner. But I also hoped Juke was taking care of the problem. If anyone could sort out a demonic man-eating snake, it was him.

Strangely, I seemed hardly bothered. My feelings were numb and a sense of unreality hung over me. Now I'd lost Theo, the world was monochrome and dull, and I didn't care about anything. After everything we'd been through, what was one more evil monster? Nothing could hurt me more than losing Theo.

I thought of his tousled blond hair and blue eyes. I couldn't believe I'd never look into them again, drowning in their depths, seeing centuries of pain and longing turn to happiness and love. Never again would I smell his skin next to mine or feel his arms around me. My future had been ripped away, all my doubts and insecurities over the past few weeks futile and meaningless. It was never meant to be. I would live a normal lifespan, alone and unhappy, then die a normal death, wizened and old, taunted by thoughts of what could have been.

The loss was so all-consuming, I could barely take it in. Shock waves kept coming, each one more ferocious than the last, hitting me with the force of a tsunami.

What made it worse was that he thought I didn't love him. He thought I'd changed my mind, that I couldn't face being with him. If only I'd been able to tell him the truth, make him see what an impossible situation I'd been in. I thought of my attackers, guessing at their identity. But what did it matter? I'd had no choice. I'd been forced into a corner and done what they asked. Now, at least my friends would live.

But they'd live for eternity, I thought bitterly, with their true loves at their side. And that set me off all over again. Missing Theo. Missing his voice. Missing his touch. Missing everything about him.

Then a fresh thought occurred. If I didn't go through the initiation ceremony, Badru would come for me. He'd said he would. Which meant I'd be dead within a few days. Well, bring it on. At least I wouldn't grow old alone. Death was preferable.

I was so caught up in my own misery, sitting in the breakfast room, I didn't hear the front door open and someone walk into the hallway. The first thing I knew about it was someone saying my name.

"Emily...."

I turned, expecting to see my mother. Instead, it was Pantera standing in the doorway, tall and magnificent, her dark eyes glittering.

"Pantera!" I gasped. "What do you want? Is Theo okay? What's happened?"

"Theo is fine," she said slowly, looking at me intensely. "I'm here because I need to speak with you."

"With me?" I repeated stupidly. "What could you possibly have to say?"

"You'd be surprised," she answered icily. "Now, is there somewhere we can go? Some place we won't be interrupted?"

## 16. Biscione Attack

Hearing the crunch of footsteps on the gravel drive, Mrs O'Briain looked up from her desk where she'd been going through the household accounts. She saw a handsome young man, with long dark hair, approaching the vicarage.

"Well, would you look at that," she murmured, looking at the tight T-shirt, well-defined muscles and handsome face. "Now that's not something you see everyday." She noticed he carried a ladder and a bucket of water. "Looks like he's a window cleaner. Thanks be to God. That will save me a job, that's for sure."

The doorbell sounded and she hurried to answer it, stopping momentarily at the hall mirror to look at herself.

"Not too bad," she said, patting her hair. "I could pass for ten years younger."

She opened the front door, admiring the young man's physique all the more now he stood in front of her.

"Good afternoon, signorina," he said in a strong Italian accent. "Barolo di Biscione at your service. I am the new window cleaner. Can I be of assistance?"

His eye seemed to pierce right through her and she shivered involuntarily, feeling almost undressed.

"Well now," she murmured, "our windows could do with cleaning, but I'm only the housekeeper. I can't employ you without the vicar's approval. He likes to know how I spend the money."

She noticed how the young man flinched slightly at the mention of the vicar, but he recovered immediately and smiled charmingly. "And is 'e 'ere?"

"No, he's at the church discussing a wedding. I wouldn't want to disturb him. Perhaps you'd like to come back?"

"I charge very reasonable rates," answered the young man persuasively. "I am 'appy to clean now and come back later for payment. I could even offer you 'alf price if you were to make me a cup of coffee…" He winked at her.

"That's very tempting," admitted Mrs O'Briain, thinking of the accounts book and how she was a little overspent. "Tell you want, you get cracking and I'll put the kettle on."

She bustled back into the house, thinking how her day had suddenly brightened up. The window cleaner watched her go and involuntarily licked his lips. She might be older, but she was succulent and her energy bright. Just how he liked them.

He lost no time in starting on the downstairs windows, dipping his cloth into the soapy water and wiping the glass, all the while examining the contents of the rooms. They revealed very little, other than the usual paraphernalia of middle class life. Mrs O'Briain watched happily as he cleaned the kitchen windows, forgetting about the coffee as she admired the athletic body moving in front of her.

Upstairs revealed little of interest, until he reached what he supposed was the vicar's room. Propping up his ladder against the wall, he climbed quickly, keen to get the cleaning over and the feeding begun. At the sight of a large, ornate, golden cross standing on the windowsill, he recoiled in horror, nearly falling off his ladder. Beads of perspiration clung to his brow and he wiped them away, chastising himself for not being more prepared.

Carefully avoiding the window, he moved on, pleased to see the next room belonged to the housekeeper. A pale pink housecoat hung off a peg on the door, and he noticed eau de cologne on the dressing table alongside a powder puff and a romantic novel. He licked his lips again. This one was going to taste all the more sweet for taking it from beneath the vicar's nose. Taking unsuspecting prey from hallowed territory had to be one of his all-time favourite pastimes.

He finished cleaning and was back at the front door, hovering on the threshold. All he needed now was an invitation. He knocked quietly and was unsurprised when the door opened immediately. She must have been waiting.

"All finished, signorina," he said, running his eyes up and down her matronly body.

"You're certainly efficient, to be sure," she laughed flirtatiously. "Why don't you come in? Coffee's ready and you can have one of my famous home-made biscuits."

Needing no further prompting, he stepped over the threshold and followed Mrs O'Briain's plump form down the hallway towards the kitchen. As she opened the kitchen door, his handsome physique began to meld and morph into serpent form, his olive skin turning black and scaly, his neck stretching upwards and his mouth enlarging, revealing rows of pointed white teeth. It happened so quickly that Mrs O'Briain was completely unaware, blithely offering him a choice of ginger or double chocolate cookies. He arched above her, mouth open wide, ready to consume her, when a noise behind startled him. He turned to see the front door opening and the Reverend James Debonair stepped into the hallway, chatting merrily away.

"I can smell the coffee, Mrs O'Briain. Just what I need before I start on my next sermon. What the...?"

At the sight of the serpent, about to swallow Mrs O'Briain, he stopped, clutching the wooden crucifix that hung around his neck.

"Holy Mother of God," he muttered.

Brandishing the cross, he rushed forward and thrust it at the snake, screaming, "Be gone, infernal creature."

Mrs O'Briain turned just in time to see the serpent's head towering above. Looking up into its gaping mouth, she screamed and made the sign of the cross. At the same time, the vicar drove his crucifix into its neck, smoke and flames appearing where it touched the scaly flesh.

"Exorciamus te, omnia incursion infernalis et secta diabolica," he cried, recalling the words from a recent exorcism and holding the cross firm. The smell of burning flesh filled the hallway.

At the sudden pain in its side, the creature swung its head around, writhing and twisting, screaming horribly. Its razor-sharp teeth brushed past Mrs O'Briain's arm, cutting through her clothing and into her flesh. Bright-red blood seeped through her cardigan, causing the creature to go wild. Once again it rose above her, its jaws snapping and snarling over her head, opening wide and bearing down. But Mrs O'Briain was too quick. Leaping to one side, she grabbed a silver letter opener lying on the hall table. "It's just a surface wound, Father. I'll survive. Hold that cross steady."

While Father James held up the crucifix, arms extended in front of him, she began stabbing at the serpent's neck, making small jabbing movements with the small, pointed letter opener.

"I've encountered one of these before," she shouted. "We need to cut off its head."

"Are you sure? Sounds a bit drastic," he shouted back, trying to avoid the creature's writhing, thrashing head.

"It's the only way," she cried, thrusting the letter opener into its neck. "Take that you vile demon. Tricking me into thinking you're the window cleaner."

Black blood spurted from the wound, spattering the hallway walls. She stabbed wildly, causing more serpent blood to flow and the creature to thrash wildly. Once more, Father James pushed his crucifix into its neck, and the smell of burning flesh filled their nostrils again.

"We're winning, Father. Keep going," ordered Mrs O'Briain.

Panicked and weakening, the biscione backed into the kitchen and they followed it, showing no remorse.

"Get the door, Father," shouted Mrs O'Briain, seeing the kitchen door standing ajar, but it was too late. The creature saw its chance and leapt for the open door. It temporarily morphed back into the form of Barolo di Biscione, a series of ugly gashes round his neck and the shape of a cross burnt into his shirt, revealing burnt, red flesh beneath. Briefly, he looked at them, hissing at the crucifix, his teeth bared and an ugly leer contorting his face. Then the serpent head returned, black blood dripping down its neck, wings growing from its scaly sides. With one quick movement, the creature disappeared through the open door, wings extended, flying up and over the trees in the vicarage grounds.

Father James chased after it, Mrs O'Briain following, but they were too late. They watched as the dark figure rose into the late afternoon sky, flying into the crimson-stained clouds and disappearing into the distance.

"He got away," said Mrs O'Briain, in disappointment.

"At least we're still alive," pointed out Father James, exhaling loudly and looking exhausted. "Must admit I didn't expect that. First feeders, then zombies and now serpents. This parish is full of surprises. Although, you seem to know what you're doing, Mrs O'Briain. How did you know to cut off its head?"

"I've seen one before, many years ago," she admitted, "when I was working as a housekeeper in Italy. Nasty type of demon. They eat you, absorb your soul and spit out the rest. The only way to kill them is to behead them."

Father James shuddered. "At least it's wounded and won't be attacking anybody for a while."

"No," agreed Mrs O'Briain. "We sent the blighter packing."

The sound of the front doorbell sent Mrs O'Briain rushing back into the hallway, Father James close behind.

"Whoever it is, don't let them in," he instructed her, seeing the hallway splashed with the dark, foul-smelling blood. "We need to clear up."

They needn't have worried. It was Juke, hot on the trail of the biscione. He took one look at the blood-stained hallway and Mrs O'Briain's injured arm.

"I take it you've had a visitor, Reverend," he exclaimed, examining the blood with his finger.

"You should have seen it," exclaimed Father James, "the most vile serpent with an enormous mouth. It nearly ate Mrs O'Briain. But we fought it off."

"You've had a lucky escape," Juke informed her. "Most people don't."

Mrs O'Briain raised her eyebrows. "I'm not most people," she said in her soft Irish brogue. "Demons don't scare me." She examined her arm, seeing where the serpent teeth had penetrated her flesh.

"Looks nasty," said Juke. "That needs treating."

"It's just a graze," she answered dismissively. "Nothing a little holy water won't sort out."

Father James surveyed the bloodbath in his hallway and couldn't help but feel a sense of triumph.

"He won't be back," he announced to Juke. "We took him by surprise."

"It's not him I'm worried about," said Juke. "It's how many other bisciones he's created that concerns me. The new bloods are the worst. They have an insatiable hunger. And every time they feed, they create more. We don't know how many other houses he's visited."

It was a thought that didn't bring them any cheer.

\* \* \*

Baby Barrowsmith was having more luck than her creator. That morning, she'd hosted a coffee morning for the Young Wives Circle and it had yielded rich pickings. As they'd sat in her lounge, enjoying coffee, biscuits and the latest gossip, she'd managed to isolate each one with some excuse.

"Oh, Mrs Davenport, could you give me a hand with the coffee, please?"

"Let me show you where the upstairs bathroom is, Mrs Higson. There's a problem with the downstairs cloakroom."

"I've a beautiful cardigan that would match your outfit, Mrs Grey. It doesn't fit me. Why don't you come upstairs and try it on?"

Each one had been lured to their deaths, turning their backs for an unfortunate second, and looking up too late, into the cavernous serpent mouth that towered above them. Baby Barrowsmith had proved to be an adept hunter, striking fast and deadly, giving her prey no chance to make a sound. Within half an hour, she'd absorbed each of their souls, regurgitating empty shells that looked and sounded just like the originals.

Now she sat in her lounge, satisfied and replete, surrounded by the nest of bisciones she'd created. She looked round the room, beaming. To all intents and purposes, they looked just as before. No one could tell they were new blood bisciones with nothing on their minds other than where to get their first meal. Her creator would be proud. Not that she really cared. Rational thought had been stripped from her. All she wanted to do was sleep then go in search of further food. And if she created more bisciones in the process, it was of no concern to her.

"Ladies," she said, looking around and beaming. "I've really enjoyed getting to know you better this afternoon. Now it's time for you to go."

Six pairs of glassy eyes looked at her.

"You'll feel better when you've had something to eat," she assured them. "May I suggest female. It's much sweeter."

Without replying, each one got up and left the room, walking out of the house without looking back.

## 17. **Near Death**

Viyesha climbed up the main stairway in the Hall deep in thought. With Seth and Tash so ill, she didn't want to burden Violet and Joseph with fresh problems, but they needed to know what had happened.

With a heavy heart she walked along the corridor leading to the bedrooms where Seth and Tash lay gravely ill. Gently, she knocked on the first door.

Joseph answered, pale and tired. "Hi Viyesha, have you come to see Tash?"

"Yes, but I need to speak to you. Violet, too. Can you join me in the library? It won't take long." She glanced at Tash, sleeping peacefully. "How is she?"

"Better, thanks to that energy transference Emily gave her, but I don't how long it will last."

Viyesha found Violet close to tears when she visited Seth's room.

"He's worse, mother. I don't know what to do. He wakes up and tries to be cheerful, then falls asleep again immediately. And he looks so pale and ill."

Viyesha glanced at Seth and was shocked at what she saw. His face had sunk, revealing his cheekbones, giving him an older, gaunt look, and his skin was tinged yellow. She could see his energy field was all but gone.

"Leave him sleeping, Violet, and join me in the library. I need to speak with you and Joseph. It won't take long."

"But mother, I can't leave him."

"As I say, it won't take long, but it's important."

Joseph and Violet sat opposite Viyesha on one of the red, leather Chesterfield sofas in the library. Briefly, she outlined her conversation with Pantera, revealing how the housekeeper, along with Aquila and Bellynda, had taken the crystal as a means of forcing Emily to split with Theo.

"They had the crystal all along!" declared Violet incredulously. "Do they know the panic they've caused? Why would they want to do that?"

"They thought Emily was taking Ahmes' place and wanted her out of the way. Once she'd split from Theo, they planned to return the crystal."

"Ahmes died a long time ago," declared Violet. "Those guys need to move on. I know they don't like Emily, but what about Theo? He's suffered enough."

"They hold him responsible," said Viyesha. "They don't think he deserves to be happy."

"Emily should have refused."

"How could she?" asked Joseph. "What about her friends?"

"So, Emily's split with Theo," said Violet. "How is he, if it's not a stupid question?"

"I don't know," admitted Viyesha. "I haven't seen him."

"But now we have the crystal, we can save Seth and Tash," said Violet hopefully.

"Unfortunately not," said Viyesha. "Events have taken a turn for the worse. Bellynda never intended to return the crystal. She duped Pantera and Aquila. She's swapped allegiance."

"What do you mean?" asked Violet, her face white.

"She's taking the crystal to the Fallen Angel."

"Then Seth and Tash are dead. We can't save them!"

"There's still hope," said Viyesha calmly. "Aquila is following Bellynda. He could return at any moment with the crystal. When he gets back, healing Seth and Tash will be our first priority."

"One black eagle is no match for a dragon, let alone one of the most evil demons in creation," said Joseph. "He may not return."

"We can only hope he intercedes before she reaches the Fallen Angel," said Viyesha. "Aquila is wily and clever. He'll find a way."

"Does Badru know?" asked Violet. "He may be our best hope of getting the crystal back."

"No," said Viyesha sharply. "Badru knows nothing of this. If he knew we'd let the crystal slip out of our grasp, he'd do battle with the Fallen Angel. Once he'd secured the crystal, he'd keep it for himself. He wouldn't trust us. And he'd never return it to us."

"What can we do?" asked Violet.

"Nothing," declared her mother, "except wait for Aquila to return. Pantera knows they were wrong to intercede. I've asked her to tell Emily the truth and how their plan went badly wrong. Hopefully, Emily will soon be reunited with Theo. I only wish I could find him. He must be distraught."

"Where's Leon?" asked Joseph. "What does he think about all this?"

"He's angry, as you can imagine. But we have another pressing problem."

"And that is?" asked Joseph, his face strained with worry.

"Juke thinks we have a biscione in the village," answered Viyesha. "Leon's gone to tell him about the crystal and find out how bad the biscione problem is."

"A biscione!" declared Violet. "Like a supernatural crocodile? I hope Juke kills it before it starts feeding, otherwise we'll be overrun."

"So, we've potentially lost the crystal to our archenemy, we're under attack from bisciones and Theo's gone missing," said Joseph. "Things couldn't be much worse."

"It couldn't get much worse for Seth and Tash…" Violet started to say.

She was prevented from speaking further by the library door opening. They looked up in surprise as Seth walked into the room.

"Hey dudes, what's happening? Did I hear my name mentioned?" He grinned at them, his face deathly pale against his dark hair, half-heartedly flicking back his fringe as it fell over his eyes.

"Seth, you should be in bed," said Violet, going to him.

"Chillax, Vi. I'm okay. Never better. It was getting a bit boring lying in that big old bed. I woke up and you'd gone, so I figured I'd come and find you."

"Sit down, Seth," instructed Viyesha. "How are you feeling?"

He sat alongside her on the red sofa.

"Top banana. A little tired. But nothing is gonna stop me playing rugby next Saturday. It's the game of the season and the guys are counting on me."

Violet glanced worriedly at Joseph.

"Of course you'll be there, Seth," he said smiling. "Just keep resting. Build up your strength."

"Would you like something to drink, Seth?" asked Viyesha, smiling kindly.

"A cold beer would go down well," he answered, sprawling out, his long legs stretched before him. "I've been lying in bed dreaming of a long, cold beer."

He sat upright suddenly, his eyes black and bright.

"Actually, I think I may go back to bed. I don't feel so good."

He stood up and tried to walk but his legs buckled beneath him. Joseph leapt up, catching him as he fell.

"Whoa there, Seth. Come on, mate, let's get you upstairs. Can you walk?"

Seth couldn't answer. He lay unconscious in Joseph's arms.

"Mother, what's happening to him?" cried Violet, feeling his brow.

Seth's skin was cold to the touch and white as parchment. As they watched, a delicate, mosaic like pattern began to appear, spreading like a spider's web across his face and body, first pale grey, then turning to black.

"What is it?" asked Joseph.

"The evil in his system is poisoning him," answered Viyesha. "The small crystal necklaces aren't strong enough to prevent it."

"Is there nothing we can do, mother?" asked Violet in desperation. "There must be something."

"I'm sorry, Violet. Without the big crystal we are powerless."

"If it's happening to Seth, then it must be happening to Tash," said Joseph. "I must go to her."

He lifted Seth, noticing how fast and shallow his breath had become and carried him back up the stairs to the upper room, placing him on the bed.

"Time's running out, Vi," he said quietly. "We have to face the fact they might not make it. Let's pray Aquila gets back with the crystal quickly."

Anxious to get back to Tash, he left Violet holding Seth's hand, tears running down her cheeks. Once in Tash's room, he gazed sadly at her sleeping form, small and vulnerable in the huge bed. She had the same mosaic-like markings covering her body.

Like Seth's, they had already turned black.

## 18. **Pantera's Story**

I led the way into the lounge, feeling Pantera's eyes on my back like two sharp daggers. I couldn't imagine what she wanted to say. This was the woman who detested me, who was surly and unpleasant every time she saw me and looked at me as if she wanted me dead. Now she was seeking me out. It didn't add up and in my current state of mind she was the last person I wanted to see.

I didn't offer her refreshments. Whatever she had to say, I wanted it done quickly and for her to leave as soon as possible. I sat on one of the sofas and she sat opposite on one of the hardback chairs, her back upright and rigid. It was the wrong thing to do. Now, she was in a more elevated position and I felt at a disadvantage, as if she was about to interview me. I shifted uncomfortably, aware of her energy field reaching across to me like a thick, dark, clinging mist.

She regarded me with glittering black eyes, her expression haughty and sneering. I stared back, willing her to speak first.

"So, this is your home?" she asked dismissively, giving a cursory look around the room.

"Yes," I replied, keeping my face expressionless, not wanting to say one word more than necessary.

She looked back at me. "There are things I have to say. You must listen."

"Actually, I don't have to do anything you tell me and I certainly don't have to listen to you." I started to get up from the sofa, but her words cut into me.

"Sit down, you fool. D'you think I would have come here unless I had to. Events at the Hall have taken a turn for the worse and you need to listen."

Something in her tone chilled me and I sat back like an obedient puppy.

"I know you've split with Theo," she began.

"How...?" I started to say.

"It doesn't matter how. I know. I also know why. You've sacrificed yourself to save your friends and the de Lucis family. For that, I commend you."

"Were you my attacker?" I demanded. "Was it you who stole the crystal and made me finish with Theo? Is that how you know?"

"I wasn't your attacker," she answered, "but I was party to it, along with others. And, yes, I admit, we used the crystal as leverage to make you leave Theo."

I stared at her aghast. "But why? I don't understand. I know you dislike me, but to throw away Theo's future doesn't make sense."

She regarded me coolly. "That is one of the things I have to explain."

My mind was reeling. "This had better be good, Pantera. You can't go around playing with people's lives. Your actions have consequences."

She laughed scornfully. "Believe me, I know. To my cost."

"Go on," I demanded.

"For you to understand, we must go back in time. Three thousand years."

"Don't tell me. 1275 BC. The reign of Rameses the Second in Egypt."

I could barely keep the sarcasm out of my voice.

She looked surprised. "Yes. How did you know?"

"A conversation I had with Theo. He told me about his wedding to Ahmes."

"And did he tell you what happened?" demanded Pantera, her face hard.

"Yes," I answered quietly. "I know how she died."

Pantera regarded me for a second, as if weighing up what to say next.

"Did he tell you about the role Aquila and I played?"

Now it was my turn to be surprised.

"You and Aquila?" I asked stupidly. "What do you mean?"

I looked into her eyes and saw torment etched deep within their black depths.

"She was our child," she said simply. "We loved her above all else. She was as beautiful as the morning sun, bright and pure. All that mattered was that Ahmes fulfilled her destiny." Her voice became chilly. "It was snatched from her while she was still a child, with everything before her. Instead of a wedding bed she had a cold tomb. And all because he couldn't wait. He doesn't deserve to be happy. Not after what he did."

"But he didn't mean to," I protested. "He didn't know what would happen."

"And you were there?" she asked scornfully. "You, the pretender. The false one, who claims to be Ahmes reincarnated."

"I never said that. Those were Theo's words."

"Said to assuage his guilt."

"You're wrong. He thought I was Ahmes reincarnated. He said I looked just like her."

"It is true, you have her look. But that makes it all the more painful. To see a living copy of the beautiful child we lost is almost too much to bear."

I frowned. "I don't understand how she was your child. She was fair and blue eyed."

A far away look came in Pantera's eyes.

"She wasn't my natural child. She was the child of a slave woman who was murdered. Her name was Nubiti, meaning golden lady, a fair-skinned woman of great beauty, with blue eyes and golden hair. She'd been abducted from a land far north by an Arab trader and sold to a wealthy Egyptian couple. They didn't know she was pregnant. Nubiti managed to hide her condition until the baby was born, on the night of a full moon. She named her daughter Ahmes, child of the moon, and took her to the temple at El-Amarna to keep her safe."

As much as I didn't want to hear anything about Ahmes, I was transfixed.

"What happened?" I asked.

"The old story," said Pantera contemptuously. "Nubiti was beautiful and it wasn't long before the rich Egyptian husband made advances to her. She never reciprocated. But his wife found out and, in her eyes, Nubiti was guilty. She accused her of sorcery, of bewitching her husband with her strange pale skin and shining blond hair. One night, Nubiti disappeared, her body never recovered. Some said she'd been fed to the crocodiles of the Nile. I don't know."

"And what of the child?" I asked. "How did she come into your care?"

"I was a handmaiden in the temple. Aquila was a priest. The new ruler Akhenaten had forced us to worship Aten, the Solar Globe, but secretly we remained true to Amun-Ra, God of Eternal Life. Nubiti begged me to take care of her child if anything should happen. She knew her time was running out, but she wanted her daughter to live. She made me swear on Amun-Ra's name that I would not reveal the whereabouts of Ahmes to the Egyptian wife. Aquila and I left the temple and went into hiding, taking Ahmes with us. It was the only way we could protect her. I had given my word. We had no choice."

"Were you and Aquila a couple?"

Pantera looked at me with disdain. "A handmaiden and a priest? That would have been unthinkable. But he wanted to help. And he knew I couldn't do it without him. And so we hid in a cave in the mountains."

"Like Viyesha?"

"Yes. Viyesha had been High Priestess in the temple. But she worshipped Amun-Ra and was forced to flee when Akhenaten introduced his new cult."

"She vowed to protect the blue crystal of Amun-Ra," I interrupted.

Pantera looked at me askance. "I see you know our history."

"Theo told me," I admitted. "Go on."

"As followers of Amun-Ra, we were in regular contact with Viyesha and Leon, who'd joined her by then. We knew the crystal was powerful, but it wasn't until the Blue Moon of 1332 that Viyesha discovered it's true power. By then Akhenaten was dead and a new ruler, Tutankhamun, the boy king, had come to power. He reinstated the religion of Amun-Ra and it was safe for us to return. Ahmes became a handmaiden in the temple. She stayed there until she was seventeen, when she left to marry Theo."

This was uneasy ground for me and I changed the subject.

"How about you and Aquila?" I asked. "How did you become shape-shifters?"

"When we were guarding Ahmes in the desert, we needed our wits about us. Aquila developed razor-sharp vision, able to detect movement in the desert many miles away. Time and again his exceptional sight saved us from being discovered. With my long limbs, I developed speed, many times getting Ahmes away from our enemies as they looked for us. Our loyalty to Viyesha and the crystal was unswerving and we came to Badru's attention. He wanted to give Viyesha more protection and, using the power of the crystal, he gave us the ability to change shape into a powerful black eagle and a black panther. We became guardians of the crystal."

She sighed deeply before continuing.

"Shortly after Ahmes died, Tutankhamun died and the family was forced to flee. Viyesha led them into the mountains and we went with them, their protectors and their guardians."

I had to ask. "About Ahmes..." I began.

Pantera's eyes filled with tears.

"She was so young, her life just beginning. To have happiness within her grasp and to have it so cruelly ripped away broke our hearts. We cared for her as if she was our own and I can never forgive Theo. Or you for taking her place."

This was too much. I had to defend myself.

"Pantera, no one could blame Theo more than himself. He's carried the guilt of her death for three thousand years. Surely he's paid the price? And when it comes to me, you're forgetting one thing. I never said I was the reincarnation of Ahmes. That came from Theo. I may have a passing resemblance but that's not my fault."

"That's all very well," declared Pantera, "but you cannot deny you've placed the crystal in danger. Since you arrived, the crystal has been under constant threat."

"And I've done what I can to make things better. I've even sacrificed my future with Theo to bring back the crystal. I've put the lives of my friends and the future of the family above my own needs."

As I spoke, realisation hit me.

"Why are you here, Pantera? I've given you what you wanted. I'm out of the family. You can return the crystal. What's the point in giving me a history lesson? It means nothing to me now."

"We don't have the crystal," Pantera said bluntly. "It was Bellynda who attacked you. Aquila and I only ever intended to frighten you. We had no intention of threatening the lives of the family. Or your friends."

"What's happened? Where is the crystal?" I demanded.

"Bellynda has taken it. She's formed an alliance with the Fallen Angel on the promise of wealth and power. She's taking the crystal to him."

"She can't," I gasped. "He'll use it to achieve human form. That's what he wants more than anything. I met him. He told me. He's a twisted, evil being, eaten up with hate and the desire for revenge. He'll destroy Viyesha and the family."

"You don't need to tell me," said Pantera. "The situation is critical."

"So, what's happening?"

"Aquila is flying after her," said Pantera. "He'll bring the crystal back."

"An eagle against a dragon? I don't hold out much hope for him."

"Aquila is clever and quite capable of out-thinking Bellynda," said Pantera curtly. "She's a dragon, all brawn and no brain, hardly the brightest of creatures."

"She can't be," I retorted. "Or why else would she be chasing after the Fallen Angel and his empty promises?" I looked Pantera squarely in the face. "I still don't understand. Why are you here? What can I do?"

She paused and I realised her words were coming with difficulty.

"Reunite with Theo. Explain why you ended things, how you were pressured into it, that it wasn't your choice." She swallowed and looked down. "Things could get ugly. We need everyone we can on our side. We especially need Juke. He's a powerful adversary and he wants to protect you. He'll fight for us if he knows you're with the family."

"So, suddenly I'm useful," I started to say, but Pantera interrupted.

"Save your words, Emily. I didn't have to tell you my story. I wanted you to understand why we acted as we did. Aquila and I are grieving parents, can't you see? We didn't want you to take our daughter's place. But now, we have no choice. We have to move on. So the question is, are you with us?"

I looked at her without smiling, disliking her now as much as ever, even having heard her story. But inside, my heart was bursting with joy. I would see Theo again. We could be together. I had a future.

"Yes, I'm with you," I answered. "I'll make up with Theo. With Juke's help, we'll get the crystal back. Or fight to the death trying."

Pantera arose. "Let's hope it doesn't come to that. For the record, Emily, it was never personal. You were in the wrong place at the wrong time. Now I must go. You know what to do."

Then she was gone, leaving the house in a mass of swirling energy.

I couldn't help it. Despite the gravity of the situation, I sat there smiling. As far as I was concerned, I'd been in the right place at the right time. It all depended on your perspective. And soon I'd be back with Theo.

I thought of Pantera, realising the effort she'd made in coming here to tell her story. At last I understood. But I couldn't share her sadness. I couldn't grieve for a girl I'd never known, no matter how sad the circumstances.

I thought of Aquila chasing after Bellynda and my smile faded. If he didn't bring back the crystal, none of this meant anything. My friends would die and Theo and I would have limited time.

I thought of Theo and how much he would be hurting. I had to find him and put things right.

The situation was more desperate than ever. But at least I would have Theo by my side.

## 19. **In The Ravine**

Aquila approached the dragon's supine form with caution, picking his way over boulders that lay strewn across the cave's floor, the results of a previous landfall. Unable to fold his injured wing into his body, he dragged it alongside, cumbersome and bulky, making progress slow and painful.

He saw the black bag containing the crystal attached to the dragon's talons and moved forward, calculating how best to extract it. The dragon appeared to be sleeping, worn out from the long journey and the injury she'd sustained. Like Aquila, she'd been hit by the lightning strike on her right side, the bolt of electricity scoring a blackened hole in the wing, which now lay at an awkward angle.

Aquila hopped forward, trying to make his body space as small as possible. The dragon's eyes were closed and her breathing came in shallow gulps. Whether this cave was her final destination or simply a stopping place along the way, Aquila had no idea. He glanced around nervously, looking for the Fallen Angel, perhaps waiting in the wings to receive the precious gift. But the cave remained dark and silent, the black shadows thick and impenetrable.

Now he was just half a metre from the dragon's head, feeling her warm breath caress his feathers as she exhaled, but this was dangerous territory. One breath of fire from her mouth would incinerate him totally. The drawstring bag was temptingly close, its black cord handles wrapped around her huge yellow talons.

Suddenly, she moved, raising her head and shifting her weight, stretching out her injured wing. He stepped back in panic, flattening himself against the cave wall, trying to make himself invisible. Nervously he watched, seeing her eyelids flicker then settle. She was still sleeping.

System on high alert, he approached again. Her sudden movement had benefited him, because now the bag lay within reach and one of the drawstrings had come loose from her talons. If he could just slip the remaining drawstring over the curved talon, the bag would be free.

He crept forward, hardly daring to breathe, unable to act with his usual speed and precision, cursing his injured wing for making him cumbersome and clumsy.

Then his beak was touching the bag and he carefully lifted the black drawstring over the curled yellow talon, sensing the proximity of the crystal. Glancing upwards to check she was still sleeping, he was horrified to see a large yellow eye open wide, watching his every move. Quick as a flash, he pulled the bag free and attempted to fly into the cave roof, where the jagged rocky outcrops would give him cover. But the dragon was too fast.

A ball of fire shot from her mouth, engulfing him in flames, and she rose up, clutching for the bag, a howl coming from deep within. Aquila felt the flames surround his body, white hot and burning. Determined to hold on to his precious cargo, he soared to the cave roof and aimed for the opening, his body lit with flames, a living torch bright against the black, ancient rock.

The dragon followed, more flames shooting from her mouth, smoke billowing from her widened nostrils. Her fire breath narrowly missed Aquila's fleeing form and he flew out of the cave, each wing movement fanning the flames that consumed him.

Unable to extend her wings within the confines of the cave, Bellynda was at a disadvantage. Howling in frustration, she struggled over the boulders to the opening, pulling her injured wing along, impervious to the ripping pain that shot through her body. Once on the ledge, she extended her wings to their full width and took off, seeing the eagle some distance below, a fast moving fireball.

Aquila tried to gain height but it was impossible. His feathers were burning and his flesh was on fire, making it impossible to stay airborne. His only chance of survival was to land in the snow, dowse the flames and take cover. But on either side, the sheer rock faces of the narrow ravine rose high into the clouds, dropping down to the valley floor, thousands of metres below. There was nowhere to land, no snowy outcrop or hidden crevasse. And now the situation was made worse by the shadow of the dragon flying above, her outstretched wings cutting out the light, creating a twilight world beneath.

Bellynda moved carefully to avoid knocking her wings against the ravine sides, but she had her quarry firmly in sight. She hovered above, watching him burn, waiting for him to drop the bag. But she hadn't allowed for the eagle's resourcefulness.

Aquila had no intention of allowing the crystal to fall from his grip. Calculating that speed and agility were in his favour, he aimed for the bottom of the ravine, flying between the sheer rock faces as fast as he could, knowing the snow below offered his only chance of survival. He knew the dragon couldn't match him for speed and her size might even prevent her from landing on the valley floor.

Beak forward, wings back and head down, he dived, aiming for the ground far below, hoping the snow would break his fall. Behind him the dragon followed, watching the diminishing fireball hurtle towards extinction, anticipating the moment she could retrieve the bag from his mutilated body and carry it to her new master.

Aquila was lucky. There had been fresh snowfall and a huge snowdrift had accumulated at the bottom of the ravine, creating a deep, soft blanket into which he plunged. The cold snow extinguished his flames immediately, taking the sting out of his burning feathers and flesh. For a short while he lay, unable to move or think coherently, luxuriating in the white coldness all around him, thankful to be rid of the heat and flames. But a dark shadow hovered above and he wasn't safe. Unaware of the pain, he clawed his way out of the snowdrift, dragging his singed wings beside him, looking for cover from the approaching dragon.

Bellynda watched him land in the snow. For a while, he disappeared from view and she carried on descending, drawing in her wings to avoid contact with the narrowing ravine sides. Then unbelievably, she saw the raw, burnt eagle claw his way out of the snow and drag himself to the ravine side, seeking cover beneath a low rocky ledge.

Neither of them noticed the black bag hanging suspended by its drawstring cords on a tiny rocky spur to one side of the ravine.

Too late, Aquila realised it was missing, as he lay exhausted and injured on the cold valley floor. Focused on her prey, Bellynda passed it by, too consumed with thoughts of killing her former friend to notice it.

Neither was aware of another dark shape, high up in the cave entrance at the top of the ravine. From his resting place deep within the mountain, the Fallen Angel had awoken, sensing the presence of the crystal. He'd made his way up through the subterranean passages into the cave, a bodiless entity craving human form.

Now he hovered on the ledge, looking down into the ravine, knowing the object of his desire was within reach, but prevented by the ancient laws that had cast him out from going after the crystal. It had to be brought to him.

## 20. **Theo Missing**

I ran all the way to the Hall, my legs heavy and slow, my mind in turmoil. I could hardly believe the story Pantera had just told me or that Bellynda had taken the crystal to the Fallen Angel. Things were looking bad and I should have felt panic or alarm. But instead, I felt euphoric. I could be with Theo. There was no reason for us to part. We could be together. Even if we didn't have long, any time with Theo would be preferable to spending the rest of my life alone.

I had to see him and explain what had happened, how I'd had no choice, how Bellynda had attacked me, and Pantera and Aquila had forced me to act.

The gravelled driveway seemed to pull my feet downwards, slowing my progress like a hideous dream sequence. Time stood still and I could feel my heart beating fit to burst. The thought of Theo's arms around me and his lips on mine was almost unbearable. I'd only seen him a short time ago, but it felt like an age. I couldn't wait to look into his eyes, see his smile, touch his skin. The thought of the pain I'd caused him made me feel sick. I had to tell him how much I loved him, how leaving him had been the most difficult thing I'd ever done.

I'd been through such a rollercoaster of emotions in the last few hours, I felt as high as a kite with nerves stretched taut. Only one person could bring back my equilibrium and every step was taking me closer to him.

At last, I was going up the front steps, opening the great oak front door and walking into the reception area. I looked around eagerly, hoping I might see him, my face flushed with anticipation. But I was to be disappointed.

"Emily," said Viyesha, gliding down the central stairway, looking divine in a blue, flowing gown. "I'm glad you're here. Has Pantera visited you?"

"Yes. She's told me everything. I know what they did. And why. I need to see Theo. To explain it wasn't my decision to finish with him, to tell him everything is all right." I checked myself. "Well, I know things aren't alright, with the crystal missing and everything. But between us, I mean."

I looked at Viyesha with expectant eyes. "I can't bear it that I caused him so much pain. I have to see him."

Viyesha looked troubled.

"I'm sorry, Emily. He's not here. I don't know where he is. I haven't seen him since this morning. He's not answering his phone."

My hand went instinctively to the blue crystal pendant hanging round my neck. I felt the cold, shiny facets beneath my fingertips and shouted his name in my mind. The energy buzzed around my system like a charge of electricity. He must be feeling it. It was my way of contacting him, telling I needed him when we were apart. Now he would know I was trying to contact him.

Viyesha watched me, a frown on her face.

"What do you feel, Emily? Can you contact him?"

I looked at her in panic as the electricity surged then died.

"I'm not feeling anything," I said in a whisper. "It's as if the connection is dead. But that can't be."

"Perhaps he's taken off his crystal," suggested Viyesha.

"Have you checked his room?" I asked.

Now the panic was in Viyesha's eyes. "Follow me," she commanded.

She led the way up the central stairway and on to the galleried landing, taking the corridor that led to the private rooms. Stopping outside one of the doors, she knocked loudly.

"Theo, are you there?"

No answer. Cautiously, she opened the door and looked in. I heard her sharp intake of breath and followed her inside.

The room was in semi-darkness, the curtains half drawn, creating an eerie glow. I saw what had made Viyesha gasp. The room had been trashed, pictures torn from the walls, vases smashed, clothes ripped from the wardrobes. A large bookshelf lay on its side, books tumbling out, torn pages scattered like confetti; a bedside lamp lay shattered and broken where it had been thrown against the wall; and one of the four posts around the bed hung at an angle, as if a giant pair of hands had tried to snap it in two.

"He must have been so angry," said Viyesha, surveying the damage.

"It's my fault," I said in a choked voice. "I drove him to it."

"You acted in our family's best interests, Emily. You're not responsible." She looked around the room. "But for Theo to lose control like this, he must have been out of his mind."

I glanced at the bed with the shattered bedpost and saw something that made my blood run cold. On the crumpled sheets was a photograph of me. It was one Tash had taken last summer. Theo had admired it and I'd given him a copy. Now, it lay torn in two, the ugly tear running straight between my eyes. With a sob, I picked up the pieces, feeling my control disintegrate. I blinked back tears, my head dizzy and faint.

But worse was to come.

Something small glinted on the bed where the torn photo had lain, and Viyesha picked it up, placing it in her open palm. It was Theo's crystal pendant.

"That's why I felt nothing," I said in a whisper, feeling empty and numb. I took it out of her hand and held it in front of me. "What have I done, Viyesha?"

I swallowed, forcing myself to breathe slowly, pushing the panic down.

"He's angry and he needs space," she answered.

"How can you be so calm, Viyesha?" I demanded, my control crumbling.

"I've seen this before," she answered. "After Ames died. He did the same. Disappeared into the desert. We didn't see him for a month. It was his way of coping. He couldn't face seeing anybody."

"But this is different. I'm not dead," I almost shouted. "If I can find him, I can make everything right again."

Viyesha spoke softly and firmly.

"I know that, Emily. But we don't know where he's gone. And the fact he's left the pendant means he doesn't want us to follow him. Our family is in crisis and I can do nothing until Aquila returns."

"No," I cried. "We have to find him. You can't just give up on him."

She fixed me with her cool, steady gaze.

"I'm not giving up on him. He's my son and I can't bear the fact he's suffering. But getting the crystal back takes precedence over everything. Especially where your friends are concerned."

Now I felt guilty. "Are they worse?"

"They're running out of time. Once Aquila has brought the crystal back, we'll look for Theo. I'm sorry." Seeing my expression, she added kindly: "He's strong, Emily. He'll survive. But your friends won't. I have to wait for Aquila."

With a breaking heart, I ran from the room and down the corridor still clutching the torn photo and Theo's crystal. I took the steps two at a time down the central stairway, running into reception and out into gravelled car park, feeling lost, not knowing what to do or where to turn.

I should have stayed and visited my friends, but I wasn't thinking straight. There in the car park stood Martha, my beautiful mini, waiting to be driven home after Joseph had fine-tuned the engine. With a cry, I wrenched open the driver's door, finding the key in the ignition.

I started her up and put my foot on the accelerator, speeding down the driveway and away from the Hall. I had some mistaken idea about searching for Theo, but realised I had no idea where to start. More than anything, I had to get away from the Hall, with its problems, its secrets and its sickness. I drove blindly, turning my phone to maximum volume, blasting Falling in Reverse 'The Drug In Me Is You' from the Fender sound system.

I drove away from the village, out into the country lanes, stopping at the place where Theo and I had lain, holding hands and looking up at the stars. It seemed like an age ago.

We'd thought we had everything to look forward to, our lives ahead of us. Now, nothing was certain and I had no idea where Theo could be. Time and again, I chastised myself for telling him it was over.

If only I hadn't acted so quickly. If only I'd delayed. Bellynda never intended to give back the crystal, so finishing with Theo had achieved nothing. But now he was gone, and the family had more pressing issues to deal with than to look for him.

I put my head forward on the steering wheel and cried until I had no more tears.

My world was falling apart and there was nothing I could about it.

## 21. **Escape**

From his hiding place beneath the ledge, deep at the bottom of the ravine, Aquila peered up. He could see the dragon hovering above, the narrow gap between the rock faces preventing her from getting any closer. He detected another presence further away and felt a shudder run through his injured, battered body. Waves of blackness and despair emanated down the ravine and he had no doubt the Fallen Angel was close by. Things were critical and he was in an impossible situation.

He looked for the black drawstring bag, realising he must have dropped it as he fell. Leaning his head to one side and extending his neck forwards, he glanced upwards. At the sudden movement, a fresh plume of flames issued from the dragon's mouth. He pulled back, but not before his eagle eyes had spotted the bag, dangling perilously from a small rocky spur just a few metres up. It was hidden from the dragon's view, giving him a small advantage, but he didn't see how he could retrieve it. If he moved from his hiding place, the dragon would torch him. And his wings were so burnt, he wasn't sure he could fly. His situation couldn't be worse.

At least the snow helped. The intense cold was taking the burn out of his wings and he moved them slightly, testing the muscles. Amazingly, he could extend his right wing to its full length, although that brought a fresh burst of flames from above and he quickly drew it in. Carefully, he turned and tested his left wing, surprised to find that too still worked. His main problem was lack of feathers and he pulled in his wings tight beside him, considering his options.

Returning to human form would achieve nothing. He would be unable to hide or escape and the dragon would destroy him in seconds. Remaining as an eagle gave him the best chance, but how to get out of the ravine? And how to retrieve the drawstring bag from under the dragon's gaze? For the moment, he had no choice but to wait and recoup his strength.

Overcome with fatigue, he drifted into sleep, unaware that an accelerated healing process had begun thanks to the proximity of the blue crystal. Feathers that were little more than charred stubs started to regenerate, a fresh blood supply entering the shaft, enabling the vanes to grow back, followed by the tiny barbs, each hooking on to one another, creating an aerodynamic surface. First, the small contour feathers grew, restoring his body shape, followed by the strong wing and tail feathers, preparing him for flight. Finally, the plume and down feathers grew, providing insulation and warmth.

As he slept, darkness fell. Still the dragon watched for signs of movement, perched halfway down the ravine on the slimmest of ledges. Finally, she too, slept, overcome with fatigue.

Up above, the dark form of the Fallen Angel waited and watched, aware of the crystal, but unable to act without human form. Until he became part of the physical world, he could operate only in the shadows. For now, he was dependent on the dragon to bring him the crystal, which meant waiting for her to destroy the eagle.

When Aquila awoke, it was still dark. He was immediately aware of the strength returned to his wings and body, of the silky feathers restored to health, giving him the power to escape. He looked up, assessing the situation. The bag still hung from the outcrop, but now the dragon slept, her breath rumbling, smoke puffing gently from her nostrils.

It was now or never. If he waited longer she would awake, and one fire breath would destroy his freshly grown feathers. Silently, he moved from beneath his protective ledge. In order to fly, he needed to take off from an elevated position, which meant climbing the ravine. Only then would he be able to fly into the open sky. But first he needed to retrieve the crystal.

He hopped on to the ledge that had given him protection and inched his way towards the bag, keeping his eyes on the dragon. Reaching the rocky outcrop, he unhooked the drawstrings with his beak, feeling the satisfactory weight of the crystal within. Still the dragon slept and he moved further along the ravine, away from its huge body, holding the precious package in his beak. When he was a good distance away, he stopped. Now it was simply a case of climbing up the rock face until there was enough altitude to fly.

Holding his nerve, he began to climb up the side of the ravine, fastening his talons around tiny outcrops, clinging on to tiny ledges, gaining ground. Things were going well until he misjudged a loose rocky spur. As he grasped it with his talons, the rock crumbled and fell to the ravine floor, the noise echoing around the ravine. It was enough to waken the dragon and with a mighty roar she let out a huge breath of flames. Thankfully, he was far enough away to miss the fiery onslaught, but she was awake and that didn't bode well.

Wings fluttering, he regained his foothold and climbed feverishly, spying a shelf high above that would serve for take off, if only he could make it. The darkness gave him cover and he knew her dragon eyes weren't as keen as his own, but the narrow ravine created a wind tunnel, allowing her fire-breath to travel further, which could prove fatal.

With one eye on the dragon, he aimed for the rocky shelf, seeing with dismay that dawn was breaking above him, silhouetting him against the first flushes of light. Soon there would no cover and it would be a race against time. He clung to the rock, knowing he would drop to his death if he fell back now. In hot pursuit, the dragon followed, exhaling fire-breath up the ravine.

At last, the shelf was above him.

Clinging to its jutting lip, he pulled himself up just as Bellynda's flames hit the underside, missing him by millimetres. Now it was simply a matter of taking off, riding the updraft and flying into the open sky. But that meant momentarily dropping down towards the dragon and potential incineration. Timing was critical. He had to time take-off between fire-breaths.

Again fire hit the underside of the shelf as the dragon moved closer. Aquila waited till the flames had subsided, then took off from the ledge, dropping downwards until his outstretched wings caught the thermals, made stronger by the dragon's hot air. Soon he was flying upwards, the top of the ravine within sight. He extended his wings, revelling in his newfound strength, flying for all he was worth.

Behind him, the dragon gave chase and again he felt the heat of her flames. But he was faster and more agile and soon he was climbing high above the ravine into the open sky, drawstring bag held firmly in his beak, feathers gleaming in the pink light of dawn.

As the dragon passed the upper ledge, a dark shadow attached itself to her back, filling her with demonic strength.

Aquila flew for his life, knowing this was his only chance to save the crystal, unaware the dragon's passenger had made her more deadly than ever.

## 22. **Recruits**

Leon caught up with Juke at the vicarage. Walking in to the hallway, he surveyed the bloodbath.

"Don't worry, Mr de Lucis," Mrs O'Briain informed him. "It's not ours. It came from that serpent creature. I can't believe he hoodwinked me. I thought I had a nose for demons. Must be losing my touch."

"If you fought off a biscione you're not losing your touch," said Leon, eyeing the blood spatter. "That takes bravery and skill."

"He's out of action for the moment, which buys us time," said Juke, "The problem is we don't know how active he's been already." He turned to Father James. "You defended yourselves well and it's given me an idea."

"It has?" said Father James suspiciously.

"If you're willing, you could help us find any other bisciones. If Leon or I look, they'll go to ground and we'll have no idea how many there are. But they won't suspect you and Mrs O'Briain."

"Sounds exciting. What do we do?" asked Mrs O'Briain.

"We know he's targeting women," said Juke. "The fact he's posing as a window cleaner gives him the perfect opportunity to knock on doors and get an invitation inside."

"Like a vampire," said Mrs O'Briain. "Has to be invited in."

"Exactly," said Juke. "And what woman is going to resist a handsome young guy who's just cleaned her windows?"

Mrs O'Briain coughed and looked at the floor in embarrassment, remembering his smouldering looks, rippling muscles and impressive physique.

"Given the majority of his victims are women," continued Juke, "you and Father James could visit the different women's groups across the village in your capacity as church people. See if you can identify any bisciones."

"There are lots of groups!" declared Mrs O'Briain excitedly, embarrassment forgotten. "The Ladies Prayer Circle, Young Wives, Women's Institute, Young Mothers, not to mention the painting, bowls, art appreciation, basket weaving classes and more."

"How do we know if we've got a biscione?" asked Father James.

"That's the difficult bit," admitted Juke. "They'll look like normal women. But they're not. They're empty shells, with the souls sucked out, looking to feed as quickly as they can."

"So how can we tell?"

Juke pointed to the cross hanging round his neck. "As soon as they see that, they'll give themselves away. You need to look for any women behaving strangely when you approach them."

"Genius!" said Mrs O'Briain in delight. "We can do this, Father! Let me go and find my silver crucifix."

She beamed at Juke and ran upstairs to her room.

"When we identify one, what do we do?" asked Father James nervously. "I know you have to cut off a biscione's head to kill it. But I can't start beheading women all over my parish. It wouldn't be right. And what if I got it wrong? The consequences would be unthinkable."

"Relax, Father," said Juke. "I'm not asking you to kill them, just identify them. As soon as you've found one, let me know and I'll take care of it. A biscione has to be in serpent form before it can be killed. There won't be any mistakes."

"And who'll clear up the mess?"

"There won't be any. When a biscione is killed, the victim resumes their human form. Their soul returns and they're saved."

"When you put it like that how can I refuse?" said Father James. "Saving souls is what I do."

Mrs O'Briain returned with a large silver crucifix around her neck.

"I've checked your diary, Father," she said excitedly. "It's the WI annual dinner in the village hall this evening and you're leading the prayers. What better opportunity? We can mix and mingle and flush them out!"

"No heroics, Mrs O'Briain," cautioned Leon. "This is dangerous work. Let Juke do the killing. And keep your crosses on you at all times."

"Don't worry, Mr de Lucis. We'll be careful. There's nothing we like better than a demon hunt, is there Father?"

"Indeed not," said Father James, sounding doubtful.

"Remember, if you identify one, make sure no one's left alone with it," instructed Juke. "We don't want them to breed. But most important, don't let the creature know you're on to it, or it could take off. Text me immediately and I'll be there. Have you got that?"

"Absolutely," said Mrs O'Briain, her eyes shining.

"Get the decanter from my study, Mrs O'Briain," instructed Father James. "Better stock up with holy water just in case."

* * *

As they left the vicarage, Leon brought Juke up to speed with recent events. He explained how the servants had stolen the crystal and tricked Emily into finishing with Theo, how Bellynda had turned to the dark side, taking the crystal to the Fallen Angel, and how Aquila had flown after her, aiming to steal it back again.

"Jeez, so the crystal was with your own servants all the time," declared Juke. "I don't get it. Why would they want to split up Emily and Theo?"

"Let's just say it's a long story," admitted Leon. "I'm hoping by now Emily knows the truth and has reconciled with Theo. Our main concern is that the crystal doesn't fall into the hands of the Fallen One."

"So it all hangs on Aquila?"

"Yes. Viyesha is at the Hall, waiting for him to return."

"An eagle against a dragon?" Juke pulled a face. "Could go either way."

"He has to bring it back," said Leon firmly. "We're depending on him. Emily's friends are in a bad way."

"Looks like they're not the only ones," exclaimed Juke, looking ahead.

By now they were approaching Hartswell Hall and Leon followed Juke's gaze. Instead of the honey-coloured Cotswold stone giving a warm welcome in the late afternoon sunshine and the small panes of glass glinting in the light, the Hall's front façade looked jaded and tired. The stone bricks were gaudy and blackened, and the windows tarnished and grimy. The carefully restored bas-relief ornamentation was chipped and discoloured, and the leering stone gargoyles broken and disfigured. Underfoot, weeds pushed up between the gravel, now flattened and sparse, revealing the ground beneath. Hartswell Hall was reverting to its derelict state, the crystal's absence exacting a terrible price.

Leon stared in horror at the building's crumbling exterior, his mouth open in shock. He ran to the large oak front door, finding it unwilling to open, the huge hinges rusted and stiff. Pushing his way in, he smelt damp and decay. Underfoot, flecks of plaster and paint littered the floor like old confetti from an ancient wedding. "This was not how I left it," he exclaimed, turning to Juke. "I must find Viyesha."

"And I must find Emily's mother," declared Juke. "She's just texted me. She's been invited to a Young Wives make-up demonstration tonight. I can't let that happen. It's too risky."

"Keep in touch, Juke," called Leon from the entrance hall. "Let me know how the biscione hunt goes. I'll text you as soon as Aquila gets back."

"Okay. If you see Emily. Tell her to stay with Theo. That way, we know she's safe. I'll text her."

He left Leon and ran from the Hall, noticing how the grounds had become even more overgrown in the few minutes since they walked up the driveway.

The Hall was degenerating at a rapid pace.

## 23. **Attack In The Air**

Aquila flew hard and fast, aware of the dark shape behind him. Against all odds, she was keeping up with him. He couldn't understand how she was flying so fast. Given her cumbersome shape, her injury and tiredness from the outward journey, she should be falling back. There again, maybe the blue crystal had regenerated the hole in her wing just as he had been healed. But if that was the case, they had the same advantage, and given that he was already faster, it didn't make sense she should match his speed.

Something wasn't right. Every instinct in his body was on high alert, his sixth sense telling him that danger was behind and closing in fast.

With horror, he saw Bellynda's form draw level. He looked down, seeing snow-capped mountains through the thin cloud layer. They were flying over the Alps, which meant there were a couple more hours to go. If Bellynda was already level with him, there was every chance he might not make it.

He glanced to the side and almost froze with fear. Riding the dragon, as if she was some kind of demonic racehorse, was a dark shadow, too vague to have form, but unmistakeable. It was the Fallen Angel, massive and monstrous, a brooding presence emanating hopelessness and despair. Aquila felt the waves of devastation hit him full force. It was like being covered with a dark, suffocating cloak, the negativity hitting so hard, it was all he could do to keep moving. He forced himself to think clearly, aware that his survival depended on keeping his head. If he allowed the Fallen Angel's presence into his thoughts, he would become disorientated and weak, and an easy target. He needed to think like a predator, use strategy and tactics to outwit his attacker, not become prey.

He flew laterally, extending the distance between himself and the dragon and immediately his head cleared. Now he understood Bellynda's flying speed. It was the Fallen Angel's power that propelled her forward, giving her an unnatural advantage. Thinking clearly, like a predator, Aquila considered his options. Overcoming a more powerful opponent was all about knowing your enemy, understanding their strengths and weaknesses, surprising them when they least expected it.

Speed had always been his strength, that and his razor sharp vision. But neither was of use in his current situation. Or were they? He couldn't out-fly Bellynda, but he might be able to outwit her. He glanced over at Bellynda and the evil force on her back, driving her forward. Whatever he did must be done quickly, before the Fallen Angel's dark thoughts infiltrated his mind, rendering him incapable. Speed and dexterity were on his side, giving him the element of surprise. They wouldn't be expecting attack.

He transferred the drawstring bag and its precious content from his beak to his talons, winding the black drawstring cords around to keep it secure. Keeping his distance, he flew upwards, almost vertically, immediately flying back in line with the dragon so she was beneath him.

Then he dived, aiming at one particular area.

As he neared his target, he felt the force of the Fallen Angel, feelings of emptiness and desolation filling his head. On he went, working on instinct. Moving so fast Bellynda had no time to react, he drove his beak into her right eye, feeling the yellow cornea burst on impact. She let out a howl, a huge plume of fire issuing from her mouth and began to spiral downwards. Now Aquila felt the darkness rush into his mind, slowing his body and clogging his thinking. He drew back, weak and disorientated, his wings heavy.

Below him, the dragon fell, the black rider on its back trying to gain control. As the distance between them grew, Aquila's mind cleared and he gained lost ground, flying upwards through the thickening clouds until he was at his earlier flying height. He had no idea how badly he'd wounded Bellynda, but he was certain he'd blinded her right eye and that had to affect her flying performance, giving him a time advantage, if nothing else.

But the Fallen Angel was a hard taskmaster and Aquila hadn't counted on Bellynda's resilience. She flew back up through the clouds, now black and heavy with rain, pursuing him with a vengeance. She may be partially blind, but with the rider on her back guiding every movement, lack of sight wasn't a problem. The Fallen Angel would be her eyes.

Picking up speed, she flew at him, exhaling a massive plume of fire. He felt his tail feathers in flames and dropped down beneath her, avoiding further incineration. Fortunately for him, the heavens opened and torrential rain began to fall, dowsing the fire on his tail. The damage was contained and his basic aerodynamics were unaffected.

Attack was everything and he climbed again, up through the tearing rain, following his earlier tactics, determined to keep up his assault. This time he went for a different tactic, dropping on to the wing that had been previously damaged, raking his talons through the scaly skin. Drops of dragon blood flew as she shook her wing, trying to dislodge him. He held on, sinking his talons in, using his curved beak to peck a hole, feeling the creeping dark energy enclose him like a glove. Bellynda shook her wing violently, and he lost his hold, falling back into the rainy sky, but he'd inflicted the necessary damage and, judging by her howls, a lot of pain.

He flew high, gaining ground, and now she was behind, definitely slower, giving him the advantage he needed to complete the journey. He was aware she followed, but her flying ability was diminished and attack no longer a concern. Now he could concentrate on getting back to the Hall and delivering the blue crystal to its rightful owner.

For Violet and Joseph's sake, he hoped it would be in time for Seth and Tash.

## 24. **Women's Institute**

A powerful rendition of 'Jerusalem' filled the village hall. When it concluded, President Elizabeth Jettison stood up and addressed all assembled.

"Ladies, welcome to the WI's July AGM. I trust everyone is well on this fine summer evening." She patted down her new loose perm, adjusted her collar and smiled at the ladies sitting before her.

"As with previous AGMs, the running order will be as follows. First, we'll hear a report on our activities. Secondly, we'll go through the accounts. And thirdly, we'll elect the committee for a further twelve months. After that, we'll have a small drinks reception, before enjoying a wonderful homemade supper of shepherd's pie and fruit salad. To finish off, Marie Moore will demonstrate how to make Parmesan and Pancetta Puffs, Cocktail Blinis and Salmon Tartlets."

She paused for a moment while she examined her notes: "And I'd like to welcome Father James, who's kindly agreed to say Grace before we eat."

She nodded in the direction of Father James, who nodded back.

"Sounds riveting. This could be a long evening," he murmured under his breath to Mrs O'Briain, sitting beside him.

"But very exciting if we can flush out a biscione," she whispered back, an excited glint in her eye.

For the next forty-five minutes, they grew increasingly bored as the committee went about its business, eventually agreeing all points on the agenda.

"Any one of the them could be a biscione," whispered Mrs O'Briain, scrutinising the ladies as they stood up to speak. "They all look soulless."

"I couldn't agree more," said Father James out of the side of his mouth. "We'll mingle in the drinks reception. Make sure your crucifix is showing. Let's see if anyone has a strange reaction."

After what seemed an age, the President eventually announced it was time for drinks. "Thank you for your patience, ladies. Mrs Moore will serve Pimms at the back. Please help yourselves before we sit for dinner."

"Thank the Lord," muttered Mrs O'Briain. "I was losing the will to live. Now let's flush out one of these creatures."

"Remember, no heroics," cautioned Father James. "If we find one, we call Juke. We can't go round beheading members of the Women's Institute willy-nilly."

"Absolutely not, Father. I totally understand."

They worked the room, chatting to as many of the assembled ladies as possible before meeting by the serving hatch.

"Nothing," said Mrs O'Briain in disappointment. "I thought I'd got one. That Mrs Riverton over there. Her eyes started streaming and her nose running, just as my crucifix swung forward. Turns out it was hay fever."

"I've had no luck, either," said Father James. "Just the usual chit chat. No one's so much as blinked at my crucifix."

Having experienced one biscione that day, they were keen to further their mission, but it seemed they were to be disappointed. Reluctantly, they sat for dinner.

"Let us bow our heads," began Father James, standing up from his seat alongside the President, Mrs Jettison. "Lord, we ask you to bless all here present. We thank you for this opportunity to celebrate our vibrant WI circle and its committed members. We thank you for their many talents, so keenly shared, and time given up for the benefit of others. As we sit down to enjoy this magnificent supper, Lord, for what we are about to receive, make us truly thankful. Amen."

There was a mumbled 'Amen' across the room, then fifty WI ladies picked up their knives and forks, and began to talk and eat with equal enthusiasm.

"Could you pass the salt, please, Father?" asked Mrs Jettison, beaming at him with large, over made-up eyes.

"Certainly," he answered, passing the saltcellar to her. As he did so, his crucifix swung forward, almost catching her hand.

Her reaction was immediate. Flinching, she pulled back her hand, with a sharp intake of breath. Father James looked at her in astonishment. Surely not the President of the WI?

"Are you all right, Mrs Jettison?"

"Fine, Father James. Fine. Why wouldn't I be?" she smiled, glassy-eyed.

He turned to face her, holding his crucifix forward in an apparently absent gesture. Again, she pulled back, her face draining of colour.

"Actually, Father, I'm feeling a little dizzy. I think I may take some air." She turned to her neighbour. "Mrs Benson, could you come with me?"

"Of course, my dear. It's a little hot in here. Let's go outside."

Clutching Mrs Benson's arm, Mrs Jettison left the room. Father James looked at Mrs O'Briain in panic. It had happened so fast, he'd been taken by surprise. And now a biscione was about to devour a victim.

Deep in conversation with the lady on her right, Mrs O'Briain didn't see. There was nothing for it. He had to act. Leaving the dinner table, he followed the ladies out of the hall, finding the corridor deserted. With heart hammering against his ribs, he ran to the door and looked outside. Nothing. And now it was dark, making his job even more difficult. He crept into the night, moving round the building, keeping close to the wooden cladding. Turning the corner to the rear of the village hall, his eyes widened in disbelief as he saw he was too late.

Mrs Jettison was no longer in human form. Instead, a huge serpent head rose up from her body, smooth scales shining in the dim light from the nearby street lamp. Her cavernous mouth was opening around her unfortunate victim, who appeared to have fainted from shock. With teeth bared, Mrs Jettison leant forward and was about to swallow Mrs Benson. Father James froze, rooted to the spot, unable to move. He'd failed in his quest at the very first hurdle. "I'm sorry," he mouthed to the unconscious form of Mrs Benson.

Just as he was crossing himself in silent prayer, a third figure leapt from the shadows brandishing a silver sword, its shiny surface glinting in the streetlight as it arced towards the serpent. With a fast, slicing movement, the figure wielded the sword, chopping clean through its scaly neck. The creature didn't have time to scream. Its hideous head fell from its body, serpent blood gushing like a fountain.

As it hit the ground, a thick, dark mist appeared, spinning round, disappearing into the night air. Where the serpent's body had fallen, lay the crumpled up figure of Mrs Jettison, seemingly dead to the world.

Father James rubbed his eyes and focused on the dark figure that had leapt from the shadows. As it turned towards him, he heard a familiar voice.

"Get back to the depths, you infernal serpent. Never show yourself again."

"Mrs O'Briain?" he asked weakly. "Is it you?"

"It is Father," she answered, carefully wiping the sword on the grassy bank.

"How did you know...?" he began.

"I saw you leave the hall after the two ladies," she answered, "and I figured out what was going on. I slipped out of the emergency exit just over there, so I was ahead of them as they rounded the corner. That gave me the element of surprise."

"And the sword? Where did that come from?"

"It's the ceremonial sword that hangs in the vicarage hallway," she explained. "I know Juke said not to fight, but I thought we'd better be prepared."

"Just as well, Mrs O'Briain," said Father James weakly.

"I hid it in the bushes," she admitted. "I figured if a biscione was going to attack, it would be done out here in the dark."

Father James recovered himself. "I can't condone you for disobeying orders, Mrs O'Briain. But I'm jolly glad you did. Mrs Benson owes her life to you."

They glanced at the unconscious form of Mrs Benson, lying on the grass.

"Looks like she's fainted," said Mrs O'Briain. "We'd better get her some brandy."

"And Mrs Jettison?" asked Father James.

"I don't know," admitted Mrs O'Briain. "I thought she'd recover once the serpent was decapitated. Maybe I did something wrong."

"I don't think there's much we can do for her. She looks pretty dead."

He felt for a pulse but found nothing. "We'll say it's a heart attack."

"Actually, I think you'd better get out of here, Father. Take Mrs Benson with you," said Mrs O'Briain, looking over his shoulder.

Around the corner of the building came two more bisciones, heads rearing, jaws snapping. Mrs O'Briain picked up her ceremonial sword, all thoughts of calling Juke forgotten.

## 25. **Degeneration**

Viyesha surveyed the tattered ballroom. The beautiful blue drapes hung faded and threadbare, the windows grimy and broken, frames blackened and rotten. Plasterwork from the ornate ceiling littered the floor and the once shimmering chandeliers were dusty and dull. The fireplace, usually ablaze with crackling flames, stood empty and cold, and the purple sofas sagged, mildewed and damp.

Leon stood behind her, his face impassive.

"All we have worked for gone in a moment," breathed Viyesha, her voice a faint whisper. "The Hall is dying."

"There is still time," said Leon. "Its life force has been removed and our power diminished, but all is not lost."

"Aquila should have returned by now," she answered. "I fear the worst. Why else would the Hall react, unless the crystal has been lost? And we will be next."

She raised her hand, revealing small wrinkles on her once smooth skin.

"See, Leon. It's started. How long before age and decay claim us? Will we go before our children? Or will they age like us? I cannot bear to ask if they have any signs. And as for their friends, it can only be a matter of hours before we lose them. We should never have allowed them into our lives."

"Aquila will return with the crystal. I am sure of it," answered Leon. "When he does, it will regenerate us and the Hall, and it will heal Seth and Tash. Be patient, my love."

She turned and smiled at him, small lines at the edge of her eyes, wisps of grey flecking her blond hair.

"I hope you're right, my love. I have the silver casket ready just in case. But we always knew one day it would end. Perhaps that day has come. I will hold hope in my heart right to the end, but I am a realist, and I have to concede what is happening. If Aquila does not return soon, it will be too late. The Hall will deteriorate beyond repair and we will crumble to dust. I thought we had until the next blue moon. But without the crystal it seems even that short time is denied us."

Leon put his arms around her and together they stood, a middle-aged couple contemplating their demise, staring sadly at the decaying ballroom. A knock on the door interrupted their thoughts.

"Yes?" called Viyesha, hope coursing through her body that this was the moment Aquila burst into the ballroom holding the crystal, breathing life into the decrepit building.

The doors opened and Pantera stood on the threshold, taking in the scene.

"What is it?" asked Viyesha, fighting disappointment. "Is there any news?"

"Of Aquila, no. I'm afraid not."

"Then what is it? Why do you look so anxious?" Viyesha could barely keep the emotion from her voice.

"You have a visitor," Pantera informed her, glancing at Leon.

"Who is it?"

"It is I, Viyesha," said an imperious voice.

A cloaked figure swept past Pantera into the ballroom, looking around. "Tut tut. Why did you not inform me of developments, Viyesha? Did you think I wouldn't be interested?"

It was Badru, flanked by his henchmen, Atsu and Ata, the twin assassins. The three stood before Viyesha and Leon, each wearing long blue cloaks, small vortexes of energy spinning around them. Each looked the same, long blond hair falling on their shoulders, dark glasses hiding their eyes, fingers adorned with jewelled rings and long, black, pointed fingernails.

"Badru," gasped Viyesha. "This is an unexpected pleasure. You didn't inform us you were coming."

"Just as you didn't inform me the crystal was missing. Or were you hoping to keep that from me?" His voice was icy, slicing the atmosphere like a knife.

"We had hoped the crystal would be returned by now," Leon informed him. "It seems we've been double-crossed by your second in command, the very person you sent to protect the crystal. Bellynda La Drach is behind this, Badru. She has allied herself with your enemy, the Fallen Angel, and taken the crystal to him."

"No," cried Badru, hitting the floor with the wooden staff he held in his hand. Bolts of lightning shot into the air, singeing the walls and furniture where they hit. "It is not possible. Bellynda would not betray me."

"It's true," said Pantera. "She has taken it to the Fallen One. Aquila is trying to rescue it as we speak."

"He must not take possession of the crystal," said Badru through clenched teeth. He gave up that right long ago. The crystal is rightfully mine."

"That's not true, Badru. You are as much a guardian of the crystal as I, and you know it," said Viyesha. "The crystal belongs to Amun-Ra, the Hidden One, God of Eternal Life. Or had you forgotten?"

Badru sneered. "He who remains hidden, who never shows himself? Please, Viyesha," he said contemptuously. "Credit me with a little intelligence. Amun-Ra died with the pharaohs. The only reality is the crystal. The only real power is that bestowed by the crystal."

"You are wrong," said Viyesha, drawing herself up imperiously. "As Amun-Ra's High Priestess, I caution you not to take his name in vain, Badru. You do so at your peril. He will remain hidden at all times, that is his nature, but his vengeance will be swift and deadly."

"Yes, yes, that's all very well," said Badru contemptuously, "and to be honest, rather academic, given the crystal's absence."

"We are hopeful it will be returned soon," Pantera informed him.

Badru turned on her. "It had better be. The Fallen Angel cannot be allowed to assume human form. If he does, heaven help humanity. He will corrupt, beguile, taint and destroy, creating a dark, evil world with himself at the helm. You and your family would cease to exist like that, Viyesha." He snapped his fingers. "Do you really think he would allow light bodies such as yourself to survive?"

Viyesha stared at him, her face pale and drained. "I cannot believe Amun-Ra would allow it," she murmured. But already the seed of doubt was planted in her mind and a shiver ran down her spine.

"So we wait for Aquila to arrive," said Badru imperiously. "And when he does, the crystal comes with me. I can no longer leave it in your possession. You have shown yourselves unable to protect it."

"And Bellynda?" asked Pantera.

"Leave her to me," he whispered, gripping his hands and cracking each of the knuckles in fury. "There can be no mercy for those who betray me."

A noise outside the ballroom attracted his attention. It was the sound of the huge, oak front door being pushed open. Footsteps sounded on the reception floor and the doors to the ballroom were flung open, crashing against the walls.

## 26. **Return To The Hall**

I must have slept from exhaustion, because when I raised my head from the steering wheel, dusk was approaching.

I checked my phone. No text from Theo but that was hardly surprising. One from Juke telling me to stay with Theo. Well, I would if I could, but it wasn't exactly an option at the moment. I sat for a moment, feeling disorientated, trying to regroup, refocus and decide what to do. Looking for Theo wasn't such a good plan. I didn't have the slightest idea where he might be. Neither was running away. It would achieve nothing, except cause further worry to the people I loved, and they'd already had enough to deal with.

Suddenly I felt weak and foolish. I'd put my concerns above the bigger issues faced by the family and my friends. I was sure Theo wouldn't stay away for long. He knew his family was in crisis and would need him. I guessed he was shocked and hurting. The state of his room showed how angry he'd been. Once he'd had time to think, I was sure he'd realise his place was with the family.

The people who really needed me were Seth and Tash. It was my fault they were in this predicament and if there was the slightest chance of Aquila returning with the crystal and healing them, I had to be there. Equally so, if their time was running out, I had to be there, even if it was to say goodbye. At the thought, my throat tightened and I fought to keep back the tears. I couldn't imagine life without Seth and Tash. We'd been friends for so long. They were part of my life. I couldn't contemplate not having them around.

"I need to be at the Hall," I declared, looking at my white face in the driving mirror. I hardly recognised the person who looked back at me. I seemed to have aged in the last couple of days, worry and heartache making my face pinched and drawn.

Then I thought of my mother and the threat posed by the handsome window cleaner. I knew he wasn't as he appeared. True, Juke would take good care of my mother, but what if the window cleaner came back and he wasn't there? Evil forces were at work in the village and my mother had no idea of the danger she was in.

I hit my fist on the steering wheel. What was I doing out here, feeling sorry for myself? Why did I always have to put myself first? Already, I might be too late. My mother may have fallen prey to the monstrous window cleaner, and Seth and Tash could be dead, overcome by the evil coursing through their veins.

I turned on the ignition, reversed onto the road and hit first gear, slamming my foot on the accelerator and shooting forward. I plugged in my phone and the sounds of 'Stolen Dance' by Milky Chance filled the car, the rhythm propelling me forward, calming my nerves.

I don't know what time it was when I arrived back at the Hall. The moon was on the rise, silvery and bright, casting its soft light over the turrets and towers, creating shadows on the honeyed stonework. I parked in front of the Hall and walked up the steps, taking in the altered state of the building. I noticed the dirty stonework, the rotten window frames and cracked panes of glass, the disfigured gargoyles, broken and grotesque.

Heart in mouth, I tried to open the ancient front door, finding it stiff and unyielding, as though the Hall was trying to keep me out. Now I panicked. Things were worse than I realised. The Hall had returned to its former state, derelict and neglected, due to the crystal's absence. Or maybe it had already fallen into the Fallen Angel's hands. Perhaps that was why the Hall now resembled something from a nightmare.

Half of me wanted to turn and run, but I had to see inside. I prepared myself for a stooped, aged family, lined and grey, as decrepit as the Hall, desperately craving the crystal to restore their youth and vitality. Deep down, I'd always known the promise of eternal youth and beauty was too good to be true. Things like that didn't happen. Now, it seemed the dream had come to an end.

With a superhuman push, I opened the front door, hearing the rusty old hinges creak and groan with the effort. Once in the reception area, I looked around. The lights were flickering and dim, casting strange shadows, and the air smelt musty and damp. The central stairway rose ahead, commanding and majestic, but the steps were chipped and stained, the spindles of the curved bannister missing or broken. Long cobwebs hung from the ceiling, draping the pictures and ornaments, creating a scene that time had forgotten.

I looked for any signs of life, but found none, just an empty checking-in desk. Inhaling sharply and forcing myself to look defiant, I crossed the reception area to the closed ballroom doors. Then, heart in mouth, I turned the double handles and threw them open.

The scene before me was just as neglected and broken, but all the more welcome for revealing a youthful Viyesha and Leon, and a sprightly, if glowering, Pantera. Some things hadn't changed and relief flooded my system. But it was short lived when I saw the other occupants.

I found myself facing Badru, flanked by his usual companions.

They all stared as I burst in to the room, and I sensed a feeling of hope and expectation rapidly replaced by disappointment and fear.

"Emily," declared Badru coldly, training un-seeing eyes, hidden by shades, in my direction. "What an unexpected pleasure. To what do we owe the honour?"

There was no mistaking the condescension in his voice.

"Badru," I said, fighting to stay in control. It didn't do to show fear in front of him, whatever the circumstances. "I could say the same to you. What brings you to Hartswell Hall?"

He mock-smiled. "Oh, stop playing, Emily." As usual, he sounded bored and uninterested. "You know full well. Tell me, have you brought the crystal back to us? You seem to have been instrumental in its disappearance. I thought maybe you'd play a part in its reappearance."

"No, I haven't," I admitted. "And it wasn't my fault it went missing. From what I've heard that's down to your sentinel, Bellynda La Drach. Your loyal second-in-command," I couldn't resist adding.

He bristled almost imperceptibly, before recovering and smiling again. "It would seem Bellynda has gone to what she believes is the highest bidder," he said drily, "using you as leverage to gain possession of the crystal. Oh, Emily. Why did you come amongst us? Life was so much simpler when you weren't around. Since you arrived, it's been problems all the way."

He shook his head.

"I should have removed you right at the start, followed my instincts, not had my head turned by your seemingly 'special powers'. But where are they now? What have you achieved? Nothing. Except to drive Theo away and get my crystal stolen."

I ignored him and turned to Viyesha and Leon, standing beyond him.

"Viyesha, what's happening? Why is the Hall falling into disrepair? Where's Aquila? Is Theo back? How are Seth and Tash?"

She held up her hands to calm me. "One thing at a time, Emily. Aquila has not yet returned, which is why the Hall is starting to age. But there is still time and we remain hopeful. Theo has not returned either and, so far, Seth and Tash are still alive, being tended upstairs by Violet and Joseph."

"Thank God for that." I exhaled loudly, relief flooding my system. "So, there's still hope?"

She smiled and I noticed she too was showing signs of ageing. "We're not giving up yet."

"It's a great shame you didn't keep me in the loop, Viyesha," said Badru, turning towards her. "I could have prevented all this happening, protected what was rightfully mine. Instead, you had to do things your way. And look where we are."

"Rightfully yours, Badru?" I questioned. "The Fallen Angel said you stole the crystal from him. That he was the rightful owner."

Now I felt the full impact of his rage. "I forgot, Emily. You met the Fallen One, didn't you? You were in his presence and enjoyed his company."

"I hardly enjoyed it…." I started to say, but Badru held up his hand.

124

"It seems he has filled your head with his lies and you take his side."

"No," I protested, but again, he held up his hand to stop me speaking.

"It seems that while we wait for Aquila to return, a history lesson is in order. I think you need to know the facts…"

His rage was palpable. I could feel it seething beneath the surface and didn't dare say another word.

Choosing his words carefully, he began to speak.

## 27. **Badru's Story**

"In the early days, there were two brothers, both blue-eyed and golden-haired, with long limbs and soft voices. The brothers lived in a garden that gave them everything they needed. It was lush and fertile, with rich, green grass, flowers blossoming all year round in a myriad of colours – red, yellow, pink and purple - and luscious fruit hanging from the trees. The sky was a rich deep blue, the sun shone throughout the day, and all was still and peaceful.

"A lazy river meandered through the garden, providing the sweetest drinking water. A waterfall fell into a shimmering pool, where they washed and swam, diving beneath the surface amidst fishes of all shapes and colours. It was a charmed existence and for many years the brothers were happy, growing into handsome young men, tall and straight, with strong physique and smooth, toned skin.

"As they grew older, the brothers began to tire of each other's company and wished for others. But no one came. They began to grow bored with the garden's perfection, each wanting to experience something beyond.

"The younger brother began to envy his older sibling, imagining he was taller, stronger, better at swimming. He took to watching him secretly, envying all that he did, a dark jealousy growing inside. The older brother had no knowledge of this, but sensed a rift he couldn't understand.

"They took to going off alone, each in a different direction, going farther into the garden, looking for a way out. Whereas once they'd shared their experiences, now they grew apart, protective of their desires. Each took up residence in a different part of the garden.

"One day, the older brother came across a cave, dark and cool, with ferns and moss growing at the entrance. He ventured inside, finding it enticing and mysterious, marvelling at the strange subterranean world into which he'd, stumbled, full of wondrous rock formations. On the far wall of the cave, he noticed a beautiful crystal growing within the rock and determined to free it. For days he toiled, using fragments of rock shaped as chisels, gradually working it free. Once it was in his hand, he carried it outside into the sunlight to take a better look. It was a beautiful blue crystal, with many facets, each shining and sparkling as it caught the light, casting a strange blue light all around. He knew his brother would want to take it, so he kept it hidden deep within the cave, going back every few days to take a look, carrying it outside and holding it up to the light, bathing in its beautiful blue light.

"Over time, he became stronger, taller and more handsome, his hair long and burnished gold, his eyes a sparkling blue and his skin translucent and shining. Wherever he walked, a golden light shone around him, giving him a magical appearance.

"Of course, the younger brother soon noticed and his jealousy began to eat away at him. He determined to find out what was giving his brother such strength and beauty, and secretly followed him to the cave. He watched in wonder as his brother came out with the crystal in his hands, holding it up to the light and bathing in its rays. He saw how his brother glowed with the radiance of youth, his ivory skin smooth and translucent, his shoulders broad and muscular.

"He could bear it no longer and decided to take the crystal. Early one morning, as his brother slept, he crept through the lush green garden to the cave and stole it.

"When the older brother discovered the crystal was missing, he was beside himself with grief that quickly turned to rage when he realised who the thief must be. He searched high and low for his brother and the missing crystal, but they had gone and he realised they had left the garden.

"He determined to follow and left the beautiful garden behind, searching for years across mountain and desert to find his lost brother and the magical crystal. He endured blisteringly hot days, burning and relentless, followed by freezing nights, the chill eating into his bones, and rain so vicious it almost broke his skin. He experienced thirst and hunger, cold and pain, and discovered the other side of paradise.

"On he toiled across swathes of scrubland, climbing sheer rock faces, stumbling through arid valleys, his skin becoming leathery and dark, his face lined and haggard, his body stooped and wizened. He was driven, dreaming only of the crystal and how he would be reborn when it was his again.

"Eventually he came to the far limits of the world, where he found a sparkling city, with glass spires twinkling in the light, shining with the brilliance of a diamond. Ragged and tired, he entered the citadel, wondering at its beauty. But the sights that met his eyes shocked him, for he found it to be a city of decadence and depravity, the occupants degenerate and wild, their beautiful exteriors hiding a nature that was ugly and wanton.

"As he walked through the streets, he heard shouts of 'the king is coming, the king is coming' and hid in the shadows, watching to see who was the ruler of this terrible place. There on a magnificent jewelled stretcher, carried by four gliding serpents and surrounded by beautiful serpent women, lay his brother, now indolent and fat, the blue crystal set in a glittering crown upon his head. It was obvious the power of the crystal had corrupted him. Satiated with pleasure and excess, weakness had taken over and he was hardly recognisable as his once beloved younger brother.

"Rage took hold of the older brother's heart and stepping in front of the depraved spectacle, he struck the ground with his wooden staff, calling out: 'Shame on you, who was once so upright and fair of nature. To have stooped to this level shames everything we once believed in.'

"The younger brother didn't recognise the bearded, bedraggled stranger before him and, taking him for a madman, called for guards to remove him. As he was dragged away, the older brother shouted back: 'You will live to regret the day you stole the crystal, my brother.'

"Hearing his words, the king commanded the guards to stop and bring the man in front of him. 'Is it true you are my brother?' he asked. 'The one who lived in the garden with me for so long?' 'It is I," answered his brother, 'come to take back the crystal that is rightfully mine.'

"Even though the man was wild and unkempt, he recognised him, and a terrible fear filled his heart. He knew the crystal was not rightfully his, but he also knew he could not live without it. If he were to lose the crystal, he would lose all that he had and would be nothing. And so, he pretended not to know his brother, shouting out, 'You lie. You are not my brother. You're an imposter', commanding the guards to take him to the dungeons and put him to death at dawn.

"As they took him away, the older brother struck the ground again with his wooden staff and called upon his god to take revenge. 'In the name of Amun-Ra the Hidden One, Giver of Eternal Life, I curse you. As morning breaks, all this will fall away and you will be left with nothing, not even human form. You will be less than the grains of sand that lie upon the earth, cast out and forever spurned, destined to exist as a shadow for the rest of your days.'

"The younger brother laughed and instructed his people to throw a massive banquet, with as much eating, drinking and debauchery as they could manage. The words of his brother didn't scare him. Over time, he had become complacent, believing himself to be invincible. He should have realised he was dealing with a power beyond his control, and that once Amun-Ra's wrath had been summoned, retribution would be swift and brutal.

"All night the revellers partied, falling eventually into a drunken stupor as dawn approached. Chained up in the dungeon, the older brother heard their music and laughter, looking up through an iron grille high above him for the first rays of the new day.

"As morning broke and the executioner sharpened his axe, a blinding flash of lightning rent the sky and a deafening clap of thunder echoed across the heavens. Immediately, a terrible blackness descended on the city and a fierce wind began to blow through the streets and alleyways. Cracks appeared in the shining towers and the glass began to splinter and break, lethal shards falling to the streets below, skewering and maiming all in their path. There was panic everywhere, people screaming and running as they tried to get away from the force that was destroying their city. But escape was impossible.

"From the mountains in the east, a huge black vortex rose in the sky, spinning towards the broken city. As it struck, it drew everything up into its midst, and the city was razed to the ground. Just as quickly as it had begun, it finished and a deathly calm fell across the land.

"Locked in the underground dungeon, the older brother pulled against his chains and they fell free. He walked out into the place where the glass city had been, and found nothing but a wasteland. Looking around, he saw something gleaming in the morning sunshine and went to investigate. It was the golden crown that his brother had worn, the blue crystal still inset in its mount. Carefully, he removed the crystal, placing it in his pocket for safekeeping, and discarded the crown.

"Of his brother there was no sign, just as he knew. Sadly, he left the empty, ruined place behind, heading once more into the desert, hoping to return to his beloved garden. He'd seen what lay beyond its walls. He'd experienced the other side of paradise and it sickened him. Now, all he craved was peace and sanctuary. And the light of the blue crystal.

"As he left the city's ruined walls, a shadow fell across his pathway and he looked up to see a dark, formless shape hovering before him. The temperature dropped and an icy whisper sounded on the breeze. 'I will return for the crystal. Human form will be mine once more. I will reclaim what was mine and my revenge will be total.'

"A gust of wind blew across the dark form and it disintegrated into dust, falling onto the desert sand. The older brother clutched the crystal in his pocket, feeling its smooth edges with his fingers, and continued on his way."

## 28. **Judgement**

There was silence as Badru stopped talking. His words lay heavy in the air.

I was the first to speak. "So you're the older brother, Badru. The younger brother is the one you call the Fallen Angel?"

He laughed. "It is an interesting story, is it not, Emily?"

I didn't know what to make of it. "You're brothers," I persisted.

Badru's smile faded. "He stopped being my brother the day he stole the crystal from me. He is nothing. A formless abomination that thrives on evil."

"And you?" I asked. "What happened to you? Did you return to the garden?"

Badru fixed me with his sightless stare and I felt a shiver down my spine.

"Oh yes," he said softly. "I returned to the garden and I replaced the crystal in the cave where I had found it. I was honour bound to Amun-Ra to do so. But I was afraid of my dark brother returning and never left the cave from that day forth. Every day and every the night, I watched the crystal, not pausing to sleep, drink or eat, drawing on its power for sustenance."

"Then how come it ended up in the temple under Viyesha's care?" I interrupted.

"There was a price to pay, Emily, for gazing continuously at the crystal."

"Your eyes," I gasped.

"Yes. Before long, my retinas burnt out. The brilliance of the crystal was too much for my weakened human state. And living in the darkness made my skin grow pale. But eyesight is overrated, you know. Thanks to the crystal, I gained in so many other ways. My other senses more than compensated for the loss, and soon I was able to smell, feel, touch and hear with the keenness of a wild animal.

My third eye gave me vision beyond the here and now, and I was able to live on light alone, not needing the baser requirements of ordinary mortals. And I stopped ageing."

He paused, as if enjoying an inner joke. "Of all the benefits bestowed by the crystal, that seems to be the most desirable. What is it, do you think, that fuels this desire for eternal youth? A fear of missing out? Of growing old? It has baffled me over the centuries, this overwhelming desire to stay young. Illness and death are not attractive, it's true. But age brings other benefits. Wisdom, clarity, serenity, inner beauty. Believe me, Emily, in my world the inner workings of the mind are so much more interesting than the superficiality of the external body. But I digress. You asked about Viyesha and the temple. Why don't you complete the tale, Viyesha?"

I looked towards her, noticing that she and Leon were somehow less vibrant, as if their life force was diminishing. I tried to concentrate on what she was saying.

"Badru lived in an underground kingdom," she began, glancing over at him, "but he lived in fear of the crystal being stolen. He decided there was only one place it would be safe from his shadow brother and others who had heard rumours of its powers. He placed the crystal in the inner sanctum of Amun-Ra's temple at Tel el-Amarna, as it was known then, Akhenaten. It was a holy place, sanctified and revered, home to the High Priest and Priestess, forbidden to all others. As High Priestess, it fell upon me to take care of the crystal. It was Badru who placed the crystal in the temple, but it was Amun-Ra who charged me to protect it with my life."

"He was real?" I asked, believing so far he'd been some kind of biblical fairy-tale figure.

"He was and still is real," she said firmly. "Amun-Ra has always been my god and I answer only to him, Giver of Eternal Life."

I'd never spoken to Viyesha about her religious beliefs and realised suddenly how little I knew about this family with whom I'd committed to spend eternity. Is this what Theo believed? Viyesha carried on speaking and I tuned in to her words.

"All was well until the heretic pharaoh, Amenhotep IV, changed his name to Akhenaten and abandoned his beliefs. He insisted we forget our gods and worship only Aten, the solar globe. He declared himself as the link to Aten, and ended the power of the priests. When he constructed a new temple dedicated to Aten, I knew it was time to leave. I escaped to the mountains, taking the crystal. The rest of the story you know, how I discovered the crystal's power and have guarded it since."

"They were trying times," said Badru, "marred by deception and duplicity, not knowing who was a true follower. And then came the death of Ahmes, child of the moon, beloved ward of Pantera."

I nodded silently, not trusting myself to speak. If it wasn't for Ahmes, none of this would have happened and we wouldn't be in this mess. As if reading my mind, Badru spoke.

"And therein, Pantera, lies the root of our current problem. Had you and Aquila not been so desperate to rid yourselves of Emily, thinking she was trying to take Ahmes' place, Bellynda would not have been put in a position of temptation."

"It was her decision to go to the Fallen Angel..." began Pantera.

"Silence!" thundered Badru. "I cannot hold with duplicity in any shape or form, most definitely when it places the crystal in danger. You stole the crystal and you know the price for what you have done, Pantera."

She stood with her head down and I looked on aghast.

"I cannot fault you for your loyalty or bravery over the years. But these last few days have cancelled any debt I owed you or Aquila. There is only one course of action open to me for your treachery. You placed personal grievances above the needs of the de Lucis family and The Lunari and for that must pay with your life."

He glanced at the cloaked figures standing at his side.

"Ata, Atsu, she's all yours."

They looked at Pantera and smiled, and I knew they were enjoying every moment. It was what they existed for. Moving forward, they stood either side of Pantera. She didn't say a word, just carried on looking down. Each put a jewelled hand on her shoulder and I shuddered in revulsion at their long, extended fingernails, tapering to vicious points.

Pantera looked up at Viyesha and in a voice that was barely a whisper, uttered just one word.

"Sorry."

They tightened their grip on her shoulders and suddenly it was more than I could bear.

"No," I shouted. "She doesn't deserve this. She's still loyal to you, Badru."

"Enough of your human emotion, Emily," he snapped. "I'm bored with it. In fact, I became bored with you a long time ago. There is nothing about you that interests me and as soon as they have dealt with Pantera, it's your turn."

I felt the room spin as Pantera began to shake between the two assassins' hands. If only I'd been able to see Theo one last time to tell him I loved him. Now, I'd never get the chance.

I gripped my fists and closed my eyes, not wanting to see Pantera's demise.

Instead, I heard the doors of the ballroom bounce against the walls as they were thrown open with force and a familiar voice spoke.

# PART TWO: FOUND

## 29. **Dark Matter**

I opened my eyes in disbelief. It was Aquila, dour and menacing as ever, holding a black drawstring bag in his hands.

"Let go of her," he said in his harsh, guttural voice. "I have what you want."

Everything stopped. The assassins relaxed their grip on Pantera's shoulders and everyone stared at him.

He was badly injured. His right arm hung uselessly against his body and I could see nasty gashes where his sleeve was cut, the congealing blood staining the material. His face was battered and bruised and a further gash across his forehead dripped blood onto a closing eye. His black jacket was ripped to shreds and he dragged one leg behind him, his foot extended at an awkward angle.

I glanced at Pantera. There was no mistaking the look of relief on her face.

Aquila spoke. "The bag contains the crystal, but it has been a tough journey. I was followed by Bellynda and the Fallen One. He was riding her like a horse. Don't worry, I inflicted as much injury as I sustained. She's in a bad way too. There was a storm over the English Channel. I took refuge on a fishing trawler. Unlike Bellynda." He grinned for the briefest of moments. "Size isn't everything, particularly when you're a stowaway." He paused to catch his breath. "I lost them. She had to keep flying. I don't know where she went. But she'll be here soon, I have no doubt. With her precious master." He spat out the words.

"Give me the bag," instructed Badru, stepping forward. He grabbed the black bag from Aquila, who stumbled, unable to stand. Leon caught him, supporting him while Badru opened the drawstring bag and looked inside.

"It would appear to be empty," he declared, holding the bag upside down and shaking it.

"It's in there," said Aquila, in his rasping voice. "Bellynda shrouded it in dark matter. An extra precaution in case it fell into the wrong hands."

"Clever," said Badru. "I have to hand it to her, she is a formidable opponent. But there again, she had the best teacher. Here, Viyesha, you know how to handle dark matter. You find the crystal." He was about to hand the bag to Viyesha, then thought better of it and handed it to me.

"On second thoughts, I'm constantly hearing about Emily's special powers. Let's see them in action." He handed me the bag.

I held it in my hands, thinking how light it felt. I expected it to be weightier.

"No, Emily," Viyesha warned me. "It's too dangerous. You have to know what you're doing where dark matter is concerned. Once you put your hand inside, it will be in a different dimension and could drag you with it. You could disappear without a trace."

"And wouldn't that be a shame," drawled Badru, "but so entertaining. We need a little diversion after all this angst, don't you think Atsu and Ata?"

They were silent as usual, grinning like Cheshire cats.

"I don't care who does it," declared Aquila brusquely. "Just open it and get the crystal out. I don't know how long we have until the dragon and her rider appear."

Badru smiled horribly and indicated the bag.

"What are you waiting for, Emily? Open the bag and use your special powers to get the crystal out."

"No, Badru. She doesn't know what she's doing," protested Viyesha.

But it was too late. I was already pulling back the opening and looking inside. As Badru had said, it looked empty. Just a black hole with nothing inside. I looked closely and as my eyes grew accustomed to the blackness, I realised it wasn't empty. There appeared to be some kind of black woolly mass inside. Carefully, I reached in and drew it out of the bag. It sat in my palm, like a loose ball of black wool. So far, so good. My hand hadn't disappeared, taking me with it. There was silence in the room as they watched me intently.

"And now the tricky bit," said Badru with enthusiasm. "See if you can find the crystal."

With one hand holding the strange black substance, I parted the top with my other hand. The black stuff fell back easily enough and I was able to look inside. I peered in and it was like looking through a hole into a universe. There were no edges or sides, just a vast empty space as far as I could see. Now I understood the danger. If I plunged my hand inside, there was nothing to grab. Just nothingness. And I didn't know how much pull it would have on me. It might be impossible to get my hand back. And more to the point, where was the crystal? I'd thought I'd see it floating around and be able to grab it. But there was no sign of it.

I hesitated, not knowing what to do.

"Don't use your eyes, Emily," said Viyesha. "They will tell you nothing. Go with your intuition. You have to feel your way to the crystal."

"Shush!" snapped Badru. "There's nothing more satisfying than seeing someone swallowed by dark matter. Don't spoil the fun, Viyesha. Carry on, Emily. Don't keep us waiting. As Aquila's pointed out, time is of the essence."

I closed my eyes and relaxed my shoulders, breathing slowly and disengaging myself from the room. There was just me and the dark matter. Correction. There was just me and the blue crystal. I had to establish a connection to the crystal. If I could do that, it was simply a matter of reaching in and grasping it. I concentrated with all my might on the large blue crystal, feeling its cold, smooth facets with my mind, experiencing the rivulets of blue energy coursing around my fingers, the feeling of well-being it engendered.

As if tuning in to my thinking, the blue crystal pendant around my neck began to vibrate and I felt an energy emanate from it, moving through my body, down my arms and into my fingertips. I was no longer a human being. I was a link in the chain, joining the energy between the small and the large crystals. Once the link was established, all I had to do was follow it with my fingertips until it led me to the large crystal. Feeling the energy flow from my fingertips, I pushed my hand further into the black hole, experiencing the most bizarre sensation, as if my hand had been cut off. There was no pain, just a complete absence of feeling. For a second, I allowed the strange experience into my thoughts, and found the energy link weakening, as if about to break.

I concentrated on strengthening the link between the crystals and there it was again, pulsating and blue. Now I felt the energy engulfing my hand, cold and beautiful, and knew I was near the crystal. I stretched out my fingers tips and there it was. I could feel its smooth, clear sides against the tip of my middle finger. Now I had to bring it closer towards me.

I concentrated like never before, existing only in this strange black world, making the energy link stronger, drawing the crystal towards me. And now my fingers were reaching around it, finding it larger than I remembered. Slowly, I drew my hand back towards the opening, not daring to think about letting go, knowing if I let the thought into my mind, I might lose the crystal and be catapulted forward into this strange black world. Now I was bringing my hand back through the hole and I was sure if I opened my eyes I would see the crystal. But instinctively I knew it was too soon. Black tentacles of anti-matter could still reach forward, wrenching the crystal from my grip and pulling me with it. I held my nerve, drawing the crystal away from the black woolly ball. Then, with a quick movement, I pulled my hand back and I'd done it.

I opened my eyes to find my hand dripping with black goo and crawling with tiny black spiders. Trying not to scream, I shook them to the floor, relieved to see they disappeared instantly. Viyesha wiped away the black substance with a handkerchief and that too, disappeared.

"Remnants of dark matter," she murmured. "They can't exist in this dimension."

I turned my hand over and there in my palm was the blue crystal, spilling light and energy down my arm, making me feel wonderful. For a second, I watched the blue energy travel towards my crystal necklace and was filled with a powerful feeling of warmth and happiness. Then I heard Viyesha's voice in my ear.

"It's okay, Emily. You've done it. Let go now."

I didn't want to, but I knew I must. I put the crystal in her outstretched palm.

"Well done," she said in a soft voice, placing it within the silver casket.

Immediately, the room was colourless and flat, like a black and white photograph. I felt weak and exhausted, as if my life force had been drained. I knew the feeling was only temporary, but it didn't lessen the impact.

"Go with the feeling, Emily," advised Viyesha. "It will soon fade. Focus on your breath."

I did as she told me and in a matter of seconds, the black feeling lifted. I looked in my hands, expecting to see the black woolly mass, but it had gone.

"Well, well," said Badru, begrudgingly. "You surprise me, Emily. I didn't think you had it in you. Perhaps I'm beginning to see what Theo sees in you."

"You'll never understand what Theo and I have," I said, glaring at him.

Badru laughed. "Perhaps not. But there again, I was never one for love's young dream. And speaking of Theo, where is he?"

"Looking after his friends," I lied, not wanting to give Badru any ammunition.

"And not with you?" taunted Badru. "Not by your side when your life was in danger? What kind of true love is that?"

"Leave it, Badru," cautioned Leon, tiring of his games. "We don't have time. We need to secure the crystal and take care of Aquila. He's weak and injured. Bellynda and the Fallen Angel could be here at any moment, possibly with reinforcements. We cannot allow the crystal to fall out of our hands again."

"We need to treat Seth and Tash before we do anything else," said Viyesha. "They need the crystal now."

"Very well," said Badru, waving his hand in dismissal. "Do what you must, but take Atsu and Ata with you to guard the crystal. Get back here as quickly as possible. We need a welcoming committee when my darker half arrives. And bring the crystal with you. I want to see it."

I watched them leave the room, feeling dreamy and vague, Badru's taunts nagging my brain. Where was Theo? Why hadn't he returned to help the family?

Then I was alone with Badru.

## 30. **Labyrinth**

For a second, we stared at each other and I had the distinct impression that for the first time in his long life, Badru didn't know what to say.

I glanced around the ballroom, aware that the Hall seemed to be regenerating now the crystal was back. The cobwebs were gone, the drapes once again a deep, rich blue and the windows beyond, clean and sparkling. The large purple sofas looked plump and inviting, the chandeliers had their sparkle back. In the fireplace, tiny flames leapt up, creating small, flickering shadows. Despite facing Badru, I felt a sense of hope. The crystal was back in its rightful place and my friends would soon be well again. I'd survived another of Badru's masochistic tests and soon, I was sure, I'd be reunited with Theo.

"You still wish to be initiated?" asked Badru, observing me closely.

I didn't like being dissected by his gaze, particularly as I knew he was looking inside rather than at me, which meant there was nowhere to hide.

"Yes," I said firmly. "As soon as the moon is full. And my friends, too. It's the only way they can stay alive after being tainted with such evil."

I was telling him rather than asking. I hoped he recognised that.

"So our ranks are to grow," he replied, his face expressionless. "I understand Violet and Joseph are, how shall I put it, emotionally involved with your friends?"

I stared back at him, unwilling to converse. Badru creeped me out big time. He was cruel and unkind, and seemed to take pleasure in watching others suffer. I didn't understand how he could compare himself favourably to his younger brother. They were as bad as each other. Any goodness or decency had long since gone.

"Yes," I answered, wondering if he had the power to stop Seth and Tash from being initiated. Whom was I kidding? This was Badru. He had the power to do what he liked. Which is exactly why he'd become this way.

"Such a shame your friends will be with their true loves, while you face eternity alone."

Now he had my full attention. "What do you mean? What do you know?"

"I know everything, Emily," he answered mockingly. "I may be blind, but there's nothing I can't see."

"I mean about Theo. Why will I be spending eternity alone?"

He smiled and I felt a chill run across my body.

"Theo thinks you don't love him any more. Poor Theo. He doesn't know you were coerced into finishing with him. He doesn't know you acted for the better good. How commendable, Emily! And how deliciously unfortunate for poor Theo."

"Stop saying that," I cried. "You know where he is, don't you?"

"Well, now," he said, cracking his finger joints, "that would be telling. There again, I can't help but enjoy the irony of the situation."

"What d'you mean?"

"Do I have to spell it out, Emily? You give Theo up to save his family. Once again he loses the love of his life. Only this time, he knows however many thousands of years he waits, you're not coming back. So, he gives up, just as you come back for him. Sweet!"

"No," I said, the colour draining from my face. "Theo wouldn't give up."

"I guess he wasn't thinking straight," answered Badru.

"What's happened to him?"

"Let's just say, he's in one of my games. I call it Labyrinth of Lost Souls."

"And how does it work?"

Badru smiled. "It's one of my favourites. I gather those who've given up and out of their misery I spin a web. I create a labyrinth of pathways and leave it to them to find their way out."

"And if they don't get out?"

"I think the clue lies in the phrases 'web' and 'labyrinth'."

My mind was working overtime trying to keep up with Badru's warped thinking. I knew he created realities and if you believed them, they were just as real and if not more dangerous than everyday reality.

"If Theo knows he has a future with me, your labyrinth won't work, will it?"

"It's possible."

"So let me tell him. You owe Viyesha that much. This is her son."

He appeared to consider my words.

"Very well. For Viyesha's sake, I'll let you into the game." He smiled again. "Although you might be too late."

"Show me the labyrinth," I instructed him. "Let me in."

He raised an eyebrow. "If that's what you want. But I have to warn you, those who enter rarely come out."

As he spoke, the room began to ripple and mist. The light faded and the air became cold. I looked around. I was no longer in the ballroom but in a dark passageway festooned with cobwebs, ancient walls hewn out of the rock rising on either side. I stepped forward and my foot crunched on something beneath. I stooped to look and found the floor littered with bones.

"Theo," I shouted loudly. "Theo, can you hear me?"

All I heard was my own voice echoing down the passageway.

"Where is he, Badru?" I screamed, knowing he was watching. This was his equivalent of a sick computer game to keep him amused.

Cautiously, I walked along the passageway, feeling my way as it grew darker. Placing my right hand forward, I felt a rough corner and realised the pathway was joining another. But which way to go, right or left? Which way led out and which to the centre, with its deadly inhabitant?

"Give me a clue, Badru," I shouted.

Again there was silence, but a thought entered my mind. If this was an alternative reality, maybe I had some control as to what it contained. Closing my eyes and concentrating as hard as I could, I imagined a torch in my hand. When I opened them, there wasn't a torch, but small candles had appeared in alcoves carved within the walls, lighting my way. I was beginning to get the gist of this game.

I took the right hand turning, pulling back just in time as a huge hole in the passageway floor opened up before me. A cold shiver ran down my spine as I gazed down into the inky blackness, wondering how deep it went. If the candles hadn't alerted me to its existence, I'd have fallen to my death.

One thing was clear. I had to stay alert every step of the way. There was no knowing what lay ahead.

I went back and took the left hand turning, pulling back cobwebs to see what lay ahead. The passageway led to another junction, flickering candles creating eerie patterns on the rocky walls. I chose to go right and now a hideous stench assailed my nostrils. It was bitter and nauseating, making it difficult to breathe. I pulled the corner of my jacket over my nose, wondering if Theo had come this way.

"I need proof, Badru," I shouted. "Give me something."

Up above, I noticed something snagged on the ledge of a candle-lit alcove and reached up. It was a lock of curly golden hair. Just feeling its softness brought a lump to my throat, as a myriad of memories flooded my mind. I pushed them away. Sentimentality wouldn't help. I had to maintain a cool head.

I knew Theo had passed this way before me, which gave me hope. I was going in the right direction. On I went, the stench getting stronger and the cobwebs thicker. Now there were fewer candles in the alcoves, making it hard to see and I was feeling my way again.

Just as I thought I was making headway, the passageway ended suddenly. I put out my hands, feeling my surroundings to see if there was a linking passageway, encountering solid rock all around. I'd reached a dead end. For a moment, claustrophobia threatened and I struggled to regain control. I would have to go back.

Taking deep breaths, I turned and had made a few tentative steps when I heard a noise. It was a rumbling sound, somewhere up the passageway, getting louder by the second, which meant it was coming towards me. Now fear took over as I realised there was nowhere to go. I moved quickly, hoping to find an adjoining passageway before I encountered whatever lay ahead. There were more candles now, enabling me to see ahead. The rumbling grew to a roar and then I saw it.

A huge black shape filled the passageway, leaving no room on either side, moving rapidly towards me. I looked around wildly, seeking an alcove or a crack in the rock where I could hide. The shape was getting closer and I could see it was a massive ball, bearing down on me, as if I'd fallen into an over-sized pinball machine. Perhaps this explained why there were so many bones littering the floor.

Well, not me, I decided. In my mind, I punched the rock to my right, sending my energy shooting forward like a sledgehammer. I was pleased to see a small hole appear and punched it again. The hole got larger. Again and again I punched, the rock dissolving with the force of my energy, making a hole about a metre square. Now the ball was upon me, threatening to crush me and with no time to spare, I squeezed into the hole, feeling it skim my shoulder as it hurtled by.

"Nice try, Badru," I shouted, watching it disappear down the passageway.

I wondered whether to continue, not knowing if the ball would hit the dead end and bounce back. I had to risk it. Staying in the hole wouldn't find Theo, and I was pretty certain there was a junction coming soon.

I stepped into the passageway and moved forward, listening for the giveaway sound of the ball coming back or another approaching. For the moment it was silent. The candles lit my way and up ahead I could see a junction. Now I heard another sound, a swishing noise as if something was passing quickly through the air. I had no idea what it might be, but knowing Badru, it wouldn't be pleasant. I had to reach the junction. That would give me a means of escaping whatever lay ahead.

I ran as fast as I could, the swishing getting louder. Then I was at the junction and the noise was filling the air. But which way to go? I looked in one direction and saw something approaching. It seemed to be another ball, moving more slowly, but this time covered in silver blades that swished through the air, retracting when they encountered a hard surface. It was basically a huge cutting machine, designed to make mince meat of anything in its path.

Making a hole in the wall wasn't an option, because the blades would shoot into any space around it, and I ran in the other direction, only to be faced with another cutting ball. I ran back the way I'd come, and now I could hear the rumbling sound of the black ball coming back along the passageway. I was trapped between a crushing ball and two cutting balls, with no chance of escape.

Think, I commanded myself. This was a game of lateral thinking and there had to be a way out. Badru couldn't win.

I couldn't go forwards or backwards, or to the side, which meant the only way was up. I glanced at the roof, seeing it formed an apex over the junction. That was it, my means of escape. But how to get up? I realised the candle-lit alcoves offered hand and footholds, and mentally thanking my rock-climbing teacher at the local leisure centre, I began scaling the rocky sides, clinging on for dear life. The rumbling of the black ball grew deafening and I knew it was right behind, while the swishing of the retractable blades grew louder. Any minute and they would all come together. Frantically, I climbed upwards, aiming for the domed roof space. Just in time, I moved my right leg up as the black ball hurtled into the junction, crashing into the two bladed balls with a huge cracking sound. Metal ground into metal and I felt shock waves hit me as energy from the collision filled the space above. Then all was quiet. I looked down, seeing how the cutting balls had driven into the crushing ball, their blades hanging uselessly, unable to retract, effectively blocking the passageway in all directions.

Now I was angry, knowing that Badru was deliberately using delaying tactics to keep me from Theo when every second counted. I resisted the urge to shout. That was only playing into his hands. This was a game of wits. I had to think myself ahead if I wanted to give Theo a fighting chance.

What I needed was an escape route. A draught of air made me realise there was a gap above and looking up, I could just make out a narrow duct leading upwards like a chimney. It was slightly wider than my body, enabling me to climb it by wedging my feet on either side and pulling myself up with my arms. It was slow going and dark, and soon my shoulder and thigh muscles were screaming with the effort. I persevered, inching my way up, cold gusts of air leading me to believe the duct led somewhere, although the higher I climbed the more the foul odour filled my nostrils. Wherever it led, I was sure more horror awaited.

At the point when my strength was all but gone and I felt I couldn't go on, I found I'd reached the top. My hands gripped a rocky lip on either side and I pulled myself up. I was aware of space above and around me. Now the acrid stench was overpowering and I guessed I was close to the centre of the labyrinth. Without thinking, I put my hand in my pocket, clutching Theo's crystal necklace, thankful I'd kept it with me.

"Theo?" I called gently, not wanting to draw attention to myself if Badru's pet was hanging around.

There was no answer. I looked up and saw vast cobwebs stretching above. To one side, there were five or six large white oval objects suspended in the cobwebs and I moved closer, trying to see what they were. Some kind of eggs or cocoons waiting to hatch? A shudder of revulsion ran across my body. If they were this big now, what would they turn into? And what size was the creature that had laid them?

I reached up and touched the base of one of the suspended objects, realising it was something wrapped up tightly in sticky, white thread. I pulled some away, trying to see what lay within, and jumped back in horror as a human foot dangled in front of me. These weren't eggs. This was prey that had been captured and wrapped, waiting to be eaten. I felt sick. Was this the fate that had befallen Theo?

"Theo," I called again, louder this time. "Are you there?"

This time, I heard something. A muffled response? Or was it something moving above me? I looked up into the chamber, trying to see through the thick cobwebs. I had no other option. I would have to climb and see what was up there. If it was Theo and he was still alive, there was a chance I could get him out.

There were plenty of small ledges and outcrops in the rocky walls, providing ample foot and handholds. Carefully, I began to climb. Soon I was a good few metres above ground level and I couldn't see the floor of the cavern. I reached up, my fingers encountering something sticky that clung to my hand. The more I tried to wipe it off the stickier it became and I pulled my hand back down, wiping the stuff against my jeans.

Without warning, a shaft of light appeared from above, illuminating the chamber, and I gasped in horror at the sight it revealed. I was at the foot of an enormous spider's web, the silver threads so thick they were like rope. The sticky substance I'd encountered was the outermost spoke of the web. Looking into its centre some thirty metres up, I could see something moving. It looked like prey caught in the web, but not yet packaged.

There was no mistaking the blond hair catching the light that flooded the chamber. It was Theo.

"Theo," I called again. "Can you hear me? It's Emily."

He wriggled and moved, managing to look down in my direction.

"Emily?" I heard him say. "Is it you?"

"Yes. I'm below, climbing up the side of the cavern to your left.

The figure moved again.

"I see you," he called out.

"We have to find a way to get you down."

"It's impossible. The more I move, the more I stick. I'm afraid to make too much movement in case the creature comes back."

"What is it?" I asked, although the answer was fairly obvious.

"Some kind of arachnid. I don't know exactly. I think it's feeding at the moment. Over to the right."

I looked across and could just make out a large black shape towards the top of the web. It was the spider. It began to eat, making squelching noises and I didn't dare think what it was doing to its victim. Something black and viscous dripped down, nearly making me wretch. I had to think quickly and we had to act fast. Time was running out for Theo.

"You're right. It's feeding. We have to do something while it's distracted."

"I can't move," said Theo. "You need to get out Emily. This thing is lethal. Save yourself."

"No," I shouted up. "Badru's given me an opportunity to save you, which means there must be something I can do."

I thought back to his words, knowing there'd be a clue in Badru's words.

"What are you doing here, Emily?" called Theo. "You told me you didn't want to see me any more."

"I was tricked," I answered. "Bellynda, Pantera and Aquila stole the crystal. They told me they'd only return it if I finished with you. Seth and Tash were dying. I didn't have any choice."

"So you still love me?"

"I never stopped. But I had to save my friends and the family."

"I thought I'd lost you. Does this mean we have a future together?"

"Yes, if we can get you out."

"Emily," he cried out in excitement. "My hand's free. Look."

I could see him moving his hand around and then I had it. I knew what to do.

"Theo, listen carefully," I called up. "Badru told me you were ensnared in a web of misery. I think it's created by your own thoughts. As long as you're miserable, you're stuck. As soon as you feel hope, the web will start to fall away. That's why you can move your hand."

"It's true," he called down. "I can move my arm."

I could see the silver threads starting to fall away from him. First one leg was free, then the other.

"Can you get to the side of the web?" I called. "If you can climb down, we can escape."

"I think so," he answered, and there was no mistaking the excitement in his voice. Cautiously, he began to climb across the mesh of the web, working his way towards me. But now we had a bigger problem.

Feeling the vibrations in the web, the spider was on the move.

"Theo," I screamed. "To your right. The spider's coming."

I saw two huge legs moving down the web, followed by an enormous head, black eyes bulging, two vicious fangs dripping with the black, viscous substance. This was worse than the stuff of nightmares. This was death approaching fast.

No matter how fast Theo climbed, he wasn't going to make it. I had to do something. My hands closed around the blue crystal necklace lying in my pocket.

"Theo, catch this," I cried. "It's your only hope."

I threw the necklace as hard as I could in his direction, praying my aim was true. I'd bargained without his superhuman reaction. Quick as a flash, his hand reached out and he caught it, holding it up in front of him, the blue crystal sparkling in the light. The creature backed off immediately, front legs waving furiously.

"It's working, Emily," he called.

Still facing the spider and holding it at bay with the shining crystal, Theo continued to work his way backwards across the web, edging towards me. The spider watched but kept its distance, unwilling to venture closer.

Theo was no more than a couple of metres from me, when the web gave way. The stickiness no longer held him and the threads had lost their strength. As he put his weight on a circular section, his foot went through and he fell rapidly through the remaining web. I tried to grab him but failed, and could only watch in dismay as he fell towards the floor. But of course, this was Theo, with lightning fast reflexes. As he fell, he twisted in mid air, grabbing a ledge on the cavern wall and pulling himself up.

Now, he was below and I was the one in trouble, as the spider hurtled towards me, segmented legs moving nimbly through the web, fangs twitching and venom dripping. The smell was unbearable, cloying and thick, overpowering.

"Use your crystal, Emily," shouted Theo.

Holding on to the cavern side with one hand, I held my crystal necklace in the spider's face. It spat at me, drops of venom hitting my face, but backed away.

"I can't move, Theo," I shouted, not daring to let the spider out of my sight, unable to look for hand and footholds.

"Okay, I'm coming up."

Now Theo was a like a spider, scuttling up the rock face, faster than humanly possible, at my side in no time, his arm around me and I knew I was safe.

He moved towards the spider, holding up his crystal, keeping it at bay.

"Climb down, Emily. Leave the spider to me."

I didn't need telling twice. As fast as my shaking hands would allow, I began to descend. It seemed to take forever to reach the bottom but at last firm ground was beneath my feet. I was aware of Theo climbing down, somehow managing to find footholds while holding up his crystal pendant. Then he was beside me.

"We need to run," I said, desperate to put as much distance as possible between the spider and us.

"No," said Theo, standing firm. "You go. I need to finish this thing off. If I don't, it will only attack other victims, and there's a chance I could save these people here. Just because they're bound up doesn't mean they're dead."

"If you stay, I stay," I declared. "I'm not going without you."

There was no time for argument. The creature was already dropping down, hanging on a thick thread just a couple of metres above, eyeing us hungrily.

"Okay, but stay back and do exactly as I say. There's no room for error."

The spider swung onto the cavern floor, facing us, and now I could see its true size. It was about three metres tall, with fine, blue fur covering its body and massive legs that extended some ten metres across. Badru's pet. Furry jaws twitched with a clicking sound and massive black eyes watched our every move.

"Don't turn your back. Keep your gaze on its head," warned Theo. "Move to the cavern entrance and stand to one side. Have your crystal ready. I'll lure it forward. When I say, hold up your crystal."

I did as he said, positioning myself at one side of the entrance and held my crystal ready. My mouth was dry, adrenalin making every moment last an eternity. I watched horrified as Theo ran in front of the spider, leaping out of the way as it shot towards him. The spider was fast, but Theo was quicker, moving so rapidly I could barely see him. Suddenly, he was at the opposite side of the entrance.

"Hold up your crystal," he shouted, as the spider ran towards us.

At the same time, he held up his crystal and an arc of blue light shot from one to the other, like a brilliant blue rainbow. The spider's momentum carried it forward and it slammed into the blue light, shrieking horribly as its fur started to burn. It moved back, trying to escape.

"Move forward," shouted Theo. "Keep the arc in place. Target its body."

I saw what he was trying to do and moved my crystal in line with his, swinging it forward, bringing the blue arc down on the spider's body. It shrieked horribly, pulling in its legs protectively as its body burnt. Again, we slammed the blue arc into its body, showing no mercy. The spider reared up, then fell backwards, legs shuddering violently, curling inwards.

"I need to finish it off," said Theo, approaching the flailing creature.

"Careful, Theo," I warned, heart in mouth.

He grasped the spider's head with both hands, black venom flowing down his arms, and wrenched quickly to the side. There was a sickening snap as he severed the head from the body and the spider was still, legs twitching in its final death throes. Black blood oozed onto the cavern floor and I gagged as its vile odour filled the room.

"I need to get these people down," shouted Theo. "Knowing Badru, this spider's not the only one."

He scaled the cavern wall, moving across the web to dislodge the trussed up cocoons, gently dropping them one by one to the cavern floor. Quickly we set about freeing the victims, pulling away the sticky thread to reveal the person inside. There were six in total, three boys and three girls, all teenagers, pale and dazed.

"Man, that was bad," said one dark-haired boy, sitting up.

"Where are we?" whispered one of the girls, looking at the dead spider.

"Listen carefully," said Theo, addressing them all. "You've had a lucky escape. It's my guess you've been through bad times, yes?"

A few of them nodded. "Let me tell you, and I speak as one who knows, the only reason you're in this dark place is because you put yourself here. You're prisoners of your own misery. Now you've been given a second chance. Start thinking positively and you'll be out of here in no time. D'you understand? You're young, with everything to live for. Now get moving while you can."

They got to their feet, each looking around warily, taking a few cautious steps, before heading towards the passageway, where a bright light had appeared. We watched as they stepped into the light, momentarily illuminated, then disappearing into its intensity.

"They've gone back," said Theo, holding out his hand to me. "Now, it's our turn. We have another chance, Emily."

"Better be quick," I said, glancing back, seeing movement in the web. "Looks like we have company."

I gripped his hand as if I'd never let go.

Together we walked into the passageway and stepped into the light.

## 31. **The Brothers Fight**

I opened my eyes. I was standing in the ballroom, the blues and purples brighter than I'd ever seen them, fire leaping in the grate. I looked down and found I was holding Theo's hand and he was there beside me, smiling and gorgeous.

He turned to me, blue eyes blazing. "I thought I'd lost you, Emily. I've never been in such a dark place. I can't believe they tricked you. Why did they do it?"

"They thought I was trying to replace Ahmes," I answered, not wanting to say too much about such a painful subject. "They were holding the crystal to ransom to make me leave you. Once we'd split up, Pantera and Aquila planned to return it, but Bellynda had formed an alliance with the Fallen Angel and tried to take the crystal to him. Aquila gave chase and got it back. Hopefully, by now Viyesha has used it to heal Seth and Tash. Aquila, too. He was pretty badly injured."

"I can't believe all this has happened. I should have been here."

I put my hand on his arm. "Let's not do this now. You couldn't, I know. And I'm the one who put you in that dark place. But there's more. Badru expects the Fallen Angel to attack at any moment."

"Badru? Since when was Badru involved?"

"Since I realised your family was incapable of looking after the crystal," said a voice behind us.

Badru stepped forward from where he'd been standing in the shadows at the edge of the ballroom. "Things had gone far enough. I had to intercede. It's clear your family can't manage. Welcome home, by the way, Theo."

"Badru," cried Theo angrily. "I've had enough of you and your sadistic games."

I grabbed his arm. "Theo, not now. There isn't time. We could be under attack at any moment."

"This isn't finished," Theo promised Badru.

Badru laughed. "Don't blame me for your misery. You put yourself there…"

He was interrupted by noises from the reception area. The double doors swung open and Seth and Violet, Joseph and Tash burst into the room.

"Hey everyone, we're back from the dead," declared Seth.

Badru stared, a look of bemusement on his face. "Seth, I take it?"

"Hey dude, you must be Badru," declared Seth loudly. "Pleased to meet you. You're every bit as badass as they said. Love the shades and the cape. Cool."

"Seth," I cried, embracing him warmly. "And Tash." I held on to her tightly. "I thought I'd lost you."

"We're okay, Emily," she said in a tired voice. "The crystal saved us."

"Never underestimate Super-Seth," declared Seth, taking up a superman pose. "Not even the dark lord can touch me."

"Oh God, he's back," I said to Tash, raising my eyes. "Thinks he's fallen into a Harry Potter film. Or is it Batman?"

"I'm just glad he's okay," she replied. "I can't tell you how bad it was, Emily. Our skin was covered with black veins."

"Yeah, totally gross," said Seth, "although kinda cool. I'm thinking of recreating it with a tattoo."

"Don't even go there," I warned. "You're lucky to be alive."

"Good to see you, mate," said Theo, stepping forward and shaking his hand.

"Hey man," said Seth, slapping Theo on the back boisterously. "Never thought I'd hear you say that."

"Wouldn't have been the same without you," answered Theo.

I wondered how long this entente cordiale would last.

"Theo," said Violet, embracing her brother. "Where've you been? We've been so worried."

"Long story. I'll tell you later. Where's mother?"

"Looking after Aquila, with Leon and Pantera," answered Joseph. "He's had a rough ride."

"This family reunion is all very touching," declared Badru coldly, "but don't forget, we're under attack. We need to prepare."

No sooner had he spoken than there was a loud crack at the window, as if a large object had been hurled at the Hall. We froze.

"Is this it?" I asked.

"Joseph, get Ata and Atsu," instructed Badru, "Leon and Viyesha, too. Tell them to bring the crystal. Get Pantera and Aquila, if he's able."

"Surely the crystal's safer in the Clock Tower Room," said Joseph.

"Last time it was left there, it was stolen. I'm not taking any chances. I want it where I can see it."

There was a further crack at the window and needing no further bidding, Joseph left the room.

I looked anxiously at Theo. "What can we do?"

"You, Seth and Tash stay back," he instructed. "If we're under attack from the Fallen Angel, you need to keep out of the way. This could get ugly."

I retreated, along with Seth and Tash to the far side of the ballroom. Tash's face was white and even Seth looked wary.

Theo turned to Badru. "D'you have a plan?"

"We need to rid ourselves of this menace once and for all," answered Badru, cracking his knuckles and drawing his cloak around him. "But this is personal. There's history between my brother and me that needs sorting. I need you all together, behind me. But you're back-up, understand? I need to do what I should have done centuries ago. Rid the world of an unwanted vermin."

Joseph returned with Leon and Viyesha. Ata and Atsu followed, menacing and silent as ever.

"Theo," declared Viyesha, running to her son's side and holding him tightly. "Are you okay?"

"I'm fine, mother, thanks to Emily. But there's no time to talk. We're under attack. The Fallen Angel is here."

"Okay, we need to stand in formation," declared Leon, taking control. "Make a force shield."

"Show me the crystal first," demanded Badru. "I need to see it."

Leon revealed the silver casket, opening it briefly to show Badru the blue crystal. Immediately, its wonderful light filled the ballroom, blue energy cascading from the casket onto the floor. With a snap, Leon closed the lid and the room was colourless.

"Protect the crystal," Badru instructed him. "But let me deal with the Fallen Angele. Ata and Atsu, stand either side of me. This is our battle."

The twins took position alongside Badru, while the family stood in a circle around the silver casket, facing outwards, fingers touching, creating a blue energy field. I looked for Pantera, but there was no sign of her, and I guessed she was staying with Aquila. I wondered which side they'd be on if it came to a choice.

Badru turned to Viyesha. "When I have defeated the Fallen One, I will take the crystal. You are no longer its keeper, Viyesha. You've been found wanting and I relieve you of your duties."

"You can't do that, Badru," declared Viyesha. "I answer only to Amun-Ra. He would not wish it."

He smiled briefly. "We'll see."

He was prevented from further words by another crash at the windows. This time, the window frames gave way, exploding into the room, the drapes billowing in, broken glass and ragged woodwork littering the floor. For a second, a huge cloud of dust prevented us from seeing anything. As it cleared, we saw a massive hole in the side of the ballroom, the cool night air flowing in.

There was a momentary silence and the family's energy field grew visibly stronger, creating a shimmering blue dome over the silver casket.

"Hold strong," commanded Leon. "We don't know what's out there."

As if to answer his question, a huge plume of flames ripped through the hole in the wall, torching the fallen curtains. Flames leapt up as the material burnt.

"Yes we do. It's Bellynda!" said Joseph.

Flanked by the twins and ignoring the flames, Badru moved to the large window on the right, still intact, and pulled back the drapes. Seth, Tash and I peered through the burning hole in the wall, seeing the shape of Bellynda, silhouetted against the nearly full moon, turning mid-air, flying back towards the Hall, flames spuming from her mouth and huge wings outspread. Then she was gone, flying upwards, and we heard the sound of falling masonry as she ravaged the Hall's turrets and towers. Around the broken window area, the fire took hold, fanned by the air, sending firebrands and smoke into the room, making it difficult to breath.

Badru continued to watch through the window, seemingly unconcerned the ballroom was burning. In the far corner, the family stood strong, keeping the force field in place, protecting the crystal.

"We can help," I said to Seth and Tash. "There are fire extinguishers in the hallway."

We crept into the reception area, ignoring calls from the family to come back

"Over there," I pointed to the cabinet where the extinguishers were housed.

Through the reception windows, we saw the eastern wing of the Hall in flames, under attack from Bellynda, falling debris landing in the courtyard.

"Nothing we can do about that," I said. "Let's concentrate on the ballroom."

We carried the extinguishers back with us, aiming them at the leaping flames, while the family held the force field in place.

"I've always wanted to do this," shouted Seth, spraying foam on the broken window frames.

"Just not under these circumstances," Tash answered, dowsing flames on the sofas and curtains.

It didn't take long to extinguish the fire and we soon felt the night breeze on our faces, blowing foam back into the room like weird snow, dissipating the smell of burnt furnishings and charred wood. Badru stood at the window, not moving, oblivious to our actions, his faithful twins behind him. It was clear he was watching and waiting.

We didn't have to wait much longer. As the last few flames fizzled and died, I felt a terrible chill and a sense of dread took hold of me. This could only mean one thing. The Fallen Angel was approaching.

The night seemed to grow darker and a deathly hush hung over the Hall. The sound of falling masonry stopped and we could no longer see Bellynda's dark shape in the moonlit sky. Badru grew rigid, like an animal detecting danger, every sense on high alert.

"Badru..." a voice whispered, with a resonance that hit deep inside. "Give me the crystal."

I felt goose bumps rise and looked across at my friends. Tash was pale and terrified, Seth grinning manically. If I wasn't mistaken, he was enjoying this.

Badru turned to Viyesha. "Keep the force field in place. Do not break the link under any circumstances. We don't know what tricks he may play. Leave him to me. This time he's history."

He stepped through the gaping hole on to the rear terrace, the twins in his wake, and spoke into the night, his voice steely and determined.

"I am here, brother. But have no thoughts of taking the crystal. It was never yours. Tonight I will finish what I should have done centuries ago. Banishment was too good for you. Annihilation is the only way. Prepare to meet your death."

There was a massive crash and a thunderbolt flew through the air, aimed at Badru. He moved just as the bolt of lightning hit the spot where he'd been standing, crashing into the ground. He stepped quickly onto the formal lawn behind the Hall, Ata and Atsu behind him, and together, they raised their arms, forming an apex, sending a massive thunderbolt upwards. There was a huge clap of thunder followed by the sound of laughing.

"You think you are a match for me? You were always the weaker, Badru. While you've been amusing yourself with your games and fancies, I've been gaining power. Even with your silent henchmen, you're no match for me."

To prove his point, a series of flaming thunderbolts hurtled through the air, one after the other, aiming for the figures on the lawn. But Badru and the twins were fast, easily dodging the fiery missiles.

I saw Viyesha and Leon looking nervously at each other and wondered if they would join the battle, but they stayed in place, maintaining the blue force around the crystal.

Seth, Tash and I crept forward, crouching among the rubble of the ballroom's ruined wall, getting a bird's eye view of the battle between Badru and his brother. This was better than the cinema. It was a blockbuster unfurling in front of our eyes.

"Emily, get back," called Theo, but I barely heard him over the noise.

The heavens had become wild and turbulent, lightning flying in all directions illuminating huge, black clouds racing across the sky. I looked for Bellynda, but couldn't see her and guessed she'd been the first part of the battle offensive. What came next was anybody's guess. Hailstones fell, creating a thick curtain, making visibility difficult. Still we crouched and watched, oblivious to the danger, intent only on seeing this battle of the Titans, fear overtaken by exhilaration and excitement.

Badru had been fighting an invisible enemy, the Fallen Angel an unseen force. Now we saw him, a dark figure towering above us, blurry and indistinct. Without warning, he dropped suddenly, falling upon Badru, covering him like a blanket. A hideous noise filled the air, like a hundred metal wheels scraping on tracks, wrenching and screeching, twisting and scraping. The blond twins threw themselves into the fray and it was impossible to tell what was happening. In the midst of the fray, the dark figure reared up, opening its hands to receive a powerful bolt of lightning from above that split into two forks, one through each palm. For a brief moment, he was illuminated and we saw clearly a man, powerful and huge, but hideously mutated, his features twisted and misshapen. The creature opened its mouth wide to reveal rows of lethal, pointed teeth, each buzzing with electrical current.

"Yowza, look at those electro-choppers!" whispered Seth. "Stabby-hot!"

"Careful, urban boy," I warned him. "Keep back. This looks bad."

With a howling sound, the dark figure leapt forward, grabbing one of the twins, it could have been Ata or Atsu. He sank his electric teeth into his neck, biting the head clean from the body, throwing it to one side. Blood spurted, thick and black in the dim light, and the head flew towards us, landing by Seth's foot, sightless eyes staring up at him, smoke pouring from its mouth and nostrils.

"Gross city!" said Seth, kicking it away.

It rolled back down the grassy bank leading to the lawn, leaving a bloody trail, sticky and gleaming.

We watched in horror as the black figure tore into the remaining twin, electric teeth biting and tearing, simultaneously electrocuting and dismembering, destroying him in seconds, leaving body parts strewn across the lawn, blood seeping into the grass.

"Don't look, Tash," I said, worried she was still fragile. "This is like one of Seth's horrible computer games."

"Only this is real," she answered, mesmerised by the carnage.

The body parts began to emit a thick, acrid smoke that circled over the lawn, before exploding into a million dark pieces, scattering into the night.

Now there were just two figures in the arena, Badru at one corner of the lawn, the black shape that was his brother at the other. Each appeared to be taking the measure of the other.

"Give up now," hissed the Fallen Angel, electric teeth shining in the darkness. "Give me the crystal and I'll let you walk. Attempt to fight and I'll chew you up and spit you out."

He gnashed his teeth in a chewing motion, sparks flying from his mouth.

"Never," shouted Badru. "The crystal is mine. Tonight you die."

At once, he grew to the same size as his brother, becoming another dark formless shape. We saw he carried a massive rope coiled around his arm and he swung the end like a lasso, releasing it suddenly in his brother's direction. As it shot forward, the end split into a hundred glowing electric eels that wrapped themselves around the dark form opposite, lighting up the night, binding the Fallen Angel's arms to his body. For a second he looked powerless. Then thrusting his arms up, he broke the bonds, showering the garden with brilliant fireworks.

"Is that your best shot?" he spat into the air, electric sparks flying.

Immediately, he flicked his arm down, casting a bolt of electricity into the ground. It sizzled across the lawn with lightning speed, heading for Badru like a long, thin snake, opening the ground as it travelled, creating a gaping, fiery wound. Badru had no time to react. A huge crevasse opened beneath him and he was swallowed in its fiery depths. We looked on horrified, as the Hall's beautiful grounds turned into a scene from Hell, the ground split open, fire leaping from the depths of the earth.

"Is he gone?" asked Tash, looking shocked.

"Na. He'll be back," said Seth confidently.

As he spoke, a winged creature rose from the gaping crevasse, flying above the leaping flames. There was no mistaking the blue cloak and blond hair. It was Badru, but not as we'd seen him before. Now he assumed a terrifying figure, huge and airborne, as much a demonic force as the Fallen Angel.

He soared into the night sky and we strained to see. As the moon reappeared from behind the clouds, we glimpsed the Fallen

Angel flying to meet him, massive wings carrying him high. They flew at each other like two enormous birds of prey, turning into a dark fireball, hissing and spitting with energy.

"What's happening?" asked Seth.

"I don't know," I answered. "I can't work out who's winning."

The figures tore into each other, clawing and biting ferociously, dark wings extended like a macabre butterfly. Then one fell backwards, spiralling down.

"Is it the Fallen Angel?" asked Tash.

"Let's hope so," said Seth. "But it could be either."

The figure crashed onto the lawn and lay motionless, seemingly wounded. The other winged creature followed, landing on top, coming in for the kill. For a second, it looked straight at us, a hideous electric grin spreading across its face, before turning to its victim.

"Time to go, brother," it hissed.

"That's the Fallen Angel," said Seth. "Oh man, Badru's down."

"This can't happen," I protested. "The Fallen Angel can't win. If he does, it's over. No crystal, no family, no initiation, no future. He'll take it all."

"Badru's not dead. I'm sure of it," said Tash.

But it wasn't looking good for Badru. His brother leant over him and fastened on to his neck, teeth shining in the darkness, making a hideous slurping noise. For a second, Badru's body flailed then was still.

We watched horrified.

"Yuksville. He's leeching him!" declared Seth.

Before our eyes, Badru's body shrank as the Fallen Angel drained his life force. Like an x-ray, his skeleton showed ultra violet, then the brightness was gone and there was nothing but a blue cloak lying on the lawn.

The Fallen Angel rose into the sky, wings outstretched, victorious, and was joined by another dark shape. There was no mistaking Bellynda's massive form.

Together they circled the Hall, before flying into the night. Badru had lost.

I turned back to the ruined ballroom, where Theo and the family held the force field in place, protecting the crystal.

"Badru's lost!" I shouted.

"No way!" called Theo, hardly comprehending my words.

This was not meant to happen. They'd thought they'd be defending the crystal against Badru, not the Fallen Angel.

"The Fallen Angel killed him. The twins, too."

"He's flown away with Bellynda," said Seth.

"Get behind the force field," called Viyesha, taking control. "It's the best protection we can give you. Move quickly. He could return at any moment."

With a backward look into the gardens, we ran towards the shimmering blue force field. Leon and Viyesha dropped their hands, breaking the link. Immediately, the shimmering blue force field disappeared, revealing the silver casket on a table. Seth, Tash and I ran into the centre of the circle and the family linked hands again, recreating the shining blue dome.

"Stand fast," Viyesha commanded the family. "We don't know when he'll strike, only that he will. It could be any second. This is our best chance of protecting the crystal. There's no time to do anything else."

Inside the force field, we huddled together.

"OMG," said Tash. "I'm scared, Emily. I don't want to die."

"No one's going to die, Tash," I answered.

"Er, I think they already have," pointed out Seth helpfully.

"I mean none of us is going to die. We're inside a force field created by immortal beings. We'll be fine. Besides, good always triumphs over evil."

"That's in the movies," said Seth.

"OMG, we're going to die," shrieked Tash.

"We're not," I said firmly. "Besides, Badru was bad news. I'm glad he's gone."

I meant it. I just wasn't sure the Fallen Angel was my enemy of choice. As the saying goes, better the devil you know.

"It's pretty cool in here," said Seth, placing his finger on the shimmering blue light that surrounded us. A small, blue electric charge leapt out at him, sizzling and flashing.

"Yikes!" He hastily drew back his hand.

It was pretty strange standing there inside the force field, looking out onto the ballroom through the shimmering blue, like being in a swimming pool, the world beyond hazy and rippling. Maybe it was the presence of the crystal or perhaps the security of the force field surrounding us, but it felt as though we were invincible. I prayed the family had the strength to withstand their mortal enemy.

* * *

From an upstairs bedroom window, Pantera watched the battle between the brothers. Aquila lay on the bed, weak and exhausted, the crystal's intervention unable to return him to strength.

"Badru is dead," she informed him, shocked. "I must go to the family. They need me."

"Where's Bellynda?" asked Aquila, his voice rasping and faint.

"Flown away with the Fallen Angel. They don't have the crystal, which means they'll be back."

She stared over the gardens, trying to comprehend the scene she'd just witnessed.

"What have we done, Aquila?" she whispered. "We've set in motion a train of events we could never have anticipated. Badru is dead. And the twins. Our life-long friend has gone to the dark side and the Fallen Angel is stronger than ever. The family has never been under greater threat."

There was no answer and she glanced towards the bed. Aquila lay still, lines of weariness etching his swarthy features, sweat building on his brow. His eyes were closed and he seemed unaware what was happening.

She watched him anxiously, aware the family needed her but not sure she dared leave him.

## 32. **Biscione Catch-up**

Juke sat on the blue chintz armchair opposite Father James and Mrs O'Briain in the vicarage drawing room.

It had been a long night. He'd had great difficulty persuading Emily's mother not to go to the Young Wives make-up demonstration and they'd had their first argument, she accusing him of trying to control her. In the end, she'd agreed to watch a DVD with him and he'd sat through a boring rom-com, aware of the storm raging outside, sensing danger, feeling the Fallen Angel's presence nearby, but unable to act. He'd heard nothing from Leon, so could only assume all was well at the Hall. His increasing anxiety he put down to the bisciones in the village and worried that Father James and Mrs O'Briain were out of their depth. As soon as Emily's mother had succumbed to the bottle of wine she'd consumed, and lay sleeping on the sofa, he crept out. At least she wouldn't be inviting anyone in to the house.

Father James and Mrs O'Briain had been busy. After the Women's Institute AGM, they'd been on a mission around the village, visiting the Knitting Circle, the Gardening Club, the Ladies Table Tennis Club and the Pudding Club. While Father James had talked to the members, secretly looking for bisciones, Mrs O'Briain had waited outside, holy water and ceremonial sword in hand.

As a result, Hartswell-on-the-Hill had experienced an unusually high level of heart attacks that night. She'd swooped and sliced with uncanny accuracy, and had succeeded in cutting off the heads of another four bisciones. In each case, the victim had returned to human form, fortunately with head in place, but no longer living.

"What a night. We could have done without the storm," said Father James. "It felt as if we'd fallen into a horror movie."

"Vicious beasts, these bisciones," Mrs O'Briain told Juke. "You need your wits about you. They'd swallow you whole as soon as look at you."

"They're dangerous creatures," agreed Juke. "I'm a little nervous that you've taken to slaying them Mrs O'Briain. These women should be recovering once you've beheaded the serpents. I'm concerned your ceremonial sword doesn't have the necessary power. What's happened to the bodies?"

"Taken to the morgue," replied Father James, looking disturbed. "All certified dead."

"They may appear dead, but I doubt they are," said Juke.

"Oh, Lord save us, what do you mean?" exclaimed Mrs O'Briain.

"I mean, unless they're decapitated with a celestial sword they'll turn back into bisciones," said Juke.

"So, I haven't really helped at all," said Mrs O'Briain, eyes cast down, looking dejected.

"On the contrary," said Juke. "You've prevented those women from breeding, albeit temporarily. And you've identified a number of potential groups. Just don't kill any more, okay?"

"The problem is, this is just the tip of the iceberg," said Father James. "We've found bisciones at every club and every meeting we've attended, which means the village is riddled with them. Given the hunger of the new ones, they could be multiplying at a vast rate. There could be hundreds out there."

"And until they choose to show themselves, we've no way of knowing where they all are," added Mrs O'Briain.

"Why did Barolo come here in the first place," murmured Juke, thinking aloud.

"By chance?" suggested Mrs O'Briain.

"No. This was planned. You don't come all the way from Northern Italy and just happen to land here. Not after all that's taken place in this village. He came here by design. I'd say the Fallen Angel is amassing his forces. The question is how big is his biscione army? And when will it strike?"

"More to the point, how do we fight it?" asked Father James.

"Exactly," said Juke. He frowned as he heard the ping of a text arrive on his phone and glanced at his messages. To his horror, he saw three texts had arrived at once.

"They're from Leon," he told Father James and Mrs O'Briain, reading them quickly. "He's been trying to get me all evening. Aquila's back with the crystal, Badru's turned up and they're waiting for the Fallen Angel. That last one was sent an hour ago. I must go. I knew something was wrong."

He stood up and placed his bush hat on his head.

"It's this storm," said Mrs O'Briain, showing him to the door. "It's playing havoc with the signal."

"I just hope I'm not too late," said Juke, stepping out into the stormy night. "Stay inside both of you, it's not safe out here. I'll be in touch when I find out what's happening. Lock your doors."

He left the vicarage and headed for the Hall, his sense of unease growing with every step.

## 33. **Protecting The Crystal**

From our hiding place inside the blue energy force field, we watched as events unfolded. Twenty minutes had gone by and we were all getting edgy.

"Mother, do we have to hold this force field in place much longer?" asked Violet. "Surely, the Fallen Angel would be back by now. Maybe he's not coming. Maybe Badru mortally wounded him."

"We stay put, Violet," her father said. "He could be watching, waiting for a chance to get to the crystal."

"If we let the force field go, it will give him the chink in our armour he's looking for," added Viyesha.

"Any sign of Pantera and Aquila?" asked Joseph.

"Doesn't look like it," said Theo darkly. "I wonder where their loyalties lie."

"Aquila brought the crystal back," pointed out Violet. "And was badly injured in the process. He's proved his loyalty."

"Except none of this would be happening if they hadn't taken the crystal in the first place," said Theo.

"They meant to replace it," said Viyesha. "This is all Bellynda's doing. Badru should never have put so much trust in her. All that power went to her head."

"I always said never trust a dragon," said Leon. "Too reptilian. No loyalty to anyone but themselves."

"Did you text Juke?" asked Viyesha.

"Yes, but I haven't heard back. Our signal's weak."

"We have to hope he's on his way. He said he'd help."

"I can't believe Badru's gone," said Violet. "I know he was vile, but I didn't think he'd be defeated."

"Badru had become weak and corrupt," said Viyesha. "We know he was planning to take the crystal for himself. Either way, we'd have had to defend the crystal against a powerful foe."

The conversation meandered to nothing and we continued to wait, keeping our eyes on the hole in the wall.

Just as we were beginning to think nothing would happen, the silence was broken by the sound of wings beating on the wind. Something was coming in to land on the lawn.

"Is it him?" asked Violet, straining to see.

The moon had disappeared behind the storm clouds and all was dark outside.

"Hold fast," instructed Leon. "This could be it."

The temperature dropped to freezing as a dark figure appeared beyond the ruined wall. It stepped over the loose brickwork and entered the room, tall and hazy, the outline of a man, but more shadow than person.

"Is it him?" whispered Violet again.

The figure spoke, holding up a dark, shadowy hand.

"I have no wish to destroy you. I wish to take only that which is mine. Give me the crystal and I will leave. You have my word."

"Except this crystal was never yours," said Viyesha. "You stole it from your brother and now, to add to your sins, you have killed him, the crystal's original protector."

"Silence," hissed the figure. Icy breath flowed from its mouth, chilling the room, killing the flames in the fireplace. The lights flickered and a gloom descended, making the blue force field shine brighter. "My brother wanted the crystal for himself. He would never have let you keep it. Relax the force field. Let me have the crystal and I will leave you in peace."

"Peace?" said Theo derisively. "You don't know the meaning of the word. You want the crystal to achieve human form and exact revenge on all the people you believe have wronged you. To create your own depraved power base."

"Do you refuse to give it up?" asked the figure, its outline fading and sharpening, as if struggling to hold on even to its shadow form. "Do you not understand the power I hold?"

172

Leon laughed. "Yours is a dark, insidious power that feeds on human weakness. Long ago, you fell from a world that was light and good, where your name Lucifer meant the shining one. You brought your fall upon yourself."

"And there you shall remain," declared Viyesha. "You will never have the crystal to further your own sickening ends. The crystal is a force for good, not evil."

Quivering with rage, the figure raised itself up, towering above them.

"Enough! The crystal is a force for good or evil. It cannot differentiate. It is only as good as the power that controls it. And your time is up."

It raised a hand, sending a bolt of lightning straight at the blue force field.

"Hold fast," commanded Leon. "Don't break the link."

They braced themselves, holding their arms out rigid, concentration etched on their faces. The force field shuddered and faded, then snapped into place.

Again, the dark figure threw a thunderbolt, aiming at the link between Violet and Joseph.

"You're only as strong as your weakest link and I've just found it," it hissed triumphantly. "The energy's already weakening. I can see it."

Again he threw a bright, white thunderbolt at the blue energy link between Violet and Joseph.

"I'm trying to hold it, mother," shouted Violet in desperation.

"Stay strong, Violet," said Joseph encouragingly. "We can do this."

But it soon became clear they couldn't. The energy link between Violet and Joseph was torn. Try as they might to keep it intact, it was failing. Again and again, the dark figure bombarded the weakening link with powerful bolts of lightning.

"I can't hold it much longer," cried Violet. "I haven't got the strength."

Viyesha glanced at Leon.

"Keep going, Violet," she encouraged her daughter.

But now, other areas of the force field were beginning to fail and the family was facing defeat.

The dark figure laughed, seeing victory within grasp.

"Did you not realise, Viyesha?" it asked mockingly. "I'm not only fighting with my own force. I have my brother's life force too. When I killed Badru, I absorbed him. The goodness in his nature was all but gone, replaced by a desire for self-glory that fed my own. Now, we are united, and together we will triumph."

His voice rose to a crescendo and he threw one final, all-powerful bolt. The blue energy field shuddered and faded, leaving the family defenceless and the blue crystal unprotected.

Now he saw what they'd been hiding, giving him the final ammunition he needed.

## 34. **Crystal Power**

"What have we here?" he asked, moving closer.

Seth, Tash and I stared up at him from our position on the floor where we crouched, hoping to remain unseen and avoid the flying thunderbolts. Instinctively, we closed ranks and I grasped the silver casket. It probably wasn't my best move.

"A would-be hero," said the Fallen Angel in his sibilant tones. "But sadly misplaced." He regarded Viyesha and Leon. "So, this is how you fight your battles, Viyesha. You use children as a shield. And you accuse me of being underhand."

"I am not a child," I said defiantly, standing up.

"Neither am I, dude," said Seth, standing along side me.

Tash wisely kept down.

"I assure you, we are not using children as a shield," said Viyesha. "We are trying to protect them. These are innocents and have no part in our fight."

"Will you stop calling us children," Seth began. A quick dig in the ribs made him stop.

"You cannot protect them," the dark figure hissed. "I can wipe them out like that." He made a snapping motion with his fingers. "So here's the deal. Hand over the crystal and I will spare them."

"No, Viyesha," I exclaimed. "He's bluffing."

The dark figure aimed his finger at my feet and a thunderbolt hit the ground millimetres from where I stood.

"Next time, I won't miss," he hissed.

White-faced, Viyesha spoke. "Give him the crystal, Emily. It's not a chance I can take."

"Never." I held the casket to me.

"Emily," said Tash from her place on the floor. "Just do it."

Leon reached over and gently took the casket out of my arms.

"We will not have the blood of innocents on our hands. This creature is quite capable of killing the three of you."

I couldn't stop the tears flowing as I saw my future with Theo snatched away once again. This emotional roller coaster was too much. Every time we were back on track something happened to derail it.

Leon placed the casket on the table and the family stood back.

"Come and get it," he said to the dark shadow.

The Fallen Angel moved forward, his shape coming and going, as if hovering between one world and another. "Open the casket!" he demanded.

Viyesha gripped the lid and threw it back, revealing the blue crystal in all its glory. The room was bathed in brilliant light and I breathed in its energy, feeling it run through my system like a drug in my veins. I couldn't believe this was the last time I'd experience this incredible feeling.

The Fallen Angel placed his hands around the crystal, about to lift it from the casket, just as the double doors crashed open. It was Pantera, a powerful, black panther primed for the kill. With a growl that almost shook the Hall's foundations, she sprang forward, claws at the ready, mouth pulled back in a savage snarl.

"I knew she'd come good," breathed Viyesha, closing the casket lid.

But her relief was short lived. Pantera leapt, expecting to tear the dark figure to shreds, but passing straight through him. There was no substance, nothing to land on. It was like attacking a shadow. She tried again, 150 pounds of rippling muscle and sinew, slamming into nothing, and now she was in trouble. The Fallen Angel aimed a powerful thunderbolt between the shoulder blades, causing her fur to singe and flesh to burn. Momentarily dazed, she struggled to her feet and launched herself again, but it was no good. He hit her with a thunderbolt mid-flight. Her electrified body dropped to the floor, resuming human form as she fell.

She lay still, stunned or dead we couldn't tell. I heard Violet stifle a sob and Joseph ran to her, placing his fingers on her neck.

"There's still a pulse," he informed Viyesha. "And she's breathing."

"Enough games," hissed the Fallen Angel, reaching for the crystal.

Before he could grasp it, a voice rang out from the darkness outside.

"You'd kill kids and animals to get what you want. This madness stops."

A blinding light filled the hole in the wall and Juke stepped over the debris, shining so brightly I had to look away. I put my hands over my eyes, peering through the gaps, desperate to see the urban angel. I heard Seth murmur "Cool".

"What have we here?" asked the Fallen Angel, turning to face Juke. "Do you seek death so much you would fight me. I can destroy you in an instant. I have tiny demons more powerful than you."

"Fighting talk," said Juke. "If you want the crystal, come through me."

"Now I recognise you," hissed the dark figure. "We've met before. In the dead zone. You came off worst. And now you're back for more?"

"Too right I'm back for more."

The Fallen Angel raised his hand and threw a thunderbolt. Juke raised his shield, neatly deflecting it, causing it to ricochet against the wall above us.

"Whoa!" cried Seth, dropping to his knees.

We followed suit, keeping our heads well down.

"If that's your best shot, I'd give up now," advised Juke.

It wasn't, of course. The Fallen Angel advanced on him, throwing thunderbolts from either hand, Juke deflecting each one, moving with agility and speed, turning and twisting his shield so fast he was a blur of shining white light, thunderbolts hitting the walls all around us. We peeked over the table, desperate for him to finish off the Fallen Angel with his shining sword. But it wasn't to be.

The Fallen Angel bore down on him, raining thunderbolts relentlessly, giving him no opportunity to attack. As Juke raised his sword to strike a blow, a powerful bolt knocked it from his hand and now defensive action was all he could muster. Time and again, he deflected the thunderbolts, but his shield was becoming damaged, and one final strike smashed it to pieces.

Juke faced his enemy, his aura glowing brightly, making the Fallen Angel look shadowy and insubstantial. It was an illusion. The power lay with the dark shadow and he raised both hands, hitting Juke with a massive bolt of lightning. Juke's figure erupted in a blaze of light, then crumpled to the floor. The urban angel was gone. Now he was just Juke, with his dreadlocks, jacket and jeans.

"Juke," I cried, trying to go to him, but Leon held me back.

The Fallen Angel stepped forward and grasped the silver casket. He threw open the lid, filling the room with blue light, and placed two shadowy hands around the crystal. Immediately, his dark body glowed electric blue. Holding it close to his chest, he moved towards the hole in the wall, stepping over Juke's body as if it was a swatted fly, stepping over the fallen masonry. He walked across the terrace to the formal lawn, no sign of the gaping fire-hole that had rent it in two.

I ran to Juke, thankful to see his eyes flickering open.

"I tried, Emily," he whispered.

"Hush. You're alive. That's what matters."

I put my arms around him, willing my energy to flow into his, feeling his life-force grow stronger. He struggled to sit up and I knew he was okay.

I saw Pantera attempting to get up, Joseph and Viyesha helping her.

"I'm okay," she growled, pushing them aside and rising to her feet. "What's happened to the crystal?"

We joined the others, watching the Fallen Angel from the terrace.

As he held the crystal, his form began to change. We saw the boy he'd once been, a blond-haired youth with muscular physique and handsome features. Next to him was a shadow boy, with similar looks, and I realised this must be Badru.

Gradually, the energy revitalised the Fallen Angel, turning dark matter into living, breathing flesh, and he flexed his muscles as his power grew. He was becoming human, achieving the desire that had eluded him for so long. Beside him, his ghost brother shadowed him.

"D'you think the crystal's brought his good side out?" I asked Viyesha. "He doesn't look evil any more."

She said nothing, just watched.

The blond boy stood on the lawn and laughed, a strong, youthful sound that spoke of hope and promise. Bathed in blue light and holding the crystal before him, he turned his face towards the heavens.

"At last I have human form," he shouted. "Hear this, those who would deny me. You will soon be as lifeless as the brittle leaves that blow in the breeze. My legions will rise and I will come to power. As I have long desired, so will I rule, raising those who serve and crushing any who oppose. To those who worship me, I give the riches of the earth. Those who deny me will be trampled underfoot."

As he spoke, white lightning flashed across the sky. His shining figure became more intense, his ghost brother too, until it became difficult to look at them.

"Viyesha, this is all wrong," I cried. "He's setting himself up as a god. Even Badru wasn't such a megalomaniac as this."

She didn't answer, just stared at the sky, murmuring a strange incantation.

A huge crack echoed across the heavens and the light began to dim. As it grew dark, the boy's brilliant light faded. He began to age rapidly, becoming corpulent and fat as the excesses of his life took hold, then turning into the misshapen, ugly creature we'd seen earlier, shrinking into old age. His muscles became thin and wasted, his skin yellowed and dry, and his beautiful blond hair grey and sparse. The ghost brother too began to age, turning from a statuesque blond boy into the figure we'd known as Badru, and then to an old man, stooped and grey.

I'd seen this happen before, when I'd witnessed the demise of the ex-glamour model, Kimberley Chartreuse. She'd turned to dust before my eyes and I expected to see the same. But this time it was different.

As the Fallen Angel grew old, his form became dark and hazy, as it had been in the ballroom. In contrast, his ghost brother glowed brighter, his light so intense I had to screw up my eyes. Then the ghost Badru seemed to pop out of existence, shrinking rapidly into a bright, white dot that shot into the sky and disappeared.

A look of disbelief crossed the face of the dark figure on the lawn. He looked down at his hands, now dark and indistinct, and at the crystal he clutched. It was nothing but a dull grey stone.

"No!" he whispered. "This cannot be!"

He turned his gaze towards Viyesha. "High Priestess of Amun-Ra. You knew the ancient laws would not allow me to be reborn."

Viyesha's voice, strong and clear, rang out in the night.

"No, Fallen Angel. I didn't know. It was not for me to decide your fate, but Amun-Ra, the Hidden One. He gave you human form, as you desired, but the evil within you was too strong and the crystal was unable to turn you into a creature of the light. Your brother has been given eternal life and is now a star in the firmament, the Great One repaying a debt incurred many centuries ago. But your chance has gone and you must remain in the dust, creeping forever amongst the shadows. This is the will of Amun-Ra."

There was a flash of light and for the briefest of seconds I swore I saw the sun burst forth from behind the clouds, bathing the sky in a golden glow. Then it was gone, making me wonder if the night was playing tricks on me.

Dropping to his knees, the Fallen Angel saw the darkness spreading across his body and knew that Viyesha was right.

"No!" he screamed.

Viyesha spoke again, ancient and all-knowing. "You have brought this sentence upon yourself. You will never know the glory of Amun-Ra but will remain a creature of darkness, bound forever to the lower planes."

He stood in front of her, sketchy and formless.

"Then hear this, Viyesha. I care no longer for human form. I embrace the darkness. But I will return with my legions and I will destroy you and your family. Already, my followers grow strong. Soon I will crush you completely. And do not think you have the crystal to protect you. Its powers are gone."

With dark wings protruding from his back, the Fallen Angel rose into the air and with all his might, hurled the crystal, now dark and dull, into the night sky. Then spinning into a flimsy, black wraith, he disappeared into the night.

Viyesha turned to Theo. "This is your moment, Theo. Run as never before. Catch the crystal. Its powers are not gone, just tarnished by the hand that held it."

Needing no further bidding, Theo took off, moving so fast I barely saw him.

Viyesha smiled at me. "Have no fear, Emily. The Fallen Angel has no use for the crystal. Theo will return it."

I strained my eyes in the direction Theo had taken, looking over the dark fields for a sign of him, but all was still.

"What if he can't find it, Viyesha?" I asked fearfully.

She smiled. "He's a light being, Emily. He doesn't see as you do."

"What d'you mean?"

"You see a world in darkness. He sees the colours of the night, and he sees the crystal shining bright and clear."

"It's a bit like sending a dog to catch a stick," explained Joseph. "Theo's your ultimate dog."

I looked over the fields, almost expecting to see a large dog returning with a crystal in its mouth. There was so much I had to learn about this strange family.

"Why didn't the crystal destroy the Fallen Angel, mother?" asked Violet. "I don't understand. If it couldn't turn him into a light being, why didn't he just crumble to dust? We've seen it happen before."

"Good cannot exist without evil," explained Viyesha. "It's universal law. Each is interdependent on one another. It is the duality of existence."

"You mean evil cannot be destroyed?" asked Joseph.

"Everything needs its mirror," she answered.

"You mean that badass is free to come back and take a pop at us?" said Seth.

"Yes. I'm afraid so."

"He said he'll return and crush us completely, mother," said Violet.

"OMG," said Tash tearfully. "We're in danger all over again."

Viyesha glanced at Leon. "D'you think he'll return?"

"We can't take any chances," he answered. "We have to prepare, make sure we're ready for him next time."

"Yay," said Seth, mock punching the air. "Fighting talk."

"Idiot," I said, then realised that was Theo's line.

Where was he? I scanned the dark fields again, looking for him. Then in the blink of an eye, he was there, standing beside me.

"Theo," I gasped. "I didn't see you coming."

"I'm a speed freak. You're not supposed to," he grinned.

"Do you have the crystal?" asked Viyesha.

He held the crystal up in his hands, its blue energy travelling down his arm.

"Yay!" said Seth.

"Idiot." This time it was Theo who said it.

Viyesha took the crystal and climbing over the masonry into the ballroom, placed it inside the silver casket.

"I'm taking it to the Clock Tower Room," she announced. "We need to charge up the coordinates. We'll take turns guarding it."

She glanced outside, as the moon appeared from behind a cloud, bathing the grounds with its silvery light. "Tomorrow night is the full moon. It's time for the initiation."

I looked at Seth and Tash.

This was it. We were about to join the dark and dangerous world of the de Lucis family.

Just as a battle was looming.

## 35. **Next Morning**

Next morning saw Juke huddled away in the library with Viyesha and Leon. He'd made a full recovery after his ordeal.

"Sorry I didn't get there earlier. I didn't receive your texts until late," he explained, adding wryly, "although I don't think it would have made much difference. I was stupid to try and tackle him alone."

"What you did was very brave," answered Viyesha. "You were there for us and that's what matters."

"D'you think he'll be back?" asked Juke.

"Without a doubt," answered Leon. "With his legions."

"Could he attack tonight?"

"I don't believe so," said Viyesha. "He was wounded in the fight with Badru and incurred further damage from the crystal. It will take him time to recover."

"What's the situation with the bisciones?" asked Leon

Juke pulled a face. "Growing in number. Father James and Mrs O'Briain have identified bisciones across the village. Actually, she killed six, but she didn't do it properly, so they'll be back. We could have a big problem on our hands."

"Picking off individual bisciones isn't going to work," said Viyesha. "We need to take out their leader, this Barolo di Biscione."

"Agreed," said Juke. "And we need to be ready for whatever the Fallen Angel throws at us, which means drawing up all the manpower we can get. How are Pantera and Aquila?"

"Pantera's made a good recovery," answered Leon. "She's a tough old cat. But Aquila's not great. He sustained some bad injuries. We can't rely on him."

"What about Emily and her friends?" asked Juke.

"They're preparing for their initiation tonight," answered Viyesha. "Seth and Tash have been lucky. They nearly didn't make it."

"But they did," said Leon, "and once they're initiated they'll be more powerful."

"It's not enough. You need more," said Juke, standing up and glancing at his watch.

"Where are you going?" asked Viyesha.

He grinned. "To get reinforcements. You're going to need all the help going, not only with the bisciones, but with what's to follow."

"Who, Juke? Who can you bring?" she queried.

He looked at her enigmatically. "Leave it to me. You concentrate on the initiation. Take care of Emily and her friends. I hope it goes well tonight. Tell Emily I'm looking after her mother."

He placed his bush hat on his head.

"I'll be back this time tomorrow. Then we prepare for the mother of all battles. We need to secure the future for our children."

He left the room, leaving Leon and Viyesha staring after him.

"What reinforcements?" she asked. "And what did he mean by 'our' children?"

## 36. **Into The Blue**

The full moon shone brightly in the cloudless sky. It was a perfect summer night, warm and still, small animals rustling in the undergrowth, the scent of honeysuckle in the air. Theo and I stood beneath the shadow of the Clock Tower, which remained intact, despite Bellynda's bombardment. It was peaceful and serene, and hard to believe that a spree of violence and killing had taken place less than twenty-four hours ago.

Theo pulled me towards him.

"This is it, Emily. This is where our futures become entwined forever."

His arms tightened around me and I felt his lips kiss my hair.

"I think that happened the moment we met," I murmured, burying my face in his shirt and inhaling deeply. I loved everything about this boy: the feel and touch of his body, his strength, his vulnerability. He only had to look at me with those deep blue eyes and I melted, desire and love creating an overwhelming need.

After all we'd been through, I could hardly believe the time was almost here when I'd bathe in the crystal's light and leave my human days behind. I looked up at him, seeing his tousled blond hair shining in the moonlight.

"It's a perfect evening, Theo," I whispered. "Surely nothing can go wrong."

"It can't," he said firmly and bent to kiss me.

As his lips touched mine, I felt sparks of energy enter my body. We were enmeshed, two beings fused together, the world outside ceasing to exist. This was my reality for now and all time, this golden boy who held me tight and filled my being with his love and energy. I felt weak in his arms, drunk with the intensity of the moment and knowledge of what was to come.

He broke away and smiled, and I melted all over again. Looking into those blue eyes was like journeying to eternity, with past, present and future merged into one. His smile made me breathless, drawing me to him like a magnet, and I was powerless to resist.

"No regrets for what you're about to give up?"

"None. What I said the other day wasn't what I was feeling. You know that. I was forced into it. It broke my heart to say the words."

"I know," he whispered. "It broke my heart to hear them. I couldn't believe you were walking away from me."

"It was the worst day of my life. I'd never felt so empty or alone."

He sighed. "To think we nearly lost everything. I can't believe I allowed myself to fall into such a pit of misery. I handed myself to Badru on a plate."

I put my finger on his lips. "Shush. He's gone. He can never hurt us again. Whatever the future holds, we face it together."

Then his lips were on mine and I felt a tidal wave of love and desire sweep through me, so strong it consumed me totally. I wanted nothing more than to be with this exquisite boy, possessed by him, consumed by him for all time.

I heard the clock above us begin to strike. Eleven chimes, heralding my last hour on earth as a mortal being. As the last chime struck, we forced ourselves apart.

"Not long, now, my darling. It's time to go. You need to prepare."

I nodded silently. The moment I'd been waiting for was upon us.

"Let's go," I murmured, taking his hand.

* * *

I stood in the Clock Tower Room wearing a flowing, blue gown that fell shimmering to the floor. I felt calm and serene, as if my whole life had been moving towards this point, without a hint of the nerves I thought I'd feel. My blond hair fell on my shoulders, brushed and shining, my face bare of make-up. As Viyesha prompted us, "Natural is best. You have no need of enhancements." My crystal necklace hung around my neck and I could feel the small blue crystal vibrating gently against my breastbone, in anticipation of the event to come.

Alongside me stood Seth and Tash, each dressed in a similar blue robe.

"You have to be kidding," said Seth when he'd first seen the gown. "I am not wearing a dress. No way. I'll look like a girl."

A word from Viyesha had soon changed his mind.

"These are sanctified garments, Seth, unsullied by human thought and emotion. The only other option is to go naked."

He'd agreed at that point, on the condition no one took photos and posted them on social media.

"Social media?" Theo had exclaimed in disbelief. "Does he really think we'll be putting pictures on Snapchat? The boy's a complete idiot. Doesn't he know how secret this is?"

"Yes, of course he does," I'd answered. "He's just nervous that's all. This is Seth, don't forget. Wisecracking, smartass Seth, who can't take anything seriously. He'll be fine. Let Violet take care of him, she knows how to handle him."

Tash had been quiet, putting on her gown without a word.

"Are you okay?" I'd asked her. "Is this what you want?"

"It's what I want more than anything in the world," she'd answered. "Not just to be beautiful for eternity, with perfect skin and teeth and nails, although that is a major plus point. But to be with Joseph. I've never felt like this about anyone else. He makes me feel happy and whole, as if it was meant to be. I couldn't imagine spending life without him. And to be with him for eternity, both staying young forever, is beyond my dreams. I can't quite believe it."

She looked amazing in her shimmering blue gown, gorgeous red Pre-Raphaelite hair falling around her shoulders, emerald eyes large and shining. She clutched Joseph's hand tightly, as if she never wanted to let go, and he gazed at her adoringly. It was all I could do not to cry. She'd been through so much and had nearly not made it. To have survived and found love was a fairy tale come true.

Seth, in comparison, loved the attention. He'd been born for this and to have the girl of his dreams by his side, head-over-heels in love with him, was a real life fantasy. They both looked like the cat that had got the cream and I hoped with all my heart it would work out for them. Seth needed to grow up, no doubt about that. But with eternity staring him in the face, he had time. And Violet had fallen in love with him as he was: funny, clever and chaotic. They had good times ahead, I was sure. She'd always be one step ahead of him, which is what he needed. With Violet, he'd never get bored. Life would be one great playground.

The moon came into view through the tall, thin windows, casting its silvery light into the room, lighting up the ancient hieroglyphics on the floor. At Viyesha's bidding, we stepped forward on to the strange green and blue markings. The family were dressed in similar shimmering blue gowns, standing in a circle around us. I glanced at Theo, blond and beautiful, and then at my friends. These were the people I loved most in the world, other than my mother. We'd been through so much together and now to be stepping into a life of true love and everlasting youth seemed unreal. I couldn't have wished for anything more.

The thought of my mother almost made me falter, but I knew she would want this for me. It was what she would have chosen given the chance. And it wasn't as if I'd never see her again. Things would just be different that's all.

As the moonlight illuminated the hieroglyphics, they began to glow, first gently, then brightly. Now Viyesha brought the ornate silver casket into the centre of the room and I realised the ancient symbols on its surface were the same as those on the floor. She opened the casket, revealing the large blue crystal, shining and beautiful. Blue light filled the room and torrents of blue energy fell onto the floor.

Viyesha placed the crystal in the centre of the symbols and immediately, they lit up like lights on a Christmas tree, piercing and bright.

"Move forward," she instructed us. "Stand on the hieroglyphics."

We did as she bid, stepping onto the glowing symbols and making a circle around the crystal. The family began to chant, *We hold eternity in our hands*', and I saw they each cupped their hands in front of them, with crossed thumbs, giving the sign of the crystal.

I heard the clock chiming midnight and could feel excitement pulsing through my veins. Already I was experiencing the most exquisite feelings of well-being and happiness, and couldn't imagine how it could get any better. It was like bathing in warm sunshine, feeling yourself drift away, light as a feather, without a care in the world. Mentally, I counted the chimes... nine... ten.... eleven...

As the clock struck twelve, everything changed.

The crystal that had been glowing brightly, now shone with an intensity that was unbearable. I felt my eyes hurting with the glare and closed them tightly. But it was no good. I couldn't escape the crystal's searing heat. It felt as if every part of my body was on fire, the flames eating through my flesh, reaching inside with fiery hostile fingers that tore me apart. I tried to scream, but no sound came and I realised there was no escape. I knew now why people didn't survive this. It was agony, like being submerged in boiling mercury. And now I was drowning, unable to breathe, the burning liquid filling my mouth, nose and lungs. Every part of me screamed in pain. I could feel the heat travelling along every blood vessel, crossing every synapse, filling every cell. My nerves screamed, my blood boiled and my mind teetered on the edge of sanity.

Then just as I could take no more of the burning pain, a chill filled my body and I was freezing cold, my blood turning to ice, shivers and shudders wracking my system. It felt now as if my blood vessels had frozen solid and I was a block of ice, immobile, unable even to blink my eyelids, the cold more painful than the burning flames. I couldn't swallow or move my fingers, everything was rigid, as if set in stone and I truly thought I was going to die.

Once more, the rolling heat flooded through my body and the pain was like nothing I'd ever experienced, like holding freezing fingers under a hot tap, the stabbing sharpness giving way to an intense, bone-hugging ache that was all-consuming.

I was so lost in the pain, so unaware of anything else, I couldn't even pray for it to stop. Pain was everywhere. In me, around me, through me… stabbing, piercing, cutting, jabbing. It was vicious, raw and ferocious, like being torn apart by wild animals, burnt at the stake and drowning in molten lava all at once.

Yet again, waves of icy cold flooded my body, hard and unrelenting, hitting with such force I lost consciousness, slipping thankfully into velvety blackness.

# PART THREE: THE BLUE

## 37. **Theo's World**

I opened my eyes to warm sunshine and looked around, not daring to move, for a moment seeing only brightness. Gradually I focused and took in my surroundings. I was lying in bed facing a window, rays of sunshine falling on the bedclothes. I glanced to one side and saw Theo, but not as I knew him. Everything had changed.

There was a vibrancy about him I'd never seen before. His hair shone with the intensity of burnished gold, his eyes danced with a million different shades of blue, his ivory skin was as smooth and translucent as alabaster.

"Hush, don't speak," he said gently. "It's too soon."

His voice was like a mountain spring tumbling over pebbles, clear and bright. I'd never heard so many different tones in a person's voice. It washed over me, comforting and cool

"Theo," I murmured. Even my voice sounded different. It was louder and more resonant. I felt as if I wanted to sing or to shout, to proclaim the amazing strength that was bubbling within me.

He smiled. "You've come through it, Emily. You've survived the initiation. The pain will soon be a distant memory. You've been reborn, your system regenerated with the crystal's power. Welcome to my world."

I lay still for a moment, then sat up with amazing speed, the world rushing to meet me.

"Whoa, Emily," laughed Theo. "You're going to have relearn everything. Slowly does it."

I reached over for his hand, nearly crushing it with my grip. "Ow!"

I let go and Theo rubbed his hand.

"Sorry," I boomed. The windowpanes rattled in their frames.

I dropped my voice to a whisper. "Oh, my God, Theo. How am I ever going to get used to this? I'm too strong and too loud."

He laughed. "You will. Give yourself time. Nobody said it was going to be easy. You've come through it pretty well unscathed. Some people don't make it."

My face fell and I felt a wave of panic rising inside.

"Seth and Tash?" I shouted. "Are they okay?"

Theo put his hands over his ears.

"Not so loud, Emily. You'll wake the dead. Yes, They're fine. They had a rough ride and it will take them longer to recover, but they're okay."

Relief flooded my system and I fell back on the bed. Immediately I heard the creaking sound of breaking wood and the mattress dropped to the floor.

"Oh my God," I shrieked. "I've broken the bed."

One of the small windowpanes cracked and shattered, showering the room with broken glass. Tears filled my eyes and I sighed loudly, blowing back Theo's hair.

"How am I going to rein it in, Theo," I whispered. "I wasn't expecting this. I'm a monster. None of your family is like this."

"Emily, you've just been initiated. I've had thousands of years to adapt. You've had minutes. You'll soon learn how to calm things down. It's like driving a Ferrari when you're used to a Mini. You need to get used to the power. Plus, you're seeing things as an immortal now. You have to readjust to everything."

Immortal. The word thundered through my head. I was immortal. I wouldn't get old and die. I would stay young forever. I'd be seventeen for the rest of my life.

"I need to see myself in a mirror," I shouted at Theo.

"Okay." He found a hand mirror on the dressing table and held it front of me. I seized it, pulling it towards me, staring at myself. The reflection that looked back was me, and yet it wasn't. Something was very different.

I looked as if I'd had the most amazing makeover. My skin shone, my eyes were bright and my hair thick and glossy. My mouth was redder and fuller, as if I'd had collagen injections. I looked healthier and a million times more glamorous.

"Oh my God. I look amazing," I gasped. "And I don't have any makeup on. Tash is going to love this. Like all her Christmases have come at once. I have to see her. And Seth."

Theo put his hand on my shoulder, stopping me from getting up.

"Like I said, they're recovering. It may take them longer. Don't forget, they've been ill and don't have your strength or resilience. I've never seen anyone handle their initiation so well as you, Emily."

I had to admit, I felt great. There was an energy pulsing through my veins that made me want to get up and discover this amazing new world I'd entered. I heard a clambering by the window and turned to see a fly running across the glass. A soft humming in an upper corner of the room was a spider spinning a web, and quiet whispering from the dressing table was a vase of flowers.

"It's magical, Theo," I gasped, my eyes wide in wonder. "Please let me go outside. And let me see the family. I can't wait to see them."

He could see the eagerness and energy bursting from me and relented.

"All right, but take things steady, okay? You don't know the strength you possess. Remember to move slowly and talk quietly while you adjust."

"Great," I shouted, jumping out of bed and landing on the floor. There was a loud cracking sound and I felt something give underneath me. "Oh my God, I've broken the floor boards!"

Theo raised an eyebrow.

Downstairs, we found Viyesha and Leon sitting in the ballroom. The fire crackled loudly in the grate and I was pleased to see the broken window and wall were as new. The drapes hung, blue and vibrant, no sign of the fire that had almost destroyed them. I took it all in, seeing the room as if for the first time. Viyesha sparkled with a bright blue aura, the large blue crystal at her throat blinding in its intensity, her cornflower-blue eyes dazzling and bewitching. I could almost see waves of sunlight emanating from her, bathing her surroundings in a soothing glow. Leon, sitting beside her, had a steely-blue aura that spoke of strength and determination. I hadn't appreciated just how invincible he was.

"Emily," said Viyesha joyously, rising and coming to meet me. "I didn't expect to see you so soon. You look amazing."

So did she, dressed immaculately as always, today in a midnight blue, flowing dress, nipped at the waist, with a tight-fitting bodice. A stunning bracelet and ring matched the crystal at her neck, her hair pinned up with a jewelled grip.

She embraced me and I purposely held back from holding her too hard. I was already learning to regulate myself. I felt her energy surround me and closed my eyes, soaking it up like a sponge.

"Gosh, Emily," she said, pulling back. "You're drinking my energy. Better be careful. You don't want to turn into an energy vampire."

I looked at her horrified.

"Sorry, I didn't mean to. It's just everything's so different, so concentrated."

"It's okay," she smiled. "You just need to learn some control."

"Try doing that with me, Emily, and you'll know about it," laughed Leon, stepping forward and embracing me.

Immediately, his energy field felt different. Whereas Viyesha's was soft and pliable, Leon's was hard and unyielding. It was like coming up against a rock face. I gently pulled at it with my own, but nothing happened.

"It's no good, Emily," he said. "However hard you try, you won't pull any energy out of me."

He stood back. "Welcome to the family, Emily. I can't tell you how glad we are you've come through the initiation. Your energy is clean and strong. Just what we need."

For a second, his expression darkened.

"What is it?" asked Theo. "What's happened?"

"Nothing's happened since the Fallen Angel left," answered Viyesha. "But the biscione numbers are growing. Juke's been monitoring the situation with Father James and Mrs O'Briain. They think there could be a small army amassing."

"We know the Fallen Angel will return," continued Leon. "We have to take seriously his threat that he'll return and destroy us. Given the number of bisciones in the village, it could be soon."

"Which means we must prepare," said Viyesha. "We need to take him down once and for all."

"So, it's all hands on deck," said Theo.

"Yes," replied his father. "We need all the manpower we can get."

"Including me, Seth and Tash?" I asked.

"Yes if you feel strong enough to fight," answered Viyesha.

I cracked my knuckles. "The way I feel, I'm strong enough to take on any number of bisciones or Fallen Angels and crush them with my bare hands. You have my support, that's a given."

"Thank you, Emily. The Fallen Angel may just have met his match," said Viyesha, looking at me fondly. " But I'm not sure about Seth and Tash."

"I want to see them, Viyesha," I said. "I need to know they're okay."

"All right. But be gentle with them. They're more fragile than you realise. Then spend some time with Theo. You deserve it, both of you. Let Leon, Juke and me do the planning. We'll involve you as soon as the time is right."

"Thank you, Viyesha. You won't find me wanting. And I'll do my best to contain myself, I promise." I grinned at Theo and took his hand. "Come on, if things are going to get tough we have to make the most of every moment."

"Ow," he cried, pulling back his hand. "Be gentle, remember?"

"Sorry, I forgot."

Instead, I threw my energy forward, forcing open the doors to the ballroom from ten feet away. I couldn't resist showing off just a little bit.

"Emily," Viyesha called after me. "You might want to change out of that blue gown."

## 38. **Consummation**

Seth lay back on the pillows with his eyes closed. Violet sat on a chair at his side, watching him carefully. Quietly, Theo and I closed the bedroom door behind us and came to stand by her.

"How is he?" I whispered. At least it was supposed to be a whisper. It came out rather louder than I intended and Seth opened his eyes.

"Hey, Emily," he croaked, his voice sounding tired. "You're looking good."

"So are you," I lied. In truth, he looked awful, dark circles beneath his eyes, skin pale and hair lank. I could see his energy field was in rags.

"I don't feel it," he tried to sit up, then fell back on the bed. "Hey, Vi, hold my hand."

She put her hand over his and I could see her transferring energy into him.

He smiled. "That feels good. Thank you."

She looked at him concerned, stroking his brow. "You need to rest, Seth. The initiation is tough. You have to give yourself time to get over it." She smiled at him, the sunshine from the window shining through her golden curls, giving her a halo. "The good news is, you've survived. And the even better news is we have fantastic times ahead."

"Fantastic, shmastic," he murmured. "No, that doesn't sound right."

"Do as Violet tells you, Seth," I told him. "Rest. You've got the whole of eternity to practise urban speak."

"God help us all," I heard Theo mutter behind me.

I smiled to myself, wondering how the two of them would get along. They were practically brothers-in-law.

Tash, on the other hand, and quite surprisingly, looked amazing. As if she'd just come through a total makeover, with Botox, collagen and any other beauty treatment you'd care to imagine. Her skin shone, her eyes twinkled and her lips were pink and full. She sat in bed, her voluminous hair falling around her shoulders, sparkling and shining in the morning sun, looking for all the world like a super model. Joseph sat beside her, holding her hand, a man besotted.

"Tash," I cried, running over to the bed. "You look fantastic. "I can't believe you've come through the initiation so well."

I embraced her, taking care to be gentle. I didn't want to crush her. I needn't have worried. As she put her arms around me, I was caught in an iron grip.

"Wow, you're strong. I thought you'd be a bit more fragile."

She smiled radiantly. "I feel really good. The process was horrible and I couldn't go through it again. But I can't believe how good I look."

I noticed the hand mirror on the bedside table. She obviously hadn't lost any time examining her face.

"To think I wasted all that money on Botox and collagen," she said, patting the skin on her cheek. "It's going to stay like this forever."

"It's not just about looks, though, Tash," I reminded her.

She gazed into Joseph's eyes. "No, I know. I'm the luckiest girl alive. I have everything I ever wanted."

She yawned suddenly. "You know what, I feel tired. I think I'll sleep for a bit. D'you mind, Em? I'll see you later."

She fell back on the pillow and was instantly asleep, looking like Sleeping Beauty.

We left Joseph with his princess and walked out into the gardens.

Now my senses went into overdrive. It was a beautiful summer's day, with clear blue skies and a gentle breeze. A million different scents assaulted my nostrils: the earthiness of the flower beds, the lushness of the dark green undergrowth, the heady aromas of Joseph's rose garden and a myriad of others, so many they were indistinguishable from one another. I gazed around, seeing for the first time the many different greens in the gardens, the shades of brown, the vibrant colours of the flowers. In the middle rose the golden walls of the Hall, nestling like a sleeping cat in the warm summer sunshine, the damaged turrets and battlements restored.

"I never realised it was so beautiful. Or so alive," I murmured, standing still, trying to take it all in.

Birdsong erupted around me, almost deafening, competing with the breeze noisily caressing the leaves. A sound to my right was a ladybird coming in to land, wings whirring like a helicopter, a bee gathering pollen buzzed with the energy of a jet engine. Everything had an intensity I'd never appreciated before, the colours, scents and sounds rushing towards me in sensory overload.

"There's so much, I don't know where to start," I whispered. "It's like being reborn into a wonderland."

"You'll get used to it, I promise," said Theo, taking my hand. "Why don't we walk down by the lake?"

"Sounds good to me," I said, falling in step beside him.

The water of the ornamental lake rippled gently in the breeze, catching the light, creating dappled patterns. Bright green lily pads graced the surface and the golden skins of koi carp were visible just below as they basked in the sunshine. We sat on a grassy bank beneath a weeping willow tree, in our own private space and I couldn't have asked for a more perfect setting. This was my own personal heaven and it was mine for eternity. I couldn't believe I was experiencing this moment, after all that had happened, after all the pain and heartache, the danger and despair. It felt dreamlike and unreal, and I wondered if I'd wake up and find myself back in my bedroom, thinking about college, wondering if I'd see Theo.

He pulled me close and I nestled against his body, luxuriating in his warmth and strength, feeling his energy around me, caring and protective.

"I need to see my mother," I murmured. "I have to explain to her. She'll know I'm different, that something's happened."

"Of course," said Theo. "But she knows you're here? You texted her?"

"Yes, I told her I was staying at the Hall. Juke was with her, so I know she's okay, specially with that serpent creature hanging around."

"There's no hurry, then," said Theo, nuzzling into my neck.

It felt fantastic. The old familiar longing rose up again and now there was nothing to stop us, no threat of Theo's energy bringing me to an early grave. Now, it was all for the taking and I gave myself to the moment, hungry for Theo, his body and the experience I'd desired and had been denied for so long.

Gently, he lay me down on the grassy bank, the grass soft and velvety, and slowly ran his hands over my body. His fingers felt electric on my skin, every nerve ending responding with an intensity I could never have imagined. I looked up into his eyes, piercing and blue, an echo of the sky above, and was pulled into their depths, drowning in a kaleidoscope of greys and blues. The sun shone through his blond hair, creating a golden halo, and I saw everything from a fresh perspective, my sensory awareness tuned to a fine level. He was sparkling and mesmeric. And he was mine.

When he kissed me, I could feel energy rising through my body, entwining with his, and could never have believed it was possible to feel so close to another being. Slowly, he undressed me, peeling back my clothes and admiring my new superhuman body. On my arm I saw I bore the mark of the crystal, the circle crossed by an infinity sign, indicating I was a true initiate.

He took off his t-shirt and I ran my fingers over his body, tracing the same mark on his arm, admiring his muscle definition, his firm skin, his perfect physique. We were young, beautiful and superhuman, fired up with need and longing for each other. He lay his body against mine and I clung to him, entwining my legs around him, wanting to draw him in and absorb every particle of his being. We'd endured so much, I'd never thought this moment would happen.

When it did, it was the culmination of everything that had gone before. We were truly together, now and for always. This was the golden boy I'd fallen in love with and given up my life for. Now we could be together in every sense of the word, discovering each other's bodies and minds with superhuman perception. I pushed my energy into his mind and he opened up and let me in, so just as he possessed me, I possessed him, body, mind and soul. It was perfect, incandescent, existential.

And from somewhere deep within my psyche, a distant memory rose to the surface. I saw a dry, hot land and bright colours. Rich reds, deep blues, vibrant ochres. I saw glossy black hair, eyes rimmed with kohl, and lean, tanned bodies dancing and singing, a banqueting table piled high with fruit and a wedding bed covered in white silk drapes. It was an ancient memory, deep and long forgotten, impacted by time and centuries gone past.

And then it was gone as I surrendered to the moment.

To the present. Here and now. For all time. With Theo.

## 39. **Juke's Secret**

It was late morning when Theo and I returned to the Hall. We walked into the ballroom to find Leon and Viyesha, Juke and my mother waiting for us. My mother sat next to Juke on one of the massive sofas, back ramrod straight and dressed in a blue dress I hadn't seen before. She looked different somehow, her features sharper, her energy more defined.

Then I got it. It was I who'd changed. I was no longer the mortal girl I'd once been. I was a light being, my body chemistry altered, no longer subject to the laws of physics. Everything I saw had a fresh intensity; looks, sounds and smells magnified a million times. It was a continual journey, new experiences at every step.

"Hi Mum," I said, aware I was speaking too loud.

I felt my cheeks blush bright red. Not only had I changed biologically, but emotionally, too. Theo and I were no longer innocent and I was sure it was written all over my face. I felt gawky and adolescent, not knowing why my mother was here, whether she knew about my initiation.

"Hi Emily." She spoke sweetly, putting my mind at rest.

"We were discussing events in the village," said Viyesha.

"You were?" I answered, baffled. I was pretty sure she didn't mean basket-weaving and coffee mornings.

"You need to speak with your mother," she said, getting up. "You can talk in here. We'll leave you in private."

Now I was worried. I hadn't meant to tell my mother about my initiation quite so soon.

Viyesha and Leon left the ballroom, calling for Theo to accompany them. He left, giving me a puzzled expression. The double doors clicked shut and there was silence. I sat on the sofa opposite Juke and my mother, eyeing them curiously.

"What is it?" I asked. "Why are you here? Are you checking up on me?"

My mother smiled calmly and now I really was spooked. This calm person before me was more like a waxwork than my mother. Was she a biscione?

"We're not checking up on you, Em. But we need to speak with you."

"We?" I questioned, looking at them closely. "Oh no, don't tell me. You're getting married."

My mother glanced at Juke and a special smile went between them.

"Not exactly."

"Juke's moving in?" I questioned.

"Emily, please don't shout," said my mother. "If you stop asking questions for a second, I'll explain."

I closed my mouth and waited for her to speak. I found my hands were gripping the edge of the sofa and forced myself to relax.

"There's no easy way to say this," she began, glancing at Juke, who nodded encouragingly. "Juke and I..." She tried again. "The thing is, I knew Juke before you were born." She looked at me hopefully.

"Okay. So he's not quite the stranger I thought he was." I spoke as softly as I could, consciously lowering my voice.

"No, he's not. In fact, he's not a stranger at all." She took a deep breath. "Emily, meet your father."

I stared at her as if she'd gone mad. Less than twelve hours after being initiated, the wheel of fortune had turned again and now I was being told I had an urban angel for a father.

"My what? I have a father already. He lives in America. I can't have two."

"You don't. Juke's your real father. Your dad in America isn't your biological father."

I looked at Juke, with his crinkly skin, twinkling blue eyes and dreadlocks. It was true I'd had an affinity with him. But for him to be my dad didn't make sense.

"I don't understand," I started to say.

My mother held up her hand. "Let me explain." She looked beyond me, into the distance. "Seventeen years ago I met a guy who was different, who travelled the world, who showed me another side of life. We fell in love and before I knew it, I was pregnant. He begged me to go with him, but I couldn't leave what was familiar to me, the life I knew. I moved in with my parents and prepared to become a single mother. Only I didn't. They had a lodger staying with them, a kind, decent man who offered to marry me. I took him up on his offer and we were married, just before you were born. I tried, Emily. I tried really hard to make it work, but it was no good. After a couple of years, we admitted defeat and he left for America. For a while, you and I lived in a small rented apartment in Birmingham. Then your granny died, leaving granddad on his own and we came to live in the village. The rest is history."

I stared at Juke, not trusting myself to speak.

"I'm sorry, Emily," she said softly. "I should have told you. I just never had the opportunity. And then it was easier not to say anything."

She looked down, a bright flush staining her cheeks.

"So, that's why I never got on with my dad," I said. "He was always distant. After he left, he didn't make much effort to keep in touch, specially as I got older."

I turned to Juke. "If you were my dad, why didn't you stick around? Was it easier just to abandon us?"

"Safer, not easier," he answered.

"What d'you mean?"

"You know what my line of work is, Emily. I fight the darkness. I rid the world of demons and devils. Sure, I wanted you and your mum to come with me. But realistically, it was no place for a mother and child. It was too dangerous."

"So, why didn't you stay?"

He paused and looked wistful. "I wanted to. But suburban life wasn't for me. I had to follow my calling. As long as you were safe, I could carry on fighting."

"Did you ever come back?"

"Yes. Once. But your mother was married by then. You had a dad and it didn't seem fair to complicate matters."

"So you left again."

"Yes."

"Then, why come back now? I don't understand."

"I never stopped watching over you. I came back because I detected danger. A few months ago, I saw a darkness descend on the village."

"You mean the Fallen Angel?"

"Yes. He was following the crystal. I saw great light and great darkness, and knew I had to protect you."

I was trying to get my head around this. "Let me get this straight. If the family hadn't come here with the crystal, the Fallen Angel wouldn't have followed. And neither would you. So, it's thanks to the de Lucis family you're here at all."

"I suppose so. In a manner of speaking."

Suddenly a million questions filled my mind. The ground was shifting and so many things were unclear.

"Did my mum know you were an urban angel?"

"Yes, she did. Not only that, Emily. She was one, too."

The surprises just kept rolling.

"Run that by me again. Mum? You were an urban angel? How come you never told me? How come you weren't off fighting dark forces?"

My mother looked helplessly at Juke. "It wasn't an option," she said softly. "Not when you came along."

"Your mother was just discovering her abilities when I met her," said Juke. "That's how I found her. There was a dark entity in the building where you lived. She blasted it to smithereens. I was on patrol and saw her in action. I fell in love there and then."

"Like I said, I had the option to go with Juke," continued my mother. "But I had to put you first. And Juke had to continue the fight. It was impossible for us to be together."

"Have you had secret powers all along?" I asked.

"No." She looked into the distance again, as if seeing the life she could have had. "If I'd continued as an urban angel, I'd have put you in danger. We decided it wasn't right for you."

"So you gave it up? Can you do that? Surely you are one or you're not."

"I allowed Juke to block my etheric memory," she answered. "To close me down. Stop any awareness of the supernatural from entering my mind. It was what I wanted. What we wanted."

"Leaving you as an ordinary person." I finished off the story for her.

"Yes. Until last night."

"And what happened last night?" I asked, thinking of my initiation. It seemed I wasn't the only one going through change.

"Juke lifted the block. The memories came back."

"And the power," added Juke. "She's got her power back."

Now I realised why my mother looked different. It wasn't just that I was seeing things with greater intensity. She had changed. Her aura was white gold, faint but there, speaking of a power beyond that of an ordinary mortal.

"You're an urban angel," I whispered, or tried to. It came out as more of a shout. "How did you lift the block, Juke?"

"A kind of energy shiatsu. Opens everything up. Gets the energy flowing."

"I see," I said, although I didn't. Not really.

Now I put two and two together. "If both my parents are urban angels, I guess that makes me one, too."

"That's the way genetics work." Juke grinned at me.

"So that explains why I can see people's energy fields, how I was able to hold the crystal without any ill effects and why I could talk with the Fallen Angel without being affected."

"The power's been dormant within you since you were born," said my mother. "There was no need to release it when you were younger. I wanted you to have a normal childhood, without feeling different or strange. It was only when you met Theo that your abilities started to show."

I thought back. She was right. There'd never been any incident in my childhood or schooldays where I'd felt different from other people. If anything, I'd always felt rather ordinary. I'd always wished there was something about me that set me apart. If only I'd known.

"I guess you know what happened here last night," I said to my mother. "About my initiation, I mean."

"Yes, I do. And you have my blessing, Emily. We live in a dark, dangerous, world. With Theo by your side, and possessing the power you have, you can make a difference. You can work alongside Juke and I, fighting the darkness."

"So, you're working as an urban angel now? Have you left the wood yard?"

She laughed. "I guess. I don't know. I haven't made any plans yet."

I looked closely at Juke, seeing his fine, silver energy skim the air. This was my father. It certainly explained a few things, but it was a massive leap to accept this rugged world-traveller as my dad. There again, how cool to have an urban angel as your father.

"Why did you restore her power last night?" I asked. "Why not the night before when you fought the Fallen Angel?"

"Because I thought I could do it alone and I didn't know for sure she wanted to become an urban angel again." His expression was grim, his eyes dark and hard. "I learned to my cost I can't fight him alone. I need other urban angels around me. And who better than my family?"

"Your family." I rolled the word around in my head. Suddenly I had two new families, both fairly high in the weirdness stakes.

"Do Viyesha and Leon know?" I asked.

"Yes, they do," said my mother. "I'm sorry, Emily, but we had to tell them. That's why they left us alone. I guess they've told Theo by now."

I sat and thought for a moment. I could go either of two ways. I could fight this, blaming my mother for living a lie all these years. Or I could accept it, going with the flow and embracing my newfound power. Speaking of which….

"Let me get one thing straight," I said, moving my gaze from one parent to the other. "If I have the genetic make-up of an urban angel and I've just been initiated in the light of the blue crystal, what does that make me?"

"We don't know, Emily," answered Juke. "We have no idea what you're capable of. But we do know you have special powers, and if anyone can fight the darkness, it's you."

My mother spoke. "You have a destiny, Emily, and it's beginning now."

"But what do I do?" I protested. "How do I harness the power?" I held up my hands. "How do I make it work?"

"The village is overrun with bisciones," said Juke. "We need to destroy them. That's where you start."

"Before the Fallen Angel returns," added my mother. "No point giving him extra ammunition."

"My first fight," I said and realised I was cracking my knuckles.

I felt energy building within and my aura expand. Overhead, tiny crystal droplets in the chandeliers started to pop, spraying the floor with glass.

Life was certainly getting interesting.

## 40. **Battling The Bisciones**

We crouched in the undergrowth outside the village hall. Inside, we could hear merriment and laughter as the Young Wives met. To my left was Juke, my father, although I didn't think I could ever call him dad. To my right was my mother, restored to her former status as an urban angel. I was still trying to get my head around it. There again, I'd changed too, which kind of balanced things out. We were all adjusting.

Theo was reluctantly absent. Viyesha had persuaded him I needed to spend time with my mother and father as we got used to our new roles, so he'd stood down, cautioning me to be careful and summon him via my crystal if I needed him.

To my mother's left was Father James and Mrs O'Briain, both seasoned biscione spotters. They'd accepted news of our changes without batting an eyelid.

"Who are we to judge?" Father James said, with remarkable acceptance. "The fight against evil takes many forms. We need all the help we can get."

Now Mrs O'Briain apprised us of the situation. "So far, we've identified two groups within the village," she whispered. "This is the first. We watched them last night doing a make-up demonstration. Sadly, there were a couple of casualties."

"Casualties?" asked my mother.

"Two women were turned into bisciones while we were there. We couldn't do anything without drawing attention to ourselves," explained Father James.

My mother shuddered, thinking how she'd nearly attended. If it wasn't for Juke, she could be a biscione by now.

"You did the right thing," whispered Juke. "They mustn't suspect. We need to take them by surprise. I propose we attack now. Once they're destroyed, we'll move on to the next group, eliminate as many as possible while we have the chance."

"What can I do?" I asked, desperate to put my new powers to the test.

"Observe and learn," advised Juke. "Watch us. Your turn is next."

"Are you up to this, mum?" I asked her anxiously. "This is dangerous stuff."

"Don't worry, Emily. I used to eat bisciones for breakfast."

"Your mother was one of the best," said Juke. "Totally fearless. Demons didn't stand a chance."

I looked at her, taut and edgy, eyes shining bright, eager for the kill. It was hard to reconcile this tough speaking warrior with the new-age creature I'd grown up with. Part of me was freaking out, but another part liked it. I'd thought I knew who my mother was. Turned out, I knew nothing. She'd had a whole life before me, dangerous and exciting, and now that life was back again.

"We've been spotted," said Father James in a low voice, as a face appeared at the window.

A woman with heavily made-up eyes stared down at us. When she saw Father James' crucifix hanging round his neck, she flinched, and for a brief second a forked tongue shot out of her mouth. Then it was gone and she backed away.

"Our cover's blown," said Juke, glancing at my mother. "We need to strike. Ready?"

"As I'll ever be," she answered.

In a flash, they'd disappeared from our hiding place in the bushes. I saw a residual wisp of silver energy where they'd been, dissipating quickly in the cool night air. I watched through the window, holding my breath as I saw them enter the hall, each wielding a shining silver sword, rays of light radiating from their bodies.

There was widespread panic and commotion among the women. Two turned instantly into ferocious, snapping serpents, open jaws revealing rows of jagged white teeth. In unison, Juke and my mother used their swords. Slicing rapidly with a wide arcing movement, their fast-moving blades cut clean through the serpent necks, causing black blood to flow and the huge heads to topple. Seeing two of their number felled, others assumed serpent form and in no time the hall was a seething nest of snakes, coiling around one another, slithering and hissing, twisting and turning, jaws outstretched, ready to bite.

My mother and Juke were shining so brightly it was hard to look at them. They turned this way and that, slicing and cutting in all directions, serpent heads flying and black blood spurting. I watched in awe as they moved through the room, agile and fluid.

But the more they destroyed, the more that came and soon they were surrounded by a circle of angry serpents bearing down on them. Juke and my mother stood back-to-back, facing their opponents, holding up bright, silver shields to fend off the serpents' snapping jaws. It was clear they were outnumbered.

"I need to help," I said, jumping to my feet. "They don't stand a chance against all those snakes. There's got to be over thirty in there."

I was on my feet, ready to go when Mrs O'Briain put a hand on my shoulder, stopping me.

"They're urban angels, Emily. This is what they do."

I hovered at the window, hardly daring to watch. My mother and Juke were in a seemingly impossible situation. But then an amazing thing happened. They began to expand their energy fields, creating a shimmering heat haze. As the energy rippled around them, their bodies began to concertina outwards, creating a number of replicas, until there were about a dozen angels wielding glinting silver swords.

I stared, awestruck. I'd heard this was how Juke fought the Reptilia singlehandedly. Now I'd seen it for myself.

The angels moved forward, so fast it was hard to make out their individual figures. Swift and agile, they stabbed and cut, attacking and killing every serpent.

Suddenly, I felt a pull within me that was too strong to ignore.

"Sorry, Mrs O'Briain," I muttered. "I have to be in there."

I ran around the building, through the main entrance and into the hall. Then I was in the midst of the mayhem, surrounded by shining angel warriors flashing powerful swords, fighting snarling serpents with ferocious teeth. Everywhere I looked serpent heads were toppling and blood was flowing. The stench was overpowering, but I felt excitement rising and threw myself into the fray, power surging through my arms. As if by magic, a sword was in my hand and I struck out as a serpent came for me, raising my arms high and slashing its neck. I cut clean through, slicing off its head. Then another came and I struck out again, felling it effortlessly. I stood back, observing my handiwork. This was too easy. No sooner had the thought gone through my head than three came at once and I was in trouble. I looked from one to the other, unsure what to do. If I attacked one, the other two would finish me off.

In panic, I looked round the room for help, but the other angels were fighting. I was on my own. Time slowed and instinct kicked in. I pushed my energy in three directions and suddenly I was fighting all three serpents at once, beheading them in unison, my arms moving intuitively, independent of my thoughts.

It took no longer than a few minutes for the massacre to be over, the serpents dead, their mutilated forms littering the room, black blood pooling on the floor and running down the walls. In an instant, the shining replicas returned to the figure that had created them and I felt my own energy draw back. Suddenly, there was just me, looking down on three grinning serpent heads.

I saw Juke and my mother standing amidst the carnage, back to normal, no sign of their swords or shining brilliance. I looked down at my hands and realised my own sword had disappeared.

"Well done, Emily. I knew you had it in you," called Juke.

"Did you see me?" I demanded. "I killed five serpents?"

"You're a natural," said my mother proudly. "I've never seen anyone replicate so easily."

The severed heads and bodies began to emit acrid black smoke that curled and looped around. As it cleared, I saw the serpents had disappeared, replaced by women lying around the room. Mrs O'Briain and Father James appeared at the doorway, peering in.

"Are they dead?" asked Mrs O'Briain.

"How are we going to explain this?" asked Father James. "We've already half a dozen bodies in the morgue."

"They're not dead," answered Juke, placing his hands over a couple of the women. "I can detect a life force."

Slowly, the women began to revive, stretching limbs and rubbing their eyes, looking dazed and confused, clearly not remembering what they'd been through.

"We need to go," said Juke. "Our work's done here. The women are safe."

Leaving the Young Wives to come round, we vacated the village hall, heading for our next destination, the Sports Hall at the far end of the village.

"Tell me about the bisciones," I said to Juke as we walked. "What happens when a biscione attacks?"

"It consumes the victim's soul," he answered. "That's how it feeds. What's left is a new biscione that sounds and acts like the person, but is just an empty shell, ready to turn into a serpent at any moment."

"The new ones are the most dangerous," added my mother. "They're hungry and desperate to feed."

"And when we cut off a biscione's head?" I asked.

"The spell is broken. The soul reconnects with the body, and the person is whole once again."

"Unless you use my sword," pointed out Mrs O'Briain. "It seems I don't have the power. The bisciones I beheaded turned back into women, but they didn't wake up."

"Unfortunately, they're still bisciones," said Juke. "The only way to kill them is with a celestial sword."

"Like mine?" I asked.

"Yes."

"What happens to the soul if we don't kill the serpent?"

"It's harvested by the head biscione, the leader of the pack," answered Juke. "Also known as the Capobranco."

"You mean Barolo di Biscione," said Father James grimly.

I remembered him cleaning windows at our house, how I'd seen him transform into a huge serpent in my mind's eye. There was no doubting his powers. He was deadly.

"We need to destroy him," I said. "He's at the root of all this."

"Agreed," agreed Juke. "The bigger his pack of bisciones, the more souls he harvests and the stronger he gets."

"The problem is we can only kill the bisciones when they're in serpent form," explained my mother. "If we kill them in female form, the women's souls have nowhere to return."

"Leaving them lost in the void," said Mrs O'Briain, crossing herself.

"Exactly."

"He's clever," said Juke. "With the energy of all those souls, he has huge power. As long as his bisciones stay in female form, he knows we won't attack. It gives him an army that will defend him to the last, that we can't touch."

"Which is exactly why the Fallen Angel summoned him," said my mother. "He's one of the oldest, wiliest demons in existence."

"And to think I was taken in by him," said Mrs O'Briain with a shiver. "He was so attractive. So personable."

"That's the nature of a demon," said Juke. "They're very convincing."

"So we have to kill as many serpents as we can to weaken the Capobranco, then finish him off," I said.

"That's about it," said Juke wryly.

"And if the Fallen Angel arrives in the middle of it? What then?" asked Father James.

"We pray," answered Juke. "Who knows what horrors he'll unleash? Now he's lost the one thing he wanted, he has only one aim. To destroy us all."

I looked at my mother, her eyes shining and face flushed, back with the man she loved, feeling alive for the first time in years. She'd sacrificed everything to keep me safe. Then I looked at Juke, weathered and battle-worn, strong and brave, and felt a rush of pride that he was my father.

I wondered whether we were capable of winning this fight. Or if I was about to lose my family, just as we'd been reunited.

### 41. **Serpent Slaying**

Time was of the essence and we had to destroy every biscione we could find, so we moved quickly to the Sports Hall. It was situated at the southern boundary of the village, surrounded by playing fields. A special dinner was being held in celebration of the village's sportswomen and we waited in the foyer while Juke assessed numbers and layout. We could hear the speaker talking of the women's commitment to their sport, and the many leagues and competitions in which the village teams participated.

"We need to attack," said Mrs O'Briain. "We don't have time to stand and listen."

"We need to plan," said Juke. "I'd say there's between sixty and seventy women in there and we don't know how many of them are bisciones."

"They're pretty virulent," said Father James. "I'd say they're all bisciones."

"Best to divide the room into three," said my mother. "We'll take a third each. Mrs O'Briain and Father James, stay at the entrance. Use your holy water and crucifixes to keep them in the room, but no beheading please, Mrs O'Briain."

I couldn't help it. Her words gave me a thrill I wasn't anticipating. I relished the prospect of killing demons, as if some primal force had taken hold of me. I'd never liked violence before. Now I was spoiling for the kill.

"Are you okay with this, Emily?" asked my mother. "You'll need to replicate many more times. Can you do it? This is good training ground."

I could feel myself glowing. It was a test. A rite of passage to becoming a fully fledged urban angel.

"Absolutely," I said. "Let me at them."

There was applause as the speaker concluded and that was our cue. At a sign from Juke we burst into the room, shining and fearsome. There was instant panic. Most of the women turned into snapping serpents, rising above us, jaws opening ferociously. I felt no fear, just a sense of power. As my energy field expanded, I pushed my consciousness forward and felt myself moving outwards many times. I was replicating and it gave me a potent feeling of invincibility.

I glanced around, seeing myself reflected like a fairground mirror. Each of my different selves leapt into action, wielding swords with deadly accuracy, cutting through serpent necks as if harvesting corn. Severed heads and spurting blood filled the room as my various selves fought on, thrusting and slicing.

I was aware of my parents doing the same, their replicated selves cutting a swathe through the room. We were shining urban warriors, moving at speed like a relentless cutting machine, existing only as extensions of the swords in our hands, mowing down all in our pathway.

The massacre was quick and bloody, and in minutes we came to a halt, looking for serpents that had evaded our blades. There were none. Any trying to escape had been contained by Mrs O'Briain and Father James wielding crucifixes.

The smoke came next, acrid and black, curling around the corpses, obscuring our view. As it cleared, we saw a roomful of women beginning to reawaken, rubbing their eyes in disbelief. I barely noticed them, focusing instead on an area by the stage, where the smoke continued to swirl, thick and dark.

Following my gaze, Juke addressed the women. "Go home! Lock your doors. You've had a lucky escape. Go and keep your families safe. "

Fearful it was some kind of terrorist attack, the terrified women ran from the hall, desperate to get out.

The swirling by the stage grew thicker, taking shape, becoming a figure I recognised. It was Barolo di Biscione, the Capobranco, sultry and beautiful, a black cloak around his shoulders, dark eyes glinting malevolently.

"So, Ahmes, you dare to cross me," he hissed sibilantly, his voice mesmerising and magnetic. He smiled, so handsome he was almost angelic.

"You think you can stop me by killing a few serpents? Are you so naïve? This is nothing compared to the forces at my disposal. When I summon, they will come. D'you know why? Because I own them. Lock, stock and soul. They're ready to destroy you, and when that's done, ready to die, while their souls live on in me. And the beauty of it is, you won't dare touch them, for fear of killing their bodies and condemning their souls. Which means I have an indestructible army."

I faced him head on, my energy glowing, my parents flanking me.

"Brave talk," I hissed back. "But pride goes before a fall, something you and your master know all about. Better get ready to fall from grace, this time forever."

I catapulted my energy forward like a fast shining arrow, aiming to take him surprise. He deflected it immediately, raising his hand to knock it away.

"Nice try, Ahmes, but too slow," he taunted. "Enjoy your last few hours. My master is waiting. I probably shouldn't say, but he has a little surprise in store."

This time, Juke and my mother hurled their energies forward. But it was too late. He'd already disappeared in a swirl of black smoke. The stage was empty.

I swallowed, my earlier feelings of invincibility gone. Was I really as capable as Juke believed? Or was his confidence in me misplaced?

Time was running out and I was about to find out.

## 42. **Girl Power**

The two orderlies manning the morgue chatted together, discussing family matters and affairs of the heart. It had been a quiet night. Just as well with so many fatalities the night before. Half a dozen heart attack victims from a local village. Bit of an anomaly, especially given the young age of the victims and the fact they were all female. But their job wasn't to question, just to store the bodies ready for the undertaker once the death certificate was signed. If anything strange was going on, the coroner would take charge. Another hour, then it was handover and home time.

"I always find it a bit spooky on the graveyard shift," said the older, a large lady with greying hair and a sagging midline.

"You read too many horror books," laughed her companion, a smart, blond-haired young woman. She examined her nails. "I must get a manicure, these are atrocious. It's my friend's wedding next week and I want to look fabulous."

"Make sure you don't steal the bride's thunder," the older woman cautioned.

"No chance of that. She's spent a fortune having everything done." She glanced at the clock. "Time for a final check. There's one lady out for viewing. She needs putting into storage. Will you do it and I'll complete the paperwork?"

"If I must, I suppose."

The grey-haired woman walked down the corridor, into the viewing room, where the deceased's body lay, still and unmoving, beneath a pale green sheet.

"Such a shame," she muttered, pulling back the sheet and looking at the dead woman's sleek black hair and attractive features. "Just shows. You never know when your number's up. Bet she never thought she'd end up in here."

She removed a clipboard from the gurney rail, checking the details, turning away from the body to face the light.

"I must get some reading glasses," she told herself, blinking.

Behind her, something moved beneath the pale green sheet. Slowly, a beautifully manicured hand stretched out.

The grey-haired woman filled in the required details, humming gently to herself, and turned back to the body, ready to wheel it from the room.

"What the...?" Her eyes opened wide in disbelief and the words died in her throat as she took in the attractive young woman with the sleek black hair sitting up.

The woman smiled beguilingly but said nothing, swinging her legs off the gurney and removing the sheet. She was dressed in a blue hospital gown.

Without thinking, the grey-haired woman crossed herself and gulped.

"Goodness, you hear of this happening, but I've never... I haven't... Hello dear. Don't be alarmed. You're at the hospital. I'll go and get someone."

She backed towards the door, still facing the woman, who took a step towards her, still smiling, now scarily so, her eyes staring without blinking.

"Wait here, dear," she started to say as the woman's face began to change.

Her scream stuck in her throat as the woman's skin became scaly and smooth, her neck stretching upwards, her mouth elongating, eyes flattening on either side of her head. Struck dumb with fear, the orderly gazed into the jaws of an enormous snake, its mouth opening wider than she would ever have thought possible. Rooted to the spot, she offered no resistance as the snake extended its jaws around her head, forcing her body down its throat. There was a brief pause as the snake absorbed what it required, then opened its mouth and regurgitated the contents.

Once again, the orderly stood in the viewing room, a vacant look in her eyes.

The snake snapped back into human form and spoke to her victim. "There, that wasn't so bad, was it? Now you need to feed.

That will make you feel better. Don't you have a friend on this shift?"

Without saying a word, the orderly left the viewing room, walking down the corridor towards her colleague. The dark-haired woman stepped into the corridor and went in the opposite direction, heading for the cold chamber where the cadavers were stored. She began opening doors, pulling out sliding drawers and examining the contents, soon locating the five bodies she sought. She waited patiently while they opened their eyes, tentatively moving hands and feet. Soon the five women who had died alongside her the previous night were standing next to her.

"Time to feed," said the dark-haired woman. "Then we have an appointment to keep. The master is summoning us."

She indicated the exit and the women silently left the chamber, gliding along the corridor as if on castors. At the reception desk, they were joined by the two orderlies, now staring ahead with blank expressions.

"You'll be hungry," the dark-haired woman said to the younger of the two. "When your craving's satisfied you can help with the task ahead."

"What d'you want me to do?" asked the woman.

"Join our master. A battle is looming. He needs his infantry."

They left the morgue and fanned out across the hospital, heading for the women's wards.

Some time later, a large group of women amassed in the hospital's main car park.

As one, they took to the road, heading out of town and onto the country lane that lead to Hartswell-on-the-Hill.

## 43. **Superpowers**

We returned to Hartswell Hall to find celebration in the air.

Viyesha shrugged. "I know you've been fighting the bisciones. And I know we need to prepare for what's to come. But just for a few minutes, please indulge them. They deserve it."

She was referring to Seth and Tash, who stood in the ballroom with Joseph and Violet. I could see them talking animatedly through the open doors.

"Cool or what?" Seth was saying.

"Do it again," shrieked Violet.

I walked in, the adults behind me.

"Hey, guys, what's going on?"

Seth had made a full recovery. He looked tall and handsome. His olive skin was smooth, his hair thick and black, and his eyes sparkling with fun and life. It was so long since I'd seen him looking this good that I stood and stared, a big grin on my face. Violet was staring at him transfixed.

"Em," he cried, "you're not gonna believe this."

"What?"

"Stay where you are and watch," he instructed.

I stood still, not knowing what to expect.

He concentrated intensely and I could see his body tensing up, becoming rigid with effort, his muscles trembling with exertion. His skin appeared to be getting darker and I could feel waves of heat coming from him.

"Careful, Seth," I warned. "You don't want to spontaneously combust."

"I'm okay," he said between gritted teeth. "Nearly there."

He relaxed and as he did, his body began to change. His nose extended, growing into a long, curved black snout. The black fringe that flopped over his face grew erect, transforming into two tall rectangular ears on top of his head, and his eyes elongated on either

223

side of his head. He resembled something between a greyhound and a jackal, with a bit of aardvark thrown in. I stared in disbelief. His body changed too, still human in shape, but now lithe and limber, his arms and legs longer and muscular, covered with a downy, brown fur. In one hand, he held a tall, thin staff. A yellow loincloth was wrapped around his middle, keeping him decent, and behind him, a long, forked tail protruded at a rakish angle.

"OMG, you've got a tail," I said, putting my hand over my mouth to stop myself giggling. I didn't know what to think.

The creature looked at me with indignant eyes, unable to speak. A mournful whine came from its mouth.

"What is he, Viyesha?" I asked, turning to gauge her reaction.

She smiled, bemused. "In Egyptian times, we called it a Set Animal. He was the son of Amun-Ra, a symbol of power and strength, whose job was to protect. The long thin staff was known as a Was Sceptre, also symbolic of power. Quite why Seth has become one, I'm not sure. It's not what I'd have expected."

"Trust Seth to turn into an ugly mutt," said a voice behind me. It was Theo. He stood by me, linking his fingers with mine. It felt good to feel him so close.

"Honestly," he exclaimed, "the rest of us develop superhuman powers. But Seth turns into an ancient zoo animal. Typical!"

"I think he's beautiful," said Violet, running her fingers across the Set Animal's furry head. A strange rolling sound came from its throat, which I think meant he liked it.

Gradually, his snout began to retract, the tall ears to fall flat and the fur to disappear. Once again Seth stood before us looking pleased.

"Whadaya think?" he asked. "Can't tell you how amazing I feel when I turn into that animal." He looked disparagingly at Theo. "Ancient zoo animal or not, I have this power running through me, like I could wrestle lions."

"It's okay apart from the tail," I joked, trying to lighten the mood.

"Okay, the tail's a bit weird, I admit," he said.

"The tail is weird?" queried Tash. "The whole thing's off the wall."

"You're a fine one to talk," countered Seth. He turned to me. "Wait till you see what Tash turns into."

"Go on," I instructed. "Let's have a look."

She stood in the centre of the room and, like Seth, concentrated hard, her eyes screwed up and her brow furrowed, willing herself to change. Slowly, her neck elongated, her arms fused to her sides and her skin became smooth and scaly. Her nose flattened and her jaws extended, while her long, red hair solidified into a huge hood around her head and neck. She was a huge, red and green serpent, with a wide, angry mouth, sharp white teeth and one large green eye in the middle of her forehead.

"Oh my God, she's a biscione," I said, looking at her in horror.

She reacted by shooting a forked tongue out of her mouth and hissing loudly. The red hood around her head expanded, making her bigger and scarier, and instinctively I backed away.

"She's not a biscione," said Viyesha. "She's a hooded cobra, revered in ancient Egypt for her power and wisdom. Many of the pharaohs had a hooded cobra on their headdress, representing Wadjet, the protector goddess."

"Like Tutankhamun," said Violet.

"Yes, he had a blue hooded cobra on his death mask," answered Viyesha.

"And what about the huge eye?" asked Seth, peering forward in fascination.

Tash reacted by rearing forward, shooting her forked tongue at him.

"Whoa, Tash," he cried, leaping backwards. "That's lethal."

"It was known as the Eye of Ra, all-seeing and all-knowing," explained Viyesha. "Wadjet protected the sun god Ra against evil and chaos."

"It's all about protection, isn't it?" said Joseph. He looked fondly at the huge hooded Cobra with the massive eye and couldn't help himself. He ran his fingers lovingly along her scaly body. I shuddered. It might be Tash, but it didn't mean I had to get near her.

"It would appear so," said Leon from his place by the door. "The crystal has given us two powerful forces from Egyptian times, but they're ancient symbols that haven't been relevant in centuries. Time will tell why we've been given them."

The snake fixed its eye on Leon and drew itself up to full height, extending its hood magnificently and shimmering for a second. Then the jaws shrank inwards, the neck grew shorter and the hood turned into flaming red hair. Instead of a terrifying cobra, Tash stood before us, her green eyes flashing.

"Wow, Tash. That was impressive but scary," I said, still standing back.

She smiled secretively. "I don't know why, but when I'm in cobra form I feel hugely powerful and I can see things in my mind."

"What do you see, Tash?" asked Viyesha.

"I'm not sure. It doesn't make any sense. I see a mirror image of myself. Only it's bigger and more powerful. And it's coming. I can feel it coming."

Viyesha glanced at Leon, a troubled look on her face.

"I don't like this," I heard her say quietly. "We know the Fallen Angel is plotting revenge. Maybe we need to look to ancient times to understand the nature of his attack and how to protect ourselves."

"What about you, Emily? What can you do?" demanded Seth.

I looked at him, not sure what to say.

"I have a sort of telekinetic power," I answered.

"Cool," he responded. "Such as…?"

I looked around the room. Last time I'd been in here, I'd smashed the tiny light fittings on the chandelier. I noticed they'd regenerated and didn't want to do that again. I fixed on one of the cushions lying on a sofa behind Seth and concentrated on pushing my energy out of the top of my head, looping it forward. I curled it around the cushion and it rose unsteadily. Seth didn't know what hit him. One minute he was looking at me, the next minute a large cushion landed on him from above.

"Yowza," he cried, jumping out of the way. "Great superpower, Emily. You can control cushions!"

"It's a work in progress," I replied. "Actually, guys, there's something I have to tell you, which kind of relates to my superpower."

I looked at Juke and my mother. They nodded encouragingly.

"Turns out I'm related to Juke," I announced.

"Cool!" Seth's eyes grew wide in admiration. "You have an urban angel in the family!"

"Actually, he's my dad."

"Excuse me?" said Tash. "Did you say he's your dad?"

"Yes, and there's more. My mum's an urban angel. They split up when I was born. It was too dangerous for them to stay together when I arrived."

Tash raised her eyebrows in disbelief. "Your new-age mother is secretly an urban angel? Now I've heard everything. No disrespect, Mrs M."

"It's true. I have the DNA of an urban angel. As well as being initiated."

"Yowza!" exclaimed Seth. "You could be a superhero."

Now Violet spoke. She'd been observing me quietly. "I knew there was something different about you, Emily. Your energy shone brighter than anyone else's. You could have more power than the rest of us put together. You could be phenomenal."

"She already is," said Theo, holding my hand.

"I hope you all are," said Father James from the ballroom doors. "I hate to be the bearer of bad news, but I think the attack has started."

"Already?" said Viyesha in alarm. "What's happening?"

"An army of zombie women is approaching up the main driveway," called Mrs O'Briain from the reception area. "And that's not all. The sky's getting very dark. I think something's approaching from the east."

I felt Theo's hand tense.

"This is it," he said under his breath. "It's begun."

"Okay everyone," said Viyesha, assuming control, her voice soft and calming. "We knew this was coming. It's just sooner than expected."

She turned to Mrs O'Briain and Father James.

"This is not your fight. You can leave by the underground tunnel. It leads from the Clock Tower to the church. If you go now, you can escape."

Glancing at Father James, Mrs O'Briain spoke. "Leave? What kind of cowards do you take us for? We don't run in the face of adversity."

"We've come this far," said Father James. "If we can assist, we will." He made the sign of the cross.

"Thank you, Father," said Juke, a glow of energy already appearing around his body. "We appreciate the support. We're going to need all hands on deck."

A buzz of energy crackled around the room. The air was alive with expectation and excitement, and I realised the inhabitants of Hartswell Hall were rising to the occasion. This might be war, but it was also a chance for the family to rid themselves of their oldest enemy.

I only hoped they weren't relying on me too much.

## 44. **Under Attack**

From the reception windows, we watched the women approaching up the driveway. It was hard to say how many there were as they just kept coming. I estimated a couple of hundred. Each had a glassy-eyed expression and it was obvious they were bisciones, summoned by their leader, the Capobranco. Of him there was no sight. But we knew he was in the shadows, watching and waiting, orchestrating the attack.

As they reached the Hall, they split in two directions, circling the Hall. Theo, Joseph, Violet and Leon set about securing the downstairs windows and doors. We didn't want any of the biscione women entering and taking us by surprise. As they remained outside we could see what they were doing.

"Why don't we go outside and finish them off, Juke?" I asked, watching their numbers grow around the Hall.

"As long as they stay in human form, there's nothing we can do," he answered. "We have to wait until they turn into serpents."

The women pressed their faces against the windows, the moonlit night giving them a dim, ethereal glow. They gazed in, their eyes dead and empty, and I shivered. They looked pretty creepy.

"What are they doing?" asked Mrs O'Briain. She held her cross up to a window, watching in satisfaction as the women recoiled.

"I don't know," answered Viyesha, "but we can be sure the Capobranco has a plan. These are his foot soldiers, acting on his orders."

Theo came back, reporting that all the windows and doors were locked and they would each stand guard at a strategic location around the Hall to ensure the biscione women didn't enter. He left to take up his vantage point in the kitchens.

"What about the crystal, Viyesha?" I asked. "Shouldn't we be protecting it?"

"It's safe in the Clock Tower," she answered. "It's of no use to the Fallen Angel. It's us he wants."

The sound of breaking glass drew our attention.

Violet's voice sounded from the ballroom. "Mother! You'd better get in here. I don't know what to do."

Leaving Seth, Tash, Mrs O'Briain and Father James to guard the reception area, Viyesha ran into the ballroom. My mother, Juke and I followed. The women had broken some of the smaller windows and their arms were reaching in, like tentacles on an octopus, dripping with blood where the glass had cut their flesh.

"What do I do, mother?" shrieked Violet. "How do I stop them?"

"I'll stop them," said a voice behind them. Mrs O'Briain stepped up to the windows, waving her crucifix. Immediately, the arms drew back.

Now the sound of breaking glass came from other areas of the house.

"It's no good, mother," said Violet. "We can't keep them at bay. There are too many."

"She's right," I said. "They're going to get in. We have to fight them."

"No," said Viyesha. "We cannot kill them in human form. I will not condemn their souls to purgatory."

"Then we're in danger of being invaded," said Violet. "We can't stop them."

"I need some help," came Father James' voice from reception.

Viyesha and I joined him in the reception area, where he was trying to stem the flow of arms punching through the small windowpanes.

"Should we turn into animal forms?" asked Seth. "Would it help?"

"I don't see what a dog or a snake could do," I answered.

"I could bite them," said Tash. "A cobra's bite is pretty lethal."

"But you'd kill them. Juke and Viyesha said we can't do that."

"Oh Lord," said Father James, looking out of the windows and into the sky. "Something else has arrived."

"It's Bellynda," I said, seeing the familiar shape of the dragon flying above, fire raging from her nostrils. "Where are Aquila and Pantera when you need them?"

"Aquila's in a bad way," Viyesha said, back in reception. "His battle with the Fallen Angel has left him mortally wounded. Pantera's recovered from her ordeal, but she won't leave him. She thinks he's dying."

Her words were drowned out by the sound of falling masonry as Bellynda attacked one of the turrets. We saw her land on the battlements of the east wing, just visible from where we stood. A massive plume of fire shot from her mouth and the building erupted into flames, bright and intense against the night sky. Instantly, she took off, ready for another onslaught.

There was more to come. In the distance, I spied what looked like a huge flock of birds flying towards us.

"What's that, Viyesha?" I asked.

Knocking back the women's hands that tried to clutch us through the broken windows, she peered out. The moon was on the wane, but still sufficiently large to cast its light over the cloudless sky, giving good visibility. There was no mistaking the dark shapes that approached the Hall, at first no bigger than birds, but rapidly increasing in size.

"They don't look friendly," exclaimed Seth.

"OMG, what the hell are they?" asked Tash.

"Hell's the right word," muttered Father James. "They look like they're straight from Hades."

I stared horrified at the legions of flying creatures that circled around the Hall. Each had bat-like extended wings, a domed head and a long, pointed tail. At the moment, they were no more than silhouettes and it was hard to see the detail but I experienced a terrible sense of dread. This was the stuff of horror movies.

"Juke!" called Viyesha. "Have you seen these creatures before?"

He joined us from the ballroom, looking through one of the reception windows and assessing the situation.

"Demons!" he said in disgust. "Tricky, but nothing we can't handle."

"But the numbers," said Viyesha. "There are so many. As well as the biscione women and who knows what else?"

"We need to keep a cool head and work out a strategy."

"Better make it quick," advised Seth. "I don't think they're going to wait."

Without warning, a hissing face appeared at the window, making Tash and I jump back screaming. It had curled horns, red glowing eyes and rows of jagged, yellowing teeth. With a hideous scraping noise, it pulled long, spidery fingernails down the windowpane, cutting into the glass. Father James thrust his cross towards its face and the demon lashed out, snarling. But it did the trick. It flew back into the night, hissing and spitting, black wings obscuring our view of the sky.

"Scary biscuits," muttered Seth. "That was one ugly brute."

Throughout the Hall, we could hear the sound of breaking glass. It was only a matter of time before the biscione women invaded. Now they started making an ominous buzzing sound with their mouths, reminding me of the Bhramari bee breath my mother did in yoga. It sounded like a swarm of bees amassing outside the Hall. Intermittently, they stopped buzzing and made clicking noises, the eerie sounds echoing through the night. It was disturbing and strange.

"What are they doing?" I asked Viyesha.

"I don't know," she answered, frowning.

My mother joined us and spoke to Juke in a low voice. I positioned myself nearby, listening.

"Between Emily, you and myself, we can manage the demons. We've overcome creatures like this before."

"But never so many."

"This time we have Emily. She's inexperienced but she has the power."

"What d'you suggest?"

"We take on the demons while the family holds back the biscione women. When we've killed the demons, we'll hunt down the Capobranco. Once we've destroyed him, the women won't be a threat."

"And the dragon?"

"We'll attend to the dragon after that."

"And the Fallen Angel?"

"There's no sign of him yet. Let's deal with the immediate threats first."

Okay. Let's bring Emily up to speed."

"It's alright," I said loudly. "I heard your conversation. Sounds like I'm about to be initiated into the art of demon fighting. You'd better give me some pointers on what to do."

Part of me was afraid. But another part was hugely excited.

Bring it on.

## 45. **Fighting The Dragon**

Aquila lay on the bed, barely conscious. His swarthy complexion was grey and the sheen of sickness gave him an unhealthy glow.

Pantera wiped his brow with a damp cloth.

"Try to sleep," she murmured.

A loud crash sounded outside and she ran to the window, pulling back the heavy drapes. Below in the courtyard, broken stonework and masonry lay where it had fallen, dust rising. Looking over to the east wing, she saw a hole in the battlement where a line of turrets had once stood. Flames poured from the building, a dark plume of smoke disappearing into the sky.

Looking down, she saw a line of women circling the Hall, making a strange buzzing noise, punching through the small windowpanes, trying to break in. Winged creatures flew overhead, demonic and threatening.

"What is it?" came Aquila's voice, croaking and cracked.

The sound of more crashing masonry echoed through the room and she knew she couldn't hide the situation from him.

"The Hall is under attack," she informed him. "The sky is full of demons and the building is surrounded by biscione women."

"We must fight," came Aquila's faint voice.

"No," she answered. "You've done your part. Leave the fighting to others."

She glanced out of the window again, seeing a large familiar figure land on the battlement opposite. Flames belched from its mouth and with a sweep of its powerful tail, a massive chunk of stonework fell into the courtyard.

"The dragon's back," she informed Aquila. "And she's not on our side."

As if she'd heard the words, the dragon looked up and rose from the battlement, her vast wings carrying her in the direction of

Pantera's window. She flew towards Pantera and for a brief second, their eyes met.

"It's not too late," Pantera called out, sliding up the sash window. "Change sides, Bellynda. Come back to us."

The dragon retorted by belching out a huge plume of flames and Pantera pulled down the window, narrowly avoiding being torched.

"There's my answer," she said angrily. "There's no coming back now."

She watched as Bellynda joined the demons circling around the Hall, their red eyes glowing ominously, forked tails flicking, dark wings outstretched.

"I have to do something," she muttered to herself. "We started this."

"We must kill her," came a croaky voice from the bed.

She turned. Aquila was sitting up, his black eyes flashing and angry.

"Aquila, don't be stupid. You don't have the strength."

He fixed his gaze on her. "Get the blue crystal."

"We've tried already," Pantera told him. "It had no effect."

"Get me the crystal," he repeated. "I have to make good what we did, even if I die in the process. If you don't, I'll get it myself."

Seeing his determination, she left the room, returning minutes later with the silver casket.

"Place it on the bed and open the lid," he instructed.

She did as he asked, revealing the crystal, blue energy spilling on to the bed. Carefully, he picked it up, placing both hands around it and held it to his face, inhaling deeply, drawing its strength into his body, feeling the energy shoot through his veins, revitalising every cell, pushing back the dark energy that threatened to consume him. For some time he didn't move, but continued to absorb the crystal's energy. Then he placed it back in the casket. Swinging his legs from the bed, he stood up, seemingly restored. Black eyes flashing, he spoke.

"It is done. I am ready. Return the crystal to the Clock Tower then join me. We will do what has to be done."

Needing no further bidding, she took the silver casket and hurried to the Clock Tower. When she returned, she found Aquila standing by the window.

"It seems the urban angels are to fight the demons," he said. "Which leaves the family to deal with the biscione women, and the dragon for us. Are you ready?"

"I am."

They left the bedroom, making their way to the Clock Tower, taking the spiral steps down to the basement room. It was here that the secret passageway led from the Hall to the church. Taking one of the keys that swung from a chain around her waist, Pantera unlocked a door, revealing a flight of stone steps.

From the shadows, Viyesha watched. She'd been on her way to ask Pantera for help when she saw them leaving. She believed she understood their purpose.

They arrived at the church unseen, ensuring they could attack from outside the Hall, giving them the element of surprise they needed. Quickly, they crept into the churchyard, shape-shifting into a large black eagle and sleek black panther.

Now, it was simply a case of hunting down their prey.

Stealthily, Pantera crept towards the Hall, keeping her belly close to the undergrowth, while Aquila flew overhead, silent and dark. He came to rest on the branch of a large tree, hidden from sight but giving a good view of the Hall's frontage and courtyard. Pantera waited beneath, concealed amongst the vegetation. They watched as Bellynda flew in from the east, aiming her tail at a decorative tower overlooking the courtyard, demolishing it with one fell swoop. Then she flew over the ruin, torching the interior with her powerful breath. For a moment, she hovered, then flew away from the Hall and circled round, ready to attack.

Silently, the black eagle rose into the air, seeing his opportunity, eyes focused on his target. He followed the dragon unseen, gaining ground until she was below him. Then without warning, he dropped, striking quickly. He aimed for the dragon's left eye, knowing he'd already blinded her right eye, and with deadly accuracy pierced the yellow pupil with his dagger-like beak. Taken by surprise and blinded on both sides, the dragon shrieked horribly, beating her wings and crashing into the Hall grounds.

That was Pantera's cue and she sprang, claws at the ready, leaping out of the undergrowth, landing on the dragon's back and sinking her teeth into the nearest wing. Her attack was frenzied and vicious, claws and teeth ripping and shredding, pulling the wing to pieces.

Realising it was a two-pronged attack, Bellynda fought back, shaking her body from side to side, trying to wrestle her wing from the panther's grasp. Pantera clung on while Aquila struck again, aiming for the other wing, sinking his beak into its scaly surface. Blinded and unable to fly, Bellynda flailed, knocking the panther to the ground. Pantera rolled out of the way as the dragon exhaled flames, turning the air into a fireball that scorched shrubs and trees, forcing Aquila back. They watched as Bellynda pulled her damaged wings behind her, panicked and in pain, leaving a trail of sticky dragon blood. Then it was in for the kill.

Pantera sprang and Aquila swooped, diving through the flames, with beak, talons, teeth and claws at the ready. Ferociously, they tore into the dragon, inflicting deep wounds. One last onslaught into the dragon's neck and their work was done. Their former friend lay dying before them, broken and battered, her lifeblood seeping away. Aquila flew to a branch overhead, his strength all but gone. Pantera lay to one side, panting and exhausted.

With a tremulous shudder, the huge dragon body exhaled one last time, swiping its spiked tail in a final defiant gesture. It was an unexpected movement, catching the panther by surprise, so quick she was unable to retreat. The vicious spikes tore across her body, cutting into her vulnerable underbelly. She howled in pain, realising the dragon had exacted the ultimate revenge. Aquila flew to her side, wings hanging down, feathers torn, beak bent and broken.

They had achieved their aim, but the cost was great.

Slowly, all three creatures returned to human form, the wounds they'd sustained all too evident. Aquila and Pantera looked over Bellynda's body, splendid in black leather, now lifeless and still.

"She was one of the best," murmured Pantera.

"Before the evil turned her head," added Aquila.

They watched as her body became dark and stone-like, a network of fine lines criss-crossing its surface, gradually disintegrating into dust, carried away by the night air until nothing remained.

Stooped and frail, Aquila helped Pantera to her feet, hands around her middle, trying to staunch the bleeding.

"We'll go back the way we came," he said. "Our final resting place needs to be inside the Hall."

A battle raged in the skies above them, as angels fought demons, but they were too battle-weary to take notice.

## 46. **Angels And Demons**

I stood alongside my mother and father at the French windows of the bridal suite, the doors open on to the balcony, assessing the situation and planning our attack. By now, the air was thick with demons, flying around the Hall, swooping down, hissing and spitting as they came near. Their smell was putrid, like decaying flesh, their skin discoloured and mottled, but their physique was muscular and strong. Huge wings propelled them through the sky, scalloped edges almost graceful, long sinewy tails snaking behind. I watched mesmerised at the shapes flying around me, until one shot towards me unexpectedly, its jaws open in a foul-mouthed snarl, jagged yellow teeth spiking outwards, breath straight from the tomb. Its tongue licked towards me, curling and lascivious, spraying viscous goo that hit me full in the face.

"OMG, that is disgusting," I said, wiping away the vile smelling stuff.

"That's demons for you," said Juke. "They play dirty. Just as well you know what you're up against."

Another flew past, its red eyes shining in the darkness, scraping its nails along the rim of the balcony and leaving a red substance that dripped down between the balustrading, corroding the stonework like acid. Yet another flew towards me, pointing its talons at me. Without warning, it fired long steel-like ribbons that lassoed around my neck. I felt the breath go out of me as they tightened, the bands of steel cutting into my skin, threatening to choke me.

Two swift cuts from Juke's sword and the creature lost its grip, both arms severed at the elbow. I watched horrified as its clawed hands dropped to the balcony, steel extensions retracting, and the creature rose shrieking into the air. Juke spun his sword, slicing into its wings and it fell screaming to earth.

I clutched my throat, bruised and sore, trying to draw in air, my body shaking with the ferocity of the attack.

"Are you okay, Emily?" asked my mother.

She put her hands, cool and comforting, on my throat and instantly the pain went away.

"Yes," I answered, breathlessly. "I wasn't expecting that."

"Chokers," said Juke. "A particularly nasty type of demon. Your first strike must take off the arms. Prevent them from attacking you. Your second strike takes off the wings, stops them from flying. If the steel bands come around you, slice across with your sword to free yourself. Got that?"

"Yes. I think so." I gulped. This was going to be trickier than I'd thought.

"We need to attack," said my mother. "Put paid to this show of strength."

"Agreed," said Juke, "but we need to make sure Emily's ready."

Before he could say any more, there was a noise below. Theo and Leon were in the courtyard beneath our window, beyond the line of buzzing biscione women. Theo had his hands around the wounded demon's neck.

"That'll teach it," he called up, kicking the lifeless body out of the way.

"What are you doing down there?" I called out. "How did you get past the biscione women?"

"Through the cellar," Theo called back.

"We're your ground force," shouted Leon. "We'll finish off any wounded demons that fall to earth."

"Sounds good," Juke called down. "Destroy them all. We're taking no prisoners."

"They're lethal," I called down to Theo. "They spit acid and fire steel rope that wraps round your neck and chokes you. Are you okay with that?"

"Nothing we like better," he answered, grinning up at me. "Don't worry about us. How about you?"

"She'll be fine," Juke answered for me. "I've seen Emily in action. She's a natural."

"Let's get started then," called up Leon.

I stood on the handrail of the balcony, alongside Juke and my mother, each of us shimmering with blinding white energy, holding gleaming swords in our hands, large wings extending from our shoulders. I wasn't quite sure when my transformation took place. One minute, Juke was telling me how to manoeuvre while airborne, the next I had wings growing from my body, a sword in my hand, and for the very first time, felt truly immortal.

I couldn't wait to fly into the night air and commence battle.

"You'll need to replicate," my mother advised me. "But you know how to do that. The main thing is to watch your back, keep your wings safe. Without them, you're in trouble, especially fighting this kind of demon."

"Ready?" asked Juke standing alongside me. "We'll cover you while you get used to flying. You take this area over the main body of the Hall. I'll take the east wing and your mother can take the west wing. If you're in trouble, pull back your replicas and return to the balcony. If your wings get damaged, they'll self-repair, but you have to give them time."

"We've all had our first battle," my mother informed me. "It's the only way to learn."

I wondered how many urban angels had cut their teeth on such mean creatures as these.

"I'm ready," I answered.

I stepped off the balcony, feeling my wings unfurl behind me. It was the most incredible sensation to have these two powerful extensions to my body, to feel them rise and fall, knowing I could keep myself airborne. Immediately, a demon swooped, claw extensions ready to rip into my bright angel wings. But Juke was too quick. Slicing his silver sword to the right and the left, he cut off its arms. First one, then the other, then arched back and cut into its wings. I watched as it fell to earth, shrieking and crying, where Theo and Leon were waiting.

The knowledge that we were a powerful, angelic force burst into my mind, filling my body with strength and making me hungry for blood. These demons were doomed, no match against our shining energy.

Immediately, a demon appeared out of nowhere, latching on to my back, hooking its spindly legs around my middle, digging needle-like claws into my flesh. Its speed took me by surprise and I struggled to keep my wings outstretched.

"Time to die," it taunted and over my shoulder I smelled its foul breath.

But my mother was there, shining and celestial, cutting into its body with her sword. With one slicing movement, she cut off a wing. Another slice and the other wing disappeared, the creature shrieking deafeningly in my ear. Then Juke swooped low, grabbing it by the huge curved horns curling from its head, and wrestled it from me, hurling it down to Theo and Leon.

"They're quick," I called to Juke. "I never saw that one coming."

"You need to replicate," he instructed. "As soon as there's more of you, you'll be better protected."

I needed no further bidding. Pushing my energy outwards in all directions, I concentrated on expanding my consciousness, taking myself beyond my physical boundaries. Then suddenly, there were lots of mirror figures alongside me, angel fighters just like me, each with a magnificent sword and silver-white wings.

"This is your time, Emily," called my mother. "Let's destroy these vermin once and for all."

She and Juke flew in opposite directions, replicating as they went, filling the sky with silver warriors, each wielding swords, turning this way and that as the demons fell on them. Their angel force was fast and ruthless, cutting off limbs, severing heads and slicing into wings, filling the air with a terrible shrieking and crying as demon parts littered the air and wounded demons fell to earth like large, brittle insects.

But there was no time to watch Juke and my mother in action. I had my own battle to fight and there was no shortage of demons coming for me. I held my sword at the ready, as my wings took me upwards, my replicated selves following. Now we were high up above the Hall, with a wide expanse of airspace as our battlefield. A screeching demon was immediately at my side, coming for me with claws outstretched, steel extensions shooting forward. I thrust with my sword, cutting off its hand. Demon blood spurted up and the demon dropped away, clutching its arm, hissing at me. Another came from below and now I found I was able to manoeuvre myself with ease through the air, using my wings to change direction, twisting at the last moment and coming in for the kill. I sliced my blade at its mottled head, cutting clean through the neck and watching it fall away. Then another demon was attacking from above, and I felt its steel extensors skim my wings. But I was too quick, turning out of the way and suspending myself mid-air while I hacked and chopped.

The more adept I became, the better my replicated fighters performed, until we were moving with grace and agility through the air. We used our blades with deadly accuracy, reacting to our adversaries with split second timing, despatching this way and that, taking first one that came from the front, then looping backwards and felling one that came from behind.

I felt my adrenalin buzz and my energy grow brighter as I did what I'd been born to do, galvanising my strength and using any trick I could to rid the skies of these foul creatures, revelling in my new-found ability to fly and fight at the same time. Theo and Leon had little to do as we slew the majority of demons in the air, only the occasional casualty falling to the ground, where they swiftly despatched it.

Eventually, there were no demons left to fight. I put my sword back in its scabbard, pulled my replicated selves back inside and came to rest on the balcony where I'd stood earlier. My mother and Juke and their replicas were still fighting, terminating the last few demons, sending them spinning to earth. I watched as they pulled their mirrored selves back and came to a halt, standing victorious on the battlements of the Hall's two wings.

I put up my hand to wave at them, grinning from ear to ear at the success of our mission, when something dropped on me from above, unexpected and fast, threatening to send me spinning below.

It was a rogue demon, clinging to my back with powerful legs, sending steel extensions around my throat, cutting my windpipe. I swung back with my sword, attempting to dislodge it, but my arm was at the wrong angle and no matter how I twisted and turned I couldn't shake it off. The steel cut into my neck, causing me to choke, blackness threatening my peripheral vision. Despite the pain, I tried to focus. My mother and father hadn't seen my predicament. I had to get out of this myself.

With the demon on my back, I attempted to climb on to the balcony's handrail, reckoning it wasn't expecting me to take flight. A searing pain knocked me back and I realised the creature was spitting acid onto my wings, the corrosive substance burning them away.

I fell back, unable to fly, unable to breathe, unable to scream, feeling the bands of steel tight round my neck. And now the creature leaned into my head, whispering in my ear, its putrid breath filling my nostrils.

"A message from my master, Ahmes. He says congratulations on destroying his demons. He didn't expect any less. But they were just an aperitif. A taster of what's to come. Enjoy your new life while you can, Ahmes. It won't last long."

Just as consciousness was slipping away, I became aware of someone else on the balcony, fighting the demon. I felt the creature pulled from my back and its grip on my throat loosen. Then the creature was gone and I could breathe again. I gulped in air, aware I'd nearly died at the hands of a demon for the second time that night. I turned to see who'd saved me and found Leon and Theo tearing the demon apart. Theo was twisting its head from its body, Leon had already removed its arms.

The creature thrashed in its final death throes and lay still. I staggered in to the room, dizzy and faint, my damaged wings dragging behind me. Then Theo was holding me in his arms and Juke and my mother were landing on the balcony.

"Emily, what happened?" said my mother, seeing my bleeding throat and shredded wings and the dismembered demon on the floor.

"I thought I'd killed them all, but I hadn't," I croaked. "A demon landed on my back. I couldn't get it off. Leon and Theo killed it."

'It took her by surprise," said Leon. "Lucky we saw it and got here in time."

"Come and lie down, Emily, get your strength back." Theo tried to lead me towards the bed.

"No." I looked at Juke and my mother. "It spoke. It had a message from the Fallen Angel. He said well done for destroying his demons, that he wouldn't have expected any less, but they were just an aperitif. That something worse is to come. He said to enjoy my new life because it wouldn't last long."

Juke smiled ruefully. "I thought it was too easy."

"It's going to get worse, isn't it?" I demanded.

A sudden weakness came over me. Then Theo was holding me in his arms, filling me with his strong energy, carrying me towards the bed and I realised I was back in human form.

I clung to him, luxuriating in his embrace, inhaling his scent, feeling his skin against mine, trying to forget the overpowering evil that had held me in its grip, trying not to think about the horrors to come.

I heard a beautiful singing in my head and fell back on the pillow, dead to the world.

## 47. **Biscione Women**

While the battle raged overhead, the buzzing continued around the Hall, growing in volume then dying away as the women's breath rose and fell, interspersed by their strange clicking sounds. Occasionally, a fist was thrust through a small window, but for the most part, the women were motionless, concentrating on making the strange sounds with their mouths.

"What's going on?" asked Violet. "That sound is creeping me out."

"It's a vibrational breath," said Joseph. "It's supposed to calm you."

"It's having the opposite effect on me."

Viyesha stared at Joseph, an idea forming.

"Bhramari was the Hindu goddess of bees," she said, thinking aloud. "She overcame the demon Arunasura with bees. So we know large numbers can generate immense power. What if the women are recreating the vibrational frequency of bees to create power?"

"To what end?" asked Violet. "It's not achieving anything. Apart from being intensely irritating."

"What if it's not aimed at us?" said Joseph. "What if it's aimed at the Hall?"

Viyesha's eyes opened wide as realisation dawned.

"Of course," she exclaimed. "They've formed a circle around the Hall. They're using vibrational power to attack the Hall."

"Which means what in plain speak?" asked Seth, listening to their conversation.

"It means they're undermining the Hall's foundations," answered Viyesha. "They're not interested in breaking in. They've punched holes in the windows to allow the sound in, not themselves."

"OMG, the whole thing's going to collapse," cried Tash.

As she spoke, the humming increased in volume then died away, replaced by the odd clicking noises. In time with the clicks, small cracks began to appear in the plasterwork of the reception ceiling. Tiny pieces of white plaster fell to the floor, covering it like fine snow.

"Lord save us," murmured Mrs O'Briain, clutching her crucifix.

Father James began muttering a prayer.

"The bee breath gets them into the Hall's auric field and the clicks chip away at its foundations," said Joseph.

"We have to fight on a vibrational level," said Viyesha. "It's the only way."

"Can animal forms help?" asked Seth hopefully.

"No, Seth, sorry."

"What d'you suggest?" Joseph asked Viyesha.

"I have the perfect antidote," she answered, turning to her daughter. "How's your singing, Violet?"

Violet smiled, understanding what was required. She turned to the others. "You're might need earplugs."

Violet stood before the huge oak door in the entrance hall, Joseph and her mother behind. They'd been afraid to open the door for fear the women would rush in. Now they knew this wouldn't happen.

Violet opened the door to reveal a line of biscione women, each staring blankly ahead, a loud buzzing noise coming from their mouths. It was like standing in the middle of a swarm of bees. Then the clicks began. There was a loud crack above as the lintel over the door broke in two. Further cracks ran along the walls of the entrance foyer and two framed pictures crashed to the floor. Beneath them the ground vibrated.

"When you're ready, Vi," said Joseph.

Violet inhaled deeply, closed her eyes and began to sing. It was a high-pitched mermaid's song, ancient and magical, crystal-clear and pure, piercing the air like an arrow. As she sang, the volume increased and the notes became higher, drowning out the buzzing and clicking. Still singing, Violet moved from the front door into the reception area. Her beautiful singing continued, powerful and sweet, increasing in volume and pitch until the air resonated with her sound.

Slowly, she walked around the downstairs rooms of the Hall. First into the ballroom, where Seth and Tash sat opposite Mrs O'Briain and Father James, each wearing earplugs, hands firmly placed over their ears. Then she moved into the library, through the glass-roofed atrium into the kitchens, the conference rooms, the private dining rooms, along each of the Hall's wings, singing as she went.

Windowpanes popped as her singing reached its crescendo. But one by one, the women ceased their buzzing and clicking until Violet's voice was the only sound, eventually diminishing until there was silence. A peaceful calm emanated through the Hall, as if it was breathing easy now the torture was over.

Now it was Viyesha's turn. She walked outside, aware the battle overhead was over and the dragon nowhere to be seen. Quietly, she moved among the biscione women, filling their empty minds with tranquillity and serenity. Eyelids closed, heads fell to shoulders and arms dropped by their sides, as they fell asleep, lulled by Viyesha's calming presence.

Once the stillness had settled over the women, Violet joined her. They touched hands, bright sparks of blue energy sizzling and crackling between them, then stood apart, pulling a line of blue energy between their fingertips. Each began to walk around the Hall in a different direction, drawing the line of blue energy behind them like a shimmering blue spider's thread. Three times they circled the Hall, crossing paths, creating a mesh of blue energy around the biscione women, silent and sleeping.

When the energy seal was in place and the Hall was protected, Joseph took over, using his powers of abundance to restore its damaged energy field. He took Violet's route, visiting each of the downstairs rooms, healing as he walked, mending cracks, smoothing plasterwork, making shattered windowpanes whole again.

Violet found Seth in the ballroom, sitting alongside the others, holding two cushions either side of his head.

"Is it over?" he shouted, seeing her enter the room.

She motioned for him to remove his earplugs.

"For now," she informed them. "We've restored the Hall's energy field and made the biscione women sleep. The demons are destroyed and it appears Pantera and Aquila have killed the dragon."

"Hoorah!" shouted Seth. "Time to party!"

In another part of the Hall, Viyesha met with Leon.

"I don't like it, Leon," she said softly. "This isn't a proper attack. It's more like a game of chess, having to outwit your opponent. Where's the Fallen Angel? Why hasn't he shown himself?"

"He sent a message to Emily," answered Leon. "He said this was for starters. That worse was to come."

"He's trying to weaken us," declared Viyesha. "Each of these attacks makes us that little bit weaker. So when the final onslaught comes, we're not strong enough to withstand him." She looked at him with troubled eyes, seeing the tiny lines criss-crossing his skin, knowing she was the same.

Leon took her hand. "There's a new generation coming, Viyesha, with the strength of youth. What we lack, they have in abundance. They'll stand up to him."

She held on to his hand, feeling his strength flow into her body.

"I hope it's enough, Leon. For their sakes, I hope it's enough."

## 48. **Dreaming**

It didn't seem as if any time had gone past when I found myself awakening and stepping out of bed. Looking back, I saw my sleeping form lying beneath the sheets, Theo beside me, and realised I was having a lucid dream. Nothing I could do about it except go with the flow.

I walked across the room and out of the door. There was no one around and it appeared to be early morning. I could hear birdsong outside and glorious sunshine flooded the corridor. It was a beautiful summer's day. I walked along the corridor towards the main staircase, and went downstairs. Strangely, the huge oak door was wide open, a gentle breeze blowing in. I walked outside looking for the biscione women but they'd gone. I looked for piles of broken masonry and smashed stonework but they too were gone. Everything was pristine, the Hall's honeyed stone bright in the early morning sunshine, the smell of vegetation in the air.

For some reason, I found myself walking towards the hidden garden, passing through the sweet-smelling rose garden towards the brick retaining wall. I saw the key in the lock of the ornate, wooden door and let myself in, closing it softly behind me. It was darker on the other side, the overgrown trees and shrubs casting shadows, creating a green, subterranean world. I pushed my way through, brambles clawing at my ankles, aware I was bare foot and wearing my blue initiation gown.

The dense undergrowth gave way to a clearing and the old Victorian folly stood before me, ivy and climbing yellow roses covering its crumbling arches. I ran my fingers over the ornate stonework, drinking in the peace and serenity, pulling my hand back sharply as I encountered a thorn on one of the rose stems. Tiny drops of blood fell from my finger where the barb pierced my skin, bright red against the yellowing stone. Briefly, I saw movement beneath the ruined arches, as if a shadow had passed through, and I stepped inside to investigate. Away from the sunshine, it was darker in the folly, with deep, green moss growing underfoot.

I looked around, sure somebody was there but seeing nothing. Then I sensed him standing behind me, soft fingertips on my neck.

"Don't turn round," I heard him say, gently caressing the soft skin between my neck and shoulder. "It's so peaceful here. Let's just enjoy the silence."

His fingers were electric on my skin, making me shiver with anticipation.

"How did you get here?" I murmured. "I thought you were sleeping."

"Shh," he said softly. "Don't speak."

His hands moved down over my shoulders and I felt his lips on my neck, kissing me gently, doing wonderful things to my insides. He stood close, his body firm and strong behind me and I tipped my head back so he could kiss my throat. It felt divine, the hidden world and sensuous touching combining to raise my senses to a new level.

"Let me kiss you," I begged.

"Very well," he said. "But keep your eyes closed. It'll intensify the experience."

I did as he bid, closing my eyes and turning to face him. I felt his lips on mine, hungrily devouring me, firm and demanding, and I responded with my own passion. His arms closed around me, pressing his body against mine and I could feel his heartbeat as if it were my own. I surrendered to the kiss, feeling our love flow and souls unite. Never had I felt such complete and utter love and never had it been so completely reciprocated. I wanted this boy with every sinew of my being. Every part of me cried out for him with a longing and intensity that was overpowering.

I broke away, pulling back from him.

"I want you," I gasped, "so much."

"Not as much as I want you," he said.

A smile spread over my face and I opened my eyes, expecting to look into the deep blue eyes I knew so well. Instead, my mouth dropped in horror and a scream stuck in my throat as I realised the deception. I was gazing into the dark, smouldering eyes of Barolo di Biscione and his arms were around me. Shock waves ran through me and I was rooted to the spot, unable to move.

"I thought you were...You even sounded like him," I gasped.

He smiled lazily, eyeing me hungrily.

"You heard what you wanted to hear," he said in his soft, lilting Italian. "But you have to admit, you were enjoying it."

Now my mind was reeling. How could I have made such a horrendous mistake? How could I have mistaken him for Theo? He was right. I had been enjoying it, but what did it say about me?

"You're just a wanton, Emily," he said softly, running a finger across my breastbone. "Forget Theo. Be with me. We'd be good together."

"Never," I shouted, pushing my hands against him. It was like hitting steel and my hands had no impact. I was locked in his embrace.

"You've already said you wanted me. You can't change your mind now," he whispered and smiled.

"You tricked me," I shouted.

"I never said I was anyone else, Emily. There was no trickery. You were responding to me. And now you're mine."

"No," I cried. "Let me go."

Up close, he was more attractive than I remembered, his eyes deep and soulful, his skin soft and tanned, his hair dark and gleaming. It was difficult to believe such beauty covered such evil.

"I can't let you go," he said softly. "You invited me in. Which means you're mine for the taking. That's how it goes."

He leant forward and began kissing me again, his lips soft and caressing, parting my lips with his tongue, exploring my mouth with its probing tip. Horrified, I found my body responding, wanting more, moving closer. My mind struggled against his overwhelming sensuality like a butterfly trapped in a jar. This wasn't right. This was the Capabranco, invincible and all-powerful, leader of the bisciones, the Fallen Angel's chosen demon.

With that thought, I finally came to my senses. What was I doing? I was an initiate of the blue crystal and an urban angel. If anyone could overcome Barolo de Biscione, I could. Anger and energy consumed me, and I pushed hard against his arms, breaking his hold on me.

He looked at me surprised. "Why Emily," he said softly, "what's wrong? Didn't it feel good?"

For a second, he morphed into Theo and I was staring into his deep blue eyes, gazing at me adoringly, a smile on his face. The vision faded and Barolo was back, only now there was an ugly leer across his features.

"You were enjoying that," he taunted.

"You were playing tricks on me," I countered, stepping back. "And don't even think of turning into a serpent. I'll turn into an urban angel and behead you. I've done it many times before. I've killed dozens of your snake ladies. You think you're more powerful than me, you're wrong."

I could feel my energy expanding and getting brighter, pushing him away.

"You think you're strong," he hissed at me. "You'll find out soon enough, you're nothing. There's one coming who's far greater than I."

"Who?" I demanded.

He smiled horribly and said nothing.

"You're bluffing, trying to scare me. Do your worst, Barolo. You won't win."

"Until we meet again, Emily. In the mean time, let me leave you with a serpent's kiss, a foretaste of what's to come."

He leapt forward and a forked tongue flicked from his mouth, catching me off guard. Instinctively, I jumped back, seeing two red marks appear on my arm. When I looked up, the folly was empty. Barolo di Biscione had gone.

Now I heard my name being called. I resisted, determined to seek him out in the shadows.

"Emily. Emily, are you okay?"

I felt a hand on my shoulder and turned to look, opening my eyes wide as I looked into Theo's face.

"Emily," he gasped. "You had me worried. Did you have a bad dream?"

I stared up at him, taking in his tousled blond hair, his cornflower blue eyes and softy, ivory skin. Reaching up, I pulled him towards me and kissed him passionately on the lips. Then, breathlessly I broke away.

"Theo, I would never, ever be unfaithful to you. You know that, don't you?"

He laughed, not understanding. "Of course. The thought never entered my head. What's happened?"

"Nothing," I said forcefully. "I was with Barolo di Biscione. He tried to seduce me but he didn't succeed. He's a vile creature."

"Emily," he laughed softly, stroking my brow. "It was a dream. Not surprising after everything you've been through, but nothing more than a dream."

I pulled the bedclothes off my body and looked down at my legs.

"Then how do you explain these bramble scratches?"

I showed him my finger, still bloody where the thorn had pricked me.

"I got that from the roses growing on the folly walls. How d'you explain that?"

Finally, I pulled up my sleeve to reveal two red marks across my arm.

"That's the serpent's kiss. It happened, Theo. It was real."

I took hold of his hands and looked into his face.

"He said there's one coming who's greater than him. D'you think he meant the Fallen Angel?"

"I don't know," said Theo, running his finger over the serpent's kiss on my arm, his eyes hard. "But one thing I do know…." His voice grew steely. "Barolo di Biscione is mine."

"No, Theo," I corrected him. "He's mine. And he is so dead."

## 49. **Goodbyes**

Viyesha knocked softly on Aquila's door. Hearing no answer, she gently pushed it open and entered the room. The drapes were closed and all was in darkness. Two figures lay motionless on the bed. Viyesha pulled the heavy curtain back a fraction. It was late afternoon and the sun was still high in the sky, allowing a few bright rays to shine in. What she saw made her gasp.

Aquila lay still, his eyes closed, his skin grey. He was barely breathing. Pantera lay by his side, her blue dress soaked with blood around her stomach. Her eyes were also closed and she too was barely breathing.

"Oh my friends, what's happened to you?" whispered Viyesha, sitting beside them.

Pantera's eyes fluttered open.

"Viyesha," she murmured.

"Hush, don't speak. I'll get the crystal. It will heal you."

Pantera shook her head. "No. We are beyond the crystal's help."

Her breathing became more laboured and Viyesha took her hand.

"You slew the dragon," she said. "Your oldest friend."

"She was a traitor. We did what we had to." Pantera's voice was barely audible. "Aquila was already weak. It took all his remaining strength. I sustained injury and now the evil permeates me."

Viyesha bit her lip, holding back the tears.

"You were the only ones who could. She was too powerful for us. We will never forget what you did, what you have done for us over the centuries. You've protected us and kept us safe, and for that we are eternally grateful."

"My strength is going," whispered Pantera, her voice ragged and faint. "Aquila's too. Until we meet again, Viyesha."

For a brief second, Aquila's eyes flickered open.

"Until we meet again," he echoed faintly. His eyes closed, his head slumped and he breathed his last. Pantera too, closed her eyes and uttered one last long breath.

Tears streamed down Viyesha's face. "Goodbye my friends," she said softly. "Until we meet again."

She sat and watched as their forms grew hazy and their features indistinct, as if they were being erased. Soon, they were little more than brief outlines. Silently, a shadowy black eagle arose from Aquila's form, stretching its wings. A shadow panther rose from Pantera's form, yellow eyes glowing bright.

Viyesha smiled and walked to the window, pulling back the curtains and raising the sash. Warm summer air streamed into the room and she inhaled deeply, smelling the scent of Joseph's roses in the air. When she turned back to the bed it was empty.

She looked out over the gardens, seeing the unmistakeable shape of a sleek black panther slipping away into the undergrowth. Overhead, a black eagle flew, elegant and majestic, disappearing between the trees.

"Goodbye my friends," she said again, tears clouding her eyes. "You were true to the last."

For a second, she was in the past, remembering a world of hot sand, bright colours and heady scents. Then she brought herself back to the present, focusing on what was to come.

## 50. **The Capobranco**

We sat in the ballroom, waiting for Viyesha. Night had fallen suddenly, a dark blackness pressing in on the windowpanes, the figures of the biscione women just visible, their sleeping forms creepy and disturbing. The door opened and Viyesha entered. I saw she held the silver casket in her hands. She shook her head.

"They've gone," she said quietly. "They slew the dragon. But they paid the price." She looked around. "Now it's just us."

"How can we manage without our guardians?" asked Violet, with a tremor in her voice. "They've always been there for us."

"We have no choice," answered Leon. "We fight in their memory."

As he spoke, there was a faint humming from outside. It was the biscione women. They were waking up.

"This can only mean one thing," said Juke, moving to the window and looking out. "Their master is here."

As before, tiny cracks began to appear on the walls and ceiling, and flakes of plaster fell to the floor. There was movement underneath us, causing a large vase to topple and break.

"OMG, it's an earthquake," shrieked Tash.

"Can you stop it, Joseph?" asked Violet.

He looked at her helplessly. "No. It's too powerful. I can repair it, but I can't prevent it from happening."

"We have to kill the Capabranco," said Juke. "It's the only way."

The ground began to move, undulating beneath us in a fluid motion, and the walls swayed, no longer the solid structures they had once been. Pictures crashed from the walls, windows smashed inwards and a huge crack ran from one end of the ballroom ceiling to the other. All the time, the women continued to hum, alternating with the dry clicking sound.

"We can't stay here," said Viyesha. "It's not safe. The Hall's falling down."

"Where can we go?" asked Violet in panic.

Leon took control. "Into the gardens. We'll decide what to do when we see what we're up against. D'you have the crystal, Viyesha?"

She showed him the casket.

"Won't we be playing into their hands if we go outside?" asked Theo. "They want to flush us into the open."

"We don't have a choice," answered Joseph. "Unless you want to stay and be crushed by falling masonry."

"Come on, we need to move," called Juke, opening the ballroom's French windows.

Biscione women surged at him, transformed into serpents, hissing and spitting, and a strong wind gusted inwards, whipping the doors out of Juke's grasp. The night pressed in, ominous and black, not a glimpse of the moon in sight. A horrible rumbling filled the air.

"I'll take care of the bisciones by the door," Juke shouted over the noise. "As soon as I've made a gap, run for it."

"What about the women?" asked Mrs O'Briain. "We can't leave them once they've changed back."

"Any that turn back into women, we'll take with us," shouted Juke. "But let's get out first."

As he spoke, there was a loud crack and the ceiling at the far end of the ballroom crashed to the floor, causing Tash to shriek.

"Shall we change into animals?" asked Seth eagerly.

"How could another snake and a weird dog possibly help?" asked Theo disparagingly. "Just get Tash out, okay?"

"Are you all right, Emily?" asked my mother.

I nodded. "The Capobranco's out there. And the Fallen Angel. How do we know they won't attack as soon as we're out in the open?"

"We don't," answered my mother. "We just have to be ready."

Already she and Juke were turning into urban angels, a bright glow around their bodies. I looked down and saw I had a similar glow. At least I'd be armed.

Juke led the way, slashing at the serpent women with his sword, cutting off serpent heads, making a gap in their circle through which we could escape. One by one, we left the ballroom, stepping over twitching serpent bodies into the gardens.

"Over here," said Leon, leading the way.

We followed him across the formal lawn, stepping down behind the ha-ha, it's low wall giving us some shelter.

"What's the plan?" asked Seth, peering into the dark bushes and jumping as a large moth flew into his face.

"The plan is to stay alive, dumbass," said Theo.

"I propose the urban angels take on the biscione women," answered Leon. "Mrs O'Briain and Father James can bring the women down here as soon as they've recovered. Violet and Joseph, I want you to make an energy shield and keep them safe. Seth and Tash, stay inside the energy field with the women. Don't let any wander off. It's too dangerous. Keep the silver casket with you. It's your job to guard the crystal."

"And the rest of us?" asked Theo.

Before Leon could answer, a terrible shrieking rent the night and flying creatures filled the sky, like a massive flock of monstrous seagulls.

"Demons," said Leon, glancing up. "That answers your question, Theo. You, me and Viyesha will fight the demons."

"What about the Capobranco and the Fallen Angel?" I asked.

"One step at a time," he answered. "We'll deal with what we can see first. Be prepared to regroup as the situation changes."

With no time to spare, we set to our allotted tasks. Seth and Tash took the silver crystal and hid behind a blue energy shield created by Violet and Joseph below the ha-ha. Leon, Viyesha and Theo crept on to the formal gardens and prepared to fight the flying demons.

Juke, my mother and I, accompanied by Father James and Mrs O'Briain, approached the hissing, snapping biscione women. My sword was in my right hand and my shield in my left, and I was shining like a neon sign. I looked over at my parents and saw they were the same. As one, we stepped towards the serpents.

"Emily, you and your mother stay on this side," instructed Juke. "I'll take the front of the Hall. You'll need to replicate. If you fight the Capobranco, stop the replication immediately. You need all your strength in one body. Okay?"

"Okay," I gulped and that was it. We were plunged into battle once again. I went to the right and my mother to the left, taking on the biscioni, still in formation around the Hall. By now, its destruction was well underway and I saw with dismay the crumbling brickwork, fallen gargoyles and jagged outline of the walls where the roof had collapsed. This wasn't degeneration. This was annihilation. I couldn't imagine the Clock Tower surviving and was glad Viyesha had removed the crystal.

Immediately, I was surrounded by serpent women, open mouths hissing, revealing rows of vicious teeth. I pulled out my sword and set about cutting and slicing through scaly necks. I could see my mother doing the same, a blur of fast moving white light, working her way along the line of serpents. I saw her replicate into three, making the job easier and did the same. We were lucky the serpents didn't crowd us, but stayed in formation around the Hall, intent on their job of destruction. Black blood flowed and heads toppled, black smoke curled around the bodies, clearing to reveal women from the village.

As soon as the women recovered, Mrs O'Briain and Father James gathered them up, escorting them to the blue shimmering force-field. I imagined Seth and Tash keeping the women safe, ensuring none wandered off, Seth relishing his role as guardian of the crystal, Tash wishing it were all over.

Taking a swift breather between biscioni, and pausing to let Mrs O'Briain and Father James do their job, I saw Leon, Viyesha and Theo fighting demons on the lawn. The creatures bored down on them at terrific speed, aiming with talons outstretched. They had a bird-like form, with a massive curved beak, a small head and enormous bat-like wings. I saw one fly towards Theo and was shocked to see its talons were metal blades, threatening to cut him to pieces. Heart in mouth, I saw Theo send a bolt of blue energy from his fingertips, causing it to explode mid-air. Thick and fast they came, like a swarm of giant locusts, so many the sky was a seething black mass. I saw Leon pull a demon apart with his bare hands and Viyesha lasso another with a line of blue energy, drawing it towards her at speed, pulling the line tight until it choked. Demons dived, blue thunderbolts flew and the family battled. They may be uber chic, but beneath the glamour they were hardened warriors, brutal and tough, intent on surviving.

Out of the corner of my eye, I saw a snake rear its head and turned speedily, catching it mid strike. It stood no chance. It's hideous head toppled to the ground, and another woman was free.

I was killing plenty of serpents and I knew my mother was doing the same, working our way around the Hall until we linked with Juke. But I knew this wasn't what I had to do. I needed to kill the Capobranco. Once he was dead, the serpents would automatically revert to human form, reuniting with the souls he'd stolen, leaving us free to help the family and kill the demons, and whatever else the Fallen Angel had in store. But where was he? He was keeping a low profile.

"Show yourself, Barolo," I shouted into the night. "Are you such a coward you'd let women do your dirty work?"

I felt the wind pick up around me and the air grow chilly. He was near, I knew. But I couldn't stop. I had serpents to kill and I continued to hack my way through the line, seeing my replicated selves move fluidly ahead of me, passing round the corner of the Hall, towards the Clock Tower.

Now I was away from the fighting, away from my mother and father. It was darker and more secluded on this side of the Hall and I knew I had to keep my wits about me and draw in my replicated selves if he appeared.

I glanced up at the Clock Tower, wondering if it too would soon be rubble, and then I saw him, perched high on its sloping black slate roof above the golden clock faces, huge dark wings outstretched, watching the fighting below.

"Come down, Barolo," I shouted. "We have unfinished business."

Quick as a flash, before I could draw in my replicas, he was in front of me. I tried to pull them in, but he blocked my energy, laughing at my endeavours.

"What's the matter, Emily? Spread yourself too thin? Don't worry. It'll be over all the quicker. Why not give up now? Make it easier all round? You know you're too weak to withstand me."

"Never," I said, trying again to pull in my energy and failing. My replicated selves continued to fight, drawing on my strength, and there was nothing I could do. I wondered if any one would come to my aid, but they were all busy fighting and couldn't see what was happening on this dark side of the Hall.

Barolo stood metres in front of me, his naked torso muscular and gleaming in the moonlight.

"Emily," he said softly, looking at me with melting brown eyes, "there's no need for us to fight. Imagine how good we'd be together. You think Theo can give you the world? It's nothing compared to what I can offer. You'd be a queen... revered and adored...beautiful and powerful...rich beyond your wildest dreams... followers at your beck and call. Come with me and it's all yours..."

His voice was coaxing and seductive, soft and sibilant, lulling me into a false sense of security, and I found myself mesmerised. Just in time, I thought of Theo and brought myself back to reality. I shook the lethargy away and faced him.

"Back off Barolo. You're nothing but a low-life serpent. What makes you think I'd ever be interested in a creature like you?"

Now he was malevolent, his eyes glittering darkly.

"Don't say I didn't give you a chance, Emily," he hissed. "I offered you the world and you turned me down. Now, face the consequences."

Immediately, he morphed into serpent form, his neck stretching and widening, his smooth skin black and scaly, his nose and mouth protruding forward, jaws open wide, revealing jagged teeth. So far, I'd only seen the biscione women turn into serpents. Now I experienced the Capobranco in all his glory. He was in a different league: taller, more ferocious and altogether more frightening. He continued to grow until he was towering above me, his huge serpent body coiling and writhing, yellow eyes fixed on me, jaws bearing down, ready to consume me.

Now I understood why prey failed to fight. His power and presence was so overwhelming, I was terrified, rooted to the spot, my arms inert by my side, watching as his mouth opened over my head and his breath caressed me.

My crystal necklace saved me, vibrating against my breastbone, burning my skin. The searing pain brought me back to my senses and I quickly stepped back, raising my sword above my head.

"I told you to back off," I shouted, jabbing my sword up into his open mouth. With a scream, he drew back and I pulled my sword down, black blood running down the hilt.

"Come on, Barolo, try again," I taunted. "Let's see what you're made of."

He lunged at me and I stabbed again, piercing his mouth in a different place. Now he was angry as well as in pain. Blood poured from the wounds and I knew I'd caused significant damage. Now he lowered himself to my level and came at me from the side, looping his long neck around me. He moved so fast I barely realised what was happening. Suddenly my arms were pinned to my side, my sword useless in my hand, and the coils of his body were around me, strong as a steel band, squeezing the life out of me. I gasped, trying to draw breath, unable to expand my lungs. I tried to call out, but no sound came, and still he continued to squeeze until I thought my bones would break. I tried to move my hand to my crystal pendant, to tell Theo I needed help, but it was impossible. Beyond me, my replica selves fought, draining my energy, leaving me weak in Barolo's clutches.

All around, the battle raged, my parents fighting the biscione women, the de Lucis family battling the winged demons, every one engaged in combat, not knowing I was in trouble. I could feel my eyeballs bulging and watering, and now he coiled around me again, squeezing my shoulders and neck, preventing me from seeing anything beyond his slippery scales. Mentally, I chided myself for thinking I could take him on, an inexperienced warrior against an all-powerful demon. I'd thought I was invincible, but I was wrong. And now I was paying the ultimate price.

He squeezed until I was losing consciousness, falling into a deep black pit. Just as I was slipping away, I felt his grip loosen and found I could draw breath. Gratefully, I gulped in air, my lungs expanding, the blackness in my head clearing. As his grip slackened, I could see again and there was Theo, his hands and body bathed in bright blue light, pulling away the serpent coils. Above him, the serpent jaws snapped, dripping blood, unable to pierce his energy field.

"Quick, Emily," he said through gritted teeth. "I can't hold him much longer. Get out, then finish him while you have the chance."

I needed no further telling. Wriggling out of the loosened coils, I pulled myself free, holding my sword aloft. Now, at last I could draw in my replicas. Concertina-style, they flew into my body and I felt my strength return. The serpent jaws snapped at Theo, held back by his energy field, and now he relaxed his grip, leaving the way free for me to attack.

With a massive cry, I swung my sword around my head, both hands on the hilt, feeling the energy flow through my body, culminating in my hands and sword. I struck the blade against the serpent's neck, feeling it cut deep. I saw the head fall to one side and swung my sword again, cutting it clean from the body, finishing the job. It fell to the ground, coils still writhing. Then Theo's arms were around me, his blue energy flowing over me, and I was safe.

Barolo di Biscione was dead and I was alive.

A huge sigh came from the serpent's mouth and a wind swept past us as the remaining souls he'd imprisoned were finally released. I glanced at the remaining line of biscione serpents, seeing them transform into human shape as body and soul reunited. The women were back, released at last from their grisly ordeal.

"How did you know I needed help?" I asked Theo, safe in his arms. "I couldn't touch my crystal necklace. I couldn't tell you."

"You've Mrs O'Briain to thank for that," he said. "She followed you round the Hall to collect the women and saw what happened. Thankfully, she didn't attempt to fight him herself. She came to get me."

He looked into my eyes, then his lips were on mine, the exhilaration of the battlefield heightening our emotions, intensifying the moment. But there was no time to relax. A battle raged and we broke away, knowing we must fight.

On the formal lawn, I saw my parents had joined the fray, replicating into a small army of shining urban angels, flying among the demons, slicing and hacking, giving the family the help it needed. I watched as Theo flung himself into battle, grabbing a demon latched on to Leon's back, pulling it to the ground and covering it with blue energy that burnt its mottled body. Shrieking and crying, the creature cowered, as Theo wrenched its head from its shoulders.

Now it was my turn. Two flying demons attacked Viyesha as she fought another, slicing into her blue energy field with their steel-like talons. Wielding my sword, I flew towards them, cutting across their wings, forcing them to drop to earth. I followed them down, cutting through their swiping talons, swinging my sword one way and the other, beheading them in two quick moves.

Everywhere I looked shining angels, led by Juke and my mother, battled dark-winged demons. It was a well-oiled machine doing what it did best, hunting, attacking, fighting and destroying. The steel cutters might look scary but they were no match for celestial swords and soon the demons were in trouble. As it became obvious they were losing the fight, the remaining stragglers took off into the night.

My parents drew the angel fighters back into their bodies and we stood alongside Theo, Viyesha and Leon, breathless and battle-weary, watching them flee. Behind us, Mrs O'Briain and Father James shepherded the women towards the blue energy shield held fast by Violet and Joseph.

"I hear you killed the Capobranco," my mother called to me. "Well done, Emily. He was a powerful demon. You released all those souls. The women have much to thank you for."

"She was amazing," called out Mrs O'Briain as she scuttled past. "He didn't stand a chance!"

"It was thanks to Theo," I admitted, "but, yes, Barolo's dead."

I glanced into the sky, now ominously quiet.

"What now, Viyesha? Is there more to come?"

"Oh, there's more," she answered, scanning the horizon. "The Fallen Angel hasn't finished with us yet. I just don't know what's coming."

## 51. **Apep**

The answer to my question came in the form of a massive shadow that fell over the Hall and grounds, making the night darker and more intense. The temperature dropped and goosebumps broke out across my flesh.

A sibilant, silvery voice echoed through the darkness, making me shudder.

"So, Ahmes, you've killed my Capobranco. He was an old friend, loyal and true, and will be greatly missed. And, Viyesha, your guardians killed my dragon. Or was she your dragon? Such a sweet moment when she changed allegiance. But they paid the price. I see you and your allies have despatched two legions of my demons, some with your bare hands. I hadn't realised the de Lucis family could be so barbaric. I had thought you were more...polished. And your urban angels have proved most adept at fighting our bisciones. It's all most impressive."

"He's playing with us," said Leon under his breath. "I don't like it. What's his game?"

"Show yourself." Viyesha's voice rang out loud and clear.

"The problem is, Viyesha, I don't have much to show any more, as well you know. I live in the shadows. Which is where you will be soon."

As he spoke, we heard a loud crash from the far side of the Hall. It sounded as though a wall or roof had collapsed.

"The Hall is dying," the Fallen Angel said. "Its foundations are destroyed, it cannot withstand any more. And neither can you, Viyesha. Admit it. These skirmishes have taken their toll. Your energies are diminished. "

I looked at Viyesha, realising what he said was true. She seemed tired and old, her posture stooped, the usual energy she emitted, ragged and fragmented. Leon, too, didn't emit his usual strength. I moved closer to Theo, taking his hand in mine, breathing easier as I felt the familiar energy surge from his body to mine.

"I know you still have the crystal, that it wasn't destroyed as I thought," the voice continued. "But it cannot help you now. Your time is nearly over."

"If you have something in mind, get on with it," commanded Viyesha. "Otherwise, be gone. Stop wasting our time."

There was a low chuckle in the air. "Very well. You asked. Let me introduce my piece de resistance...."

All was still and dark for a moment and we looked around anxiously. Then a hissing filled the air and a wind sprang up, whipping my hair back, making it difficult to stand upright. Theo put his arm round me, trying to shield me.

"What is it?" I asked.

"I don't know?" he answered. "Stay close to me."

The wind grew in intensity, chasing away the clouds, and the dark sky brightened, allowing us to see. But what we saw made my blood run cold. Something large and dark approached from the west, like a dark storm cloud, propelled forward by the wind, quickly taking shape. As it got nearer, the hissing increased and I realised it came from the thing in the sky.

"What is it?" I asked again, but no one answered.

I saw Viyesha glance over to the blue energy shield, checking Violet and Joseph held it strong, and the occupants were protected.

Horrified, we watched as the dark shape approached the Hall, taking the form of a giant serpent head, bigger than anything I could have imagined, prehistoric in scale, its skin mottled and aged. Behind it, a long serpent body coiled and writhed, possibly two kilometres in length, trailing back into the sky. The hideous mutation wormed its way towards us, increasing in size as it grew closer. It was possibly half a kilometre across, bigger than Hartswell Hall, rendering us totally defenceless. For a moment, it hung in the sky, suspended above us, staring without blinking through one massive yellow eye in the centre of its forehead. I'd never seen anything more terrifying in my life and felt my legs buckle. I held on to Theo, my breath panicky and shallow.

Without warning, the creature opened its mouth, revealing rows of primeval fangs, crooked and yellow, jagged and vicious. A massive roar erupted from the cavernous opening, causing the ground to shake and masonry to fall. The enormous jaws opened wider and I realised with horror that it meant to devour the Hall, taking us with it. The air became thick and putrid as it exhaled, its cadaverous breath straight from the tomb, releasing foul-smelling sulphurous fumes that had lain dormant for centuries.

Viyesha stared, petrified.

"You've released Apep!" she cried out. "What you have done?"

There was no answer from the Fallen Angel, just another massive roar from the terrifying monster.

"Who's Apep?" I shouted at Theo, trying to make myself heard

He looked at me wide-eyed, hardly believing what he was seeing.

"Apep was an ancient demon that took the form of a huge serpent. He threatened to eat Ra, the sun god, every night as he disappeared over the horizon. He lived in eternal darkness, an enemy of the light, the embodiment of chaos and evil, feared and loathed by the ancient Egyptians."

"That was thousands of years ago," I said. "What's happened? How come he's here now?"

"Ra fought him and won." Viyesha spoke clearly, turning to face us. "Apep was imprisoned in a mountain in the west known as Bakhu and has remained there ever since."

"Until now." Leon finished her sentence. "The Fallen Angel is exacting a terrible revenge, as he said he would."

I stared at the horror in the sky, its mouth opening wider, as it prepared to devour us.

"Can't we do something?" I demanded. "Can't Ra kill it again?" I clutched Theo's hand, realising these may be our last moments together.

"Not until sunrise," shouted Leon, raising his voice over the roaring and hissing.

"What's going on dudes?" called a voice. "Are we having some kind of natural disaster?"

Seth appeared beside us, accompanied by Tash.

"Seth," I cried, "You're supposed to be in the energy shield looking after the crystal and the women."

"We were. But it was getting pretty crowded in there and we wanted to see what was happening. Don't worry, the crystal's safe with Mrs O'Briain."

"Er, Seth, I think the crystal's safety is the least of our problems," said Tash, taking in the form of Apep towering above us. "Perhaps we should have stayed put."

"Holy moly," cried Seth, looking up into the gaping jaws of the monster. "That is one big mother."

"Tell me I'm dreaming," said Tash. "I am so not ready to be eaten by a giant snake."

"Is it time to turn into our animal forms?" suggested Seth.

"Like weird animals are really gonna help now," shouted Theo. "Don't you get it? This is the end of the line. Nothing can help."

Viyesha turned to face Seth, recognition on her face.

"Of course," she cried. "In the legend, the Eye of Ra transfixed Apep, while Set, lord of the desert, slayed him. I see it now. This is the gift of Amun-Ra. Yes, Seth, it's time."

"You mean this is our chance?" declared Seth, his eyes alight. "It's up to Tash and me to save the day? Are you kidding?"

"Seth! Does she look like she's kidding?" I shrieked. "For God's sake, turn into your weird animals. Time's running out."

The serpent reared up, about to strike. The ground shook, thunder echoed and huge hailstones rained down. The Hall continued to creak and groan as timbers snapped and walls crumbled.

"Holy wackamoly..." said Seth, looking up.

They were the last words he uttered before changing into the strange dog-like shape of the Set animal. Seth the boy was gone, replaced by an exotic creature with a long black nose, tall square ears and a brown muscular body. In his hand he held a huge spear. Tash too was gone, replaced by a large, hooded cobra, rising up in front of us, one massive green eye in the centre of her forehead.

Now she reared up high, facing Apep, the gaze from her eye locked on the giant eye before her. A low, sinister hissing issued from her throat and she opened her red hood in all its glory. There was nothing we could do but stand and watch. Slowly she rose upwards, as if rising from a snake charmer's basket, never taking her gaze from the huge eye above, growing in height until she was nearly as tall as the Hall.

Now she was the snake charmer, seductive and beguiling, swaying fluidly from side to side. The sounds from Apep died away, the ground stopped shaking and the hailstones dispersed. Mesmerised by the beautiful, red creature before it, the monster closed its vast mouth, creating a long, crooked line between its jaws, giving the appearance it was smiling. For the moment, it was entranced.

Seth saw his chance and took it. Taking aim with his spear, he threw it with all his might. It flew like a silver streak through the sky, piercing the soft skin under the monster's jaw. Taken by surprise, the creature uttered a deafening shriek and shook the spear loose. It fell close to Seth's feet and he picked it up, taking aim. Once again, he pierced the soft skin beneath its jaw and now the creature was in trouble. Its head crashed down into the Hall grounds, destroying Joseph's rose garden and demolishing the wall of the hidden garden.

"All yours, mate," cried Juke, passing Seth his celestial sword. "Finish the job!"

Seth stepped forward and I could have wept with joy. Holding the sword tightly and raising both hands above his head, he brought the blade crashing down on Apep's neck. Again and again he struck as the serpent screamed, cutting deep into the flesh, creating a deep gash. With every blow, the snake shrank in size and Seth kept going until he'd completely severed the head from the body. Then he stood back proudly, black ears high, panting from the exertion.

Apep was destroyed and Seth was the destroyer.

As quickly as he came, the Set animal was gone and Seth was back, fringe flopping over his eyes. He turned to us, demanding: "Did you see that? Did you see me in action? Seth saves the day. I always knew I'd be a super hero."

"OMG," I heard Theo mutter. "He's going to be insufferable."

Tash too had returned to human form, looking more graceful and beautiful than ever, green eyes sparkling, red hair tumbling over her shoulders.

The giant serpent continued to shrink, reducing in size until it was no more than a small grass snake, rapidly drying out and blackening, crumbling to dust.

For a minute nobody moved or spoke, scarcely believing our narrow escape. Then, as one, we breathed a collective sigh of relief.

The Fallen Angel's revenge had failed. We were safe.

"Thanks be to Amun-Ra," declared Viyesha. "In our hour of need he was there for us."

She stood alongside Leon, surveying the damaged grounds and the crumbling Hall.

"We have much rebuilding to do…," she started to say.

Before anyone else, I saw the movement above. I saw a dark shadow rise in the sky, turning into a black thunderbolt that hurtled with lightning speed, silent and deadly, in the direction of Viyesha and Leon. There was no time to think, only to react. Instinctively, I drew my energy to a point above my forehead, creating a force field that shot towards the thunderbolt with equal speed. White energy collided with black matter and there was a huge explosion, white sparks and black light firing in all directions, in a bizarre fireworks display.

Viyesha and Leon could only look on in surprise. The attack was unexpected and potentially lethal in power and intent.

"The Fallen Angel," gasped Viyesha. "Why did I not see that coming? Am I losing my touch? Thank God you had your wits about you, Emily."

She was visibly shaken, her face deathly white in the pale moonlight.

Another thunderbolt hurtled towards her and again I thrust my energy forward, creating a force-field that collided with the missile, exploding it mid-air.

"You think you can destroy all that is mine," shrieked a broken voice from somewhere above. "You're wrong Viyesha. Vengeance will still be mine."

"This finishes now," declared Juke, glowing bright white, huge wings outstretched, sword at the ready. He looked at my mother and me. "Are you ready?"

We joined him in the sky, our angel wings propelling us high, our bright light illuminating the form of the Fallen Angel, a dark, sketchy figure in the vague shape of a man, huge black wings outstretched, suspended in front of us.

The battle was hostile and vicious, as dark battled light. Together we fended off his black thunderbolts, using our shields, feeling the force as his missiles exploded on impact. While my mother and I faced him, luring him towards us, Juke flew behind, celestial sword outstretched. He plunged it in to the figure's back, hoping to surprise him. The figure turned on him, spitting out venomous words.

"You think you can wound me, urban angel! D'you have any idea how far down the evolutionary chain you are? You're like flies. You can never destroy me."

He hurled a thunderbolt at Juke, which he fended with his shield, dark pieces of matter scattering around him. Together, my mother and I charged, trying a double-edged approach, sinking our swords into his shadowy form. But it was like stabbing air. There was nothing there. He was a shadow man in every sense. He hurled more missiles and again we protected ourselves with our shields.

"What do we do?" I cried to my mother. "This isn't working."

"I have an idea," she called back. "I need to ask Viyesha. Can you and Juke hold him back?"

We signalled agreement and she disappeared from our side, flying to the ground. My father and I continued to fight, alternately shielding missiles and flying in to attack, although by now I was tiring, unsure how long I could continue this ineffective strategy. We needed a fresh approach.

Then my mother was back, flying alongside.

"We can't destroy him. He's too powerful. The only way is to contain him. The family will create an energy web for us to mesh around him. Then Theo and Juke can take him to Bakhu and imprison him in the mountain. Follow my lead."

Still shielding the dark missiles that rained down on us, we watched as my mother flew low, collecting a blue thread of energy from Viyesha's fingertips. She flew back up towards the Fallen Angel, pulling the energy thread that continued to flow from Viyesha's fingers, circling around him, flying faster, creating a mesh of blue energy. He saw what was happening and tried to clear it with his hands, but the more he struggled the more enmeshed he became. Juke and I followed, flying to the ground, collecting energy threads from Leon and Theo, pulling them behind us and joining my mother circling the Fallen Angel.

He soon became imprisoned in a ball of blue energy, which grew thicker by the second as we flew around him, interweaving with one another to mesh the threads together. He struggled to free himself but to no avail. He was contained, unable to fight, incapable of inflicting further damage.

Once complete, we flew back to the family, gathering the threads and twining them together to form a shining blue rope. Juke made a loop that he wrapped around his wrist.

Then he and Theo set off on their strange mission, Theo speeding over the ground, Juke keeping pace in the air, leading their diabolical prisoner in his impenetrable blue energy cage. Once they reached Bakhu, they'd take their prisoner into a cave deep inside the mountain and place him inside the leaden tomb that had once held Apep. They'd protect it with a further energy seal, before blocking the entrance with rocks and boulders. Finally, they'd invoke the protection of Amun-Ra, ensuring he would guard the tomb and prevent its inhabitant from ever leaving.

It wasn't fool proof but it was the best we could do.

When they'd departed, I turned to Viyesha. "Was there no way we could destroy him? Ensure our safety forever?"

"No," she answered. "Universal law dictates good is balanced with evil. Without one, the other cannot exist. Destroy him and we destroy ourselves. The best we can do is imprison him. With Amun-Ra's protection, he'll never return."

I was shocked to see how weary and old she looked. Small lines criss-crossed her face, her shoulders slumped and her eyes had lost their shine. I looked at Leon and saw he was the same.

"You two need some crystal energy," I told them. "Let's get the crystal and see if the Clock Tower's still standing."

"Very well," she agreed. "I hope it's safe. The biscione women too."

Seth, standing with Tash, pulled a face.

"Biscione women versus big snake and the Fallen Angel." He weighed them up with his hands. "I know which I'd prefer to take on. And it's not the biscione women. I've spent too much time with them. Those ladies are scary. I hope the reverend's still in one piece."

Smiling at Seth and glancing briefly towards the west, I followed him down to the lower levels of the garden. I hoped Theo and my father would return soon.

## 52. **Age**

We found Father James and Mrs O'Briain on the lower lawn, surrounded by a crowd of animated women. Violet and Joseph had finally let the force field go and sat to one side, exhausted by their efforts. Other than being panicked by the apparent earthquake, the women appeared none the worse for their ordeal.

"Look at the state of the Hall," Mrs Hilden was saying. "It's a wonder we're still alive. Thank goodness we were out here."

"Ladies, please," said Father James, holding up his hands for silence. "As you can see, there's been a minor earthquake. The Hall's sustained some damage, but thankfully there are no injuries. Can I ask you to go home quietly?"

"Have a cup of sweet tea," suggested Mrs O'Briain. "You've had a shock."

Chattering excitedly, the women drifted away across the gardens, pausing to look at the ruined Hall as they went.

"They think they were here for some kind of meditation session," said Mrs O'Briain, "and the blue force field was some kind of laser effect. Amazingly, they have no memory of being bisciones."

"And Apep, the giant snake? Were they not terrified?" asked Viyesha.

"Didn't see it," answered Mrs O'Briain. "None of us did. Thanks to the force-field." She handed Viyesha the silver casket. "I think you'll be wanting this."

"Thank you, Mrs O'Brian" breathed Viyesha, holding it close. "Your help has been invaluable, both yours and Father James'. We are forever in your debt."

She smiled, but it was a tired smile, her eyes crinkling into a myriad of tiny lines, her usually smooth alabaster skin now crepey and thin.

"Mother," called Violet. "Is it over? Is it really over?"

"It is," said Viyesha, sitting alongside and embracing her tightly. "We came through. You and Joseph did an amazing job keeping all the women safe."

"We didn't fight," said Joseph. "It doesn't feel like we did much."

"Winning a battle is down to everyone playing their part," said Viyesha. "You protected Father James and Mrs O'Brian, you kept the crystal safe and you looked after the women. Thanks to you there were no casualties."

"Are you okay, Mother?" asked Violet. "You look tired."

"Nothing a little crystal energy won't fix. Your father's gone to see how badly damaged the Hall is."

As she spoke, Leon returned, walking over the lawn towards them.

"The Hall's taken a battering," he informed them. "There's a lot of damage, but amazingly the Clock Tower's still standing."

"If anything could survive it would the Clock Tower," said Viyesha. "It was protected by the crystal's energy."

Leon put his arm around her protectively.

"We've come through, Viyesha," he said quietly. "We've done it."

She looked into his face. "Do you think Theo and Juke are up to the job? I can't face another battle."

"They're strong and powerful. They'll return soon."

I watched them, seeing how they supported one another, drawing strength from each other, and hoped that Theo and I would be the same in years to come.

"You both look tired," said Violet. "You need to get in front of the crystal."

"Perhaps we should wait until Theo returns?" suggested Leon

"No. I think we should go now," answered Viyesha.

Something in her tone alerted my instincts. All was not well.

"Shall Violet, Joseph and I come with you?" I asked.

She smiled at me. "Thank you, Emily. Yes, please."

We left Seth and Tash telling Father James and Mrs O'Briain about the giant snake, how the hooded cobra and the Set animal had won the day.

"D'you want to come with us?" I asked my mother.

"No," she answered. "I'll wait for Juke. I can't relax until I know he's safe. You go with Viyesha and Leon. They look as if they need some help."

Slowly we made our way to the Clock Tower room. Passing through the Hall was a distressing experience. Walls were collapsed, plasterwork littered the floor and parts of the roof had fallen in, revealing dark rafters and the open sky above.

The Hall was bad enough, but it was Viyesha and Leon that concerned us more. I saw a look of worry pass between Violet and Joseph but said nothing. I hoped the crystal would do the trick.

We entered the Clock Tower room and Viyesha placed the silver casket on the hieroglyphics in the centre of the room. Walking up the spiral stairs had been hard. She moved like an old woman, stooped and slow. I was shocked to see her hands were gnarled and arthritic, her hair grey and her skin sagging and lined. Leon was like an old man, his muscles wasted, head drooping and face tired.

She opened the casket and took out the crystal. Immediately, its beautiful blue light filled the room and cascades of blue energy ran down her hands.

"Join me, Leon," she whispered.

He stepped towards her and together they embraced the crystal, holding it jointly between their hands. It flared bright blue, encompassing their bodies in a shimmering effervescence so strong I was forced to turn away. Shielding my eyes against the glare, I looked at the floor, seeing the hieroglyphics glow green and blue. There was no denying the crystal's power, even though the full moon was past.

"Is it working?" I asked Joseph, who seemed able to withstand the glare.

"Time will tell," he answered.

Violet said nothing, just continued to watch the blue energy work its magic.

They seemed to hold the crystal for a long time until its power began to wane. Only then could I look.

The crystal was lacklustre and dull and the room dark, even before Viyesha returned it to the casket. Once it was safely in place, she turned to us.

"We need to rest. Allow our energy fields to repair."

She held on to Leon's arm and he helped her from the room and back down the spiral stairs. They still looked like an old couple and I felt my heart hammering in my chest as I realised the crystal hadn't worked its magic.

We helped them to one of the bedrooms, leaving them lying on the bed, looking up at the open sky through the broken roof rafters. Then we waited downstairs in the ruined ballroom, the night air chilling the room.

"They're not okay are they?" I asked.

"No," said Joseph. "The crystal's not working. It hasn't rejuvenated them."

"Perhaps they need a full moon," I suggested.

"Don't be stupid," Violet snapped. "They were fully regenerated at the blue moon. They need a top up, that's all."

"Emily's only trying to help, Vi," said Joseph gently.

"Sorry," said Violet. "I'm just so worried. This has never happened before." She looked out into the grounds. "Where's Theo? He needs to be here."

I glanced at Joseph. "How bad is it?" I whispered.

He shook his head and said nothing.

My mother joined us, standing next to me, placing her hand in mine, then Seth and Tash took their places by Violet and Joseph, telling us Father James and Mrs O'Briain had returned to the vicarage. Together we waited.

After what seemed an age, a figure appeared on the rear lawn running towards us, accompanied by another flying above. They were back.

I ran to Theo's side as he walked into the ballroom, Juke coming in to land behind him. I heard my mother breathe a sigh of relief.

"Mission accomplished?" asked Joseph, his voice tight and strained.

"Absolutely," said Theo. "He's deep inside the mountain, held in by so many energy seals he'll never break out."

He put his arm around me, strong and protective, and I felt his energy wrap around me.

"We make a good team," declared Juke. "We work well together. You should join me on a mission, Theo."

There was a cough from my mother and Juke looked over. "Sorry. You should join us on a mission," he said with a grin.

"Too dangerous," I declared. "I want him here with me. I've had enough danger to last a lifetime."

"It's been a tough fight," agreed Theo. "But we did it. The demons are gone and our future is secure. Where are mother and father? I need to tell them."

"They're upstairs resting," said Joseph cautiously.

"You may as well know," said Violet, her eyes filling with tears. "They tried to rejuvenate using the crystal but it didn't work. It's not looking good, Theo."

We stood around the bed where Viyesha and Leon lay. Gone were the handsome, sparkling couple I'd come to know and it took all my strength to remain with them, looking at their shrivelled forms. It was only a matter of time before they faded away.

"This isn't supposed to happen," said Violet, tears streaming down her cheeks. "We're supposed to be immortal, with eternal youth."

Viyesha sat up stiffly, propping herself against the pillows, and clutched Violet's arm with a claw-like hand.

"Even immortals have a shelf-life," she said in a dry, croaking voice. "This is our time."

"No," said Theo, sitting alongside his father. "We need you."

Leon spoke, clutching Theo's hand. "You'll be fine, Theo. It's time for us to step aside. You each have partners and angels to guide you. A new order is born."

"We'll return one day," said Viyesha faintly. "Until then, stay safe. Protect the crystal and it will protect you. "

She closed her eyes and fell back on the pillow. I could hardly bear to look as the ageing process accelerated rapidly and they wizened before us, skin stretching over their skulls, eyes sinking into their sockets, chests dropping into their bodies. It was over in seconds. They turned from old people into corpses, flesh shrinking back over bones, skeletons crumbling to dust. A gust of wind from above blew the dust into the air and for the briefest of moments I saw the people they had been rise up from the bed, hand in hand, glowing blue and ethereal.

Then they disappeared and the people I'd known as Viyesha and Leon were gone.

## 53. **Aftermath**

The days after Viyesha and Leon left us were strange. Not for the first time in his life, Theo was bereaved. But losing his parents was a different experience and he struggled, lost without their wise words and guiding hands.

But one thing his long life had taught him, time moves on relentlessly, and although he grieved, gradually he began to heal.

Violet and Joseph too. At first they were lost, particularly Violet. But these were immortals, possessed of exceptional strength and purpose, with a desire to survive and succeed. With Seth, Tash and me by their sides, life had its joys as well as its sorrows and we began to ease into our new lives.

Our first task was to rebuild Hartswell Hall. Its fabric had been eaten away by evil and it required much crystal healing and cleansing before Joseph could begin the regeneration process. With the next full moon, we charged up the crystal, allowing ourselves the luxury of bathing in its nourishing blue rays. I stood next to Theo in the Clock Tower Room, feeling the blue energy cascade around us, filling us with well being and happiness, knowing I was with my soul mate and that as long as we had each other, life would be good.

My mother and father moved in to the Hall, deciding it was a more suitable abode for urban angels than Granddad's old house. We knew they wouldn't stay, that they were guiding us through our transitional stage before leaving to continue the fight. But for the moment, it was good to have them around. It also made things easier with Seth's mother and father, and Tash's mother, who were remarkably accepting of the new arrangements.

Seth and Tash came into their own, moving into the uncharted territory of coupledom. I wasn't sure either would cope with the demands of serious relationships but I was wrong. Their relationships with Violet and Joseph were the making of them, as were their experiences with Apep. Seth learned he had the strength of character to rise to the occasion when it was demanded of him. Tash learned that beauty is a gift to be used for the good rather than simply decoration.

Don't get me wrong. Seth was still as annoying as ever, testing Theo's patience to the limit. And Tash could still be vain and flaky. But the difference was each had proved themselves and had a depth of character that had been lacking before. Although, never again would they assume their animal forms.

There was unexpected news of Father James and Mrs O'Briain. Something had happened in their fight against the bisciones, altering their DNA. We allowed them to bathe in the light of the crystal at the next full moon and each emerged as a very different creature, able to shape-shift.

Father James emerged as a great white owl, wise and all-seeing, Mrs O'Briain a huge white wolf, fearless and savage. Both offered their loyalty and protection, moving into the Hall as the crystal's new guardians.

And so the new order was established.

The Hall regenerated, the crystal kept us young and, as a final bonus, the biscione women found their desire for bitching and back-stabbing had disappeared with the serpents. Each became a force for good, intent on selfless devotion and charitable works. Even Baby Barrowsmith.

# Epilogue

*51 years later.*

The sun burns down on the hot desert sand and the heat rises in a rippling haze. I sit beside the pool, under the shade of the trees, my feet dipping in the cool water. Theo joins me, his blond hair tousled and curled, his blue eyes mirroring the intense blue of the water. Our children, a boy and a girl, the image of myself and Theo, splash in the pool, playing with Violet and Seth's three boys and Joseph and Tash's two girls. Each will be initiated when they reach seventeen.

Joseph is tending the grounds with Tash, teaching her the rudiments of horticulture. Seth and Violet have taken the four-by-four into the desert, exploring nearby caves.

We came to live here a couple of years ago when it became impossible to continue the regeneration of Hartswell Hall. Like its previous owners, the Hall had lived its allotted time, forcing us to move on. Both Seth's and Tash's parents were dead, succumbing to the natural ageing process, and there was little to stay for in Hartswell-on-the-Hill.

My parents are somewhere across the world, doing what they do, banishing demons and fighting for the light. They come to visit every so often, more so now there are grandchildren. Of course, they would visit wherever we lived. And so we chose Egypt, with its special memories for Theo, Violet and Joseph.

Upstairs, in one of the turreted towers of the cool white building, a large white owl and an enormous white wolf lie in the shade, protecting the precious contents of an inner room.

We have an important event coming up. In five days, it will be the Blue Moon and we have a party planned, attended by friends from across the globe. I look at the faint wrinkles appearing on the back of my hand and know this event cannot come soon enough.

And somewhere in the shadows, far away from this place, our enemy lies imprisoned. We know he cannot be destroyed and so we stay vigilant, protecting ourselves and our children, and the crystal that gives us life.

THE END

**Thank you for reading Into The Blue**

**If you have enjoyed reading True Blue, please leave a review on Amazon/Goodreads. Thank you! Pat Spence**

**Follow The Blue Crystal Trilogy:**

On Facebook at https://www.facebook.com/bluecrystaltrilogy

And on Twitter at https://twitter.com/pat_spence

Website: www.patspence.co.uk

**See the Blue Moon trailer at**

https://www.youtube.com/watch?v=SFvsXlPem4Q

# Acknowledgements

## Thanks go to ...

...Steve for reading through the many drafts, copy editing, cooking, ironing and washing up, Andrew Aske for cover design, Amelia for help with formatting, Beryl Henley for proof reading, Danusia Hutson for proof reading and all the friends and family who have provided encouragement. Not forgetting George, for furry sustenance.

## Other titles by Pat Spence

**Blue Moon** (Book One in The Blue Crystal Trilogy)

**True Blue** (Book Two in The Blue Crystal Trilogy)

**Abigail's Affair** (A quirky love story set in the UK and Australia)

**Find Your Sparkle! (The 30-day Sparkle Plan)**

A self-help guide to looking good and feeling great.

**Pat Spence** is a freelance writer and previously a magazine editor. She has also worked as a copywriter in advertising agencies, a freelance trainer in personal development and jobsearch skills, and a massage therapist/aromatherapist. She is married with one child, has a degree in English Literature, reads Tarot and is learning banjo.

Into The Blue

Printed in Poland
by Amazon Fulfillment
Poland Sp. z o.o., Wrocław